"Look at me."

As he spoke, he gave her arms a gentle tug.

Bit by bit, as if she were expecting it to be a trick, she did as he commanded while her mind recanted the litany that this man had killed her husband.

Common sense prevailed. *If he hadn't shot Elton, Colt would be dead and you'd probably be dead yourself. He did it for you. To save you. To save Colt.*

His crystalline eyes clouded with remorse. "I'm sorry. I didn't mean to frighten you. I was only going to get a twig out of your hair."

Holding one palm up in a "stop" gesture, he reached out with the other to pluck the harmless twig from her tangled hair. Without a word, he held it out to show her.

She felt like a fool for overreacting. "Th-thank you," she whispered, daring to let her gaze make contact with the disturbing intensity of his.

He nodded. "I know you don't have many reasons to believe anything a man says, but I want you to know that I have never raised my hand against a woman, and I never will. You have no reason to be frightened of me. Ever."

Penny Richards has been publishing since 1983, writing mostly contemporary romances. She now happily pens inspirational historical romance and loves spending her days in the "past" when things were simpler and times were more innocent. She enjoys research, yard sales, flea markets, revamping old stuff and working in her flower gardens. A mother, grandmother and great-grandmother, she tries to spend as much time as possible with her family.

Books by Penny Richards

Love Inspired Historical

Wolf Creek Wedding
Wolf Creek Homecoming
Wolf Creek Father
Wolf Creek Widow

Love Inspired

Unanswered Prayers

Visit the Author Profile page at Harlequin.com for more titles.

PENNY RICHARDS

Wolf Creek Widow

HARLEQUIN® LOVE INSPIRED® HISTORICAL

Recycling programs
for this product may
not exist in your area.

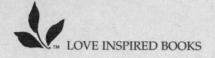 LOVE INSPIRED BOOKS

ISBN-13: 978-0-373-28326-2

Wolf Creek Widow

www.Harlequin.com

Printed in U.S.A.

In His favor is life: weeping may endure for a night,
but joy cometh in the morning.
—*Psalms* 30:5

This book is for Ace Allen Richards,
first great-grandchild and Adventurer Extraordinaire.
I hope to have many more "'ventures" with you,
precious blue-eyed boy.

Acknowledgments

Thanks to Benjamin Neeley
for telling me about "thin places."
Now I know what to call those special moments.

Chapter One

Wolf Creek, Arkansas, 1886

Thunk!

   Thunk!

   Thunk!

The dull, rhythmic sound penetrated the light layer of sleep shrouding Meg Thomerson's consciousness. She lay on her side, her knees pulled up to her chest as far as her injured ribs and healing arm would allow. Her hands, palms pressed together as if she were praying, were tucked beneath her cheek. Even now, dull pain pulsed in her side with every slow beat of her heart, a persistent reminder of the last time she'd been in this room.

   Thunk!

Restless, she moved her head on the pillow, not ready to face the day just yet. Not ready to face what might be left of her life. The lonely night had been made worse without her children there to cheer her.

She'd thought of going into their room, but knew it would only make their absence harder to bear. Besides, she was filled with the certainty that if she started sleeping in their room for comfort, she would never again find the courage to stay alone at night. Meg knew she might be many things, but she didn't think she was a coward.

It was almost dawn before she'd fallen into a light sleep filled with echoes of Elton's mocking voice and vivid dreams of him hitting her.

Thunk!

Her eyelids flew upward against her will. She didn't want to wake up, didn't want to remember the last time she was here. Too late. Her gaze collided with the battered chest of drawers that sat next to her bed. Elton had hidden some cash and a gun there. The same gun he'd used to try to kill Sheriff Colt Garrett almost six weeks ago after escaping from prison, where he'd been sent earlier in the year for a series of robberies in the area and almost killing Gabe Gentry and Sarah Van-Sickle. The attempted murder had taken place on the same day Elton had been shot and killed.

It was that decision, one of the many bad choices he had made through the years, that led to his own death. Meg moved her head restlessly on the pillow. If she let herself remember, she would be filled with that wonderful, horrible, *sinful* feeling of relief that had swept through her when the sheriff broke the news that Elton was dead.

Surely she was bound for hell to feel as she did.

Thunk!

She shoved the shameless thought aside. She would take Doc Rachel's advice and try to keep her mind occupied with other things. The lady doctor had assured her that in time, her inner wounds would heal, just as her physical ones were healing, and her joy in living would return. Meg hoped the doctor was right, but for now, she would not think; she would do. As tempting as it was to stay in bed and lick her wounds, she would get up and see what on earth that irritating noise was.

Using her uninjured arm to lever herself, she sat up. Though she had more or less healed, it was hard to break the habit of moving as if her bones were made of delicate crystal, like that she'd once seen at Sarah VanSickle's fancy house.

Meg eased her legs over the edge of the mattress and sat straight and still, waiting for her still-tender ribs to accustom themselves to the new position before putting her feet to the floor.

She didn't have to get dressed. When Doctor Gentry and her husband, Gabe, had brought her home from their place the evening before, Meg had been too tired to put on a nightgown. She'd pulled the hairpins from her hair, kicked off her shoes and curled up fully dressed on the threadbare quilt.

Now she crossed the wood floor to the window at the rear of the little three-room house. The bare planks were cool through her thin stockings. Faded blue-patterned curtains, hand-stitched from flour sacks and hanging from tautly stretched twine wrapped around a couple of sixpenny nails, were drawn against the night. Moving slowly, Meg raised her arms and pushed the curtains aside.

A familiar scene greeted her. The sun was already making its debut above the tree line in the eastern sky, hens scratched in the dirt with an industriousness Meg envied and the big white rooster flapped his wings, puffed out his chest and welcomed the day with a prideful crowing, as if it were all his doing. A lone pig rooted around near the small shack that served as a barn and her ancient gray mare nibbled at the stubs of green grass in the rickety corral.

Sunrise had always been her favorite time of day, an almost sacred time. A time when night and day merged, heaven and earth seemed to mesh and God seemed so near she could feel Him. From watching the world awaken and the animals working so hard, each new morning had seemed like a promise, filling her with warmth and hope and a chance to start over as the soft glow of the rising sun urged her to get up, move on, work harder and just maybe, things would get better.

They never had.

Today she found no joy in the familiar setting. No connection with God. All hope had been taken from her. Not even Elton's death and the knowledge that he was no longer a threat could fill the emptiness in her heart.

Please, Lord, let Doc Rachel be right. Let me find hope and peace in Your presence once more.

The brief entreaty crossed her mind before she could give it thought, a habit so ingrained that not even the guilt that kept her from voicing a proper prayer could halt the habit of a lifetime.

Thunk!

The sound drew her attention to the couple attacking the woodpile—a man splitting the logs and a small woman with a long braid hanging down her back who was stacking the split wood beneath the lean-to.

He was a big man: tall, broad through the chest and shoulders, long-legged and lean-hipped. Even from where she stood, it was easy to see that he radiated raw power and brute strength. Perfect for chopping wood.

Or battering a woman.

A shudder shivered through her, and her knees threatened to buckle, forcing her to lean against the window frame for support.

The movement must have caught his attention. He turned and, resting the ax on his shoulder, fixed her with a penetrating stare. It was the Indian—well, part-Indian—man who had helped her with her laundry baskets a few times.

She'd never noticed how intimidating he was. His hair, so dark it was almost black, hung just past his shoulders and was held away from his face by a bandanna tied around his forehead. Though she couldn't see their hue from where she stood, his eyes, in contrast to his swarthy skin, were so light they looked almost colorless.

His features were rough-hewn, and his face was all sharp angles, harsh planes and deep shadows. Heavy eyebrows were set in a straight line above a bladelike nose and a square chin and jaw. The combined effect should have rendered him ugly, but even though his face was fierce and a bit frightening, he possessed a harsh beauty. There was a noble look about him, something in the way he stood with his denim-clad legs slightly apart and the tilt of his head that seemed to shout that he was much more than what she saw standing there.

He looked magnificent and proud and wild.

Nothing at all like a killer.

Feet apart, shoulders back, his expression showing none of the turmoil churning in his gut, Ace Allen stood in the growing warmth of the September morning and stared at the woman whose husband he'd killed. Though the shooting was justified, done to save the sheriff, he was still responsible for taking a life and making the woman at the window a widow and her children orphans.

He wondered where that put him with God.

Maybe everyone was right and Elton Thomerson had deserved his fate, but Ace was having trouble making peace with what he'd done. For good or ill, his actions had forced him and the woman together and would take their lives in new directions. Wherever their paths might lead, they would forever be bound by Elton's death.

Seeing the woman—Meg—made his guilt even harder to bear. A small woman, she looked insubstantial since her ordeal. She hadn't braided her hair for the night and gold-blond tresses fell straight and silky from a side part, framing a too-thin face with almond-shaped eyes that he knew from previous encounters were green. A wide mouth, round chin and straight nose combined to make her one of the loveliest women he'd ever seen.

Almost as if she'd heard his thoughts, she ducked her head, reached up and swept the golden mass over one shoulder and began to weave it into a careless plait. The utter femininity of the gesture took his breath away.

"She's awake."

Ace turned toward his mother. There was a curious expression in the dark eyes regarding him. "Yes."

"I'll go to her, see what she needs," Awinita Allen said, adding the wood in her arms to the neatly stacked pile.

Ace looked toward the window once more, but Meg was gone. "I want to talk to her." His tone was more forceful than was necessary.

Nita placed a gentle hand on his arm. "Let me tend to her needs first. I'll call you when breakfast is ready."

Meg used the moment when the woman spoke to the man to break the strange trance gripping her. No. He was not just a man, she reminded herself. He was the man who had shot Elton. It was important that she remember that.

Ace. His name is Ace Allen.

Sheriff Garrett and Rachel had told her his name… among other things that had been mostly lost in the laudanum-laced world she'd drifted in and out of those first couple of weeks. Ace Allen had been in prison before. She'd heard that somewhere. She didn't remember why he'd been sent away, but he was out now and chopping wood for the upcoming winter. For her.

Meg wondered again how she had allowed herself to be talked into such a thing. She'd been shocked when the sheriff and doctor had approached her together and suggested that Ace and his mother would be the perfect ones to help her around the farm until she was strong enough to handle things on her own, possibly until cold weather settled in. Rachel added the argument that the self-sufficient Allens could keep her laundry business going so that she wouldn't lose her main source of income.

"I can't afford to hire them or anyone else," she'd said, though the thought of maintaining her income was tempting. "And I'm sure no red-blooded man is going to want to do laundry."

Sheriff Garrett laughed. "Actually, Ace did a lot of laundry while he was in the penitentiary."

"They live off the land, Meg," Rachel told her. "Ace hunts and traps and fishes and they sell produce and fruit to the mercantile in season. They're the kind of people who would do it for nothing, but you can give them meals, and I'm sure we can have a benefit or something to bring in some money. You know how people stand by each other here. No matter how strapped for cash they may be, they always manage to come up with something to help out."

Meg couldn't deny that. She wasn't sure she'd ever seen a more giving community than the one in Wolf Creek. She'd just never been the recipient of their generosity before. She'd always stood on her own two feet and "scratched with the chickens" for her living, as her aunt would say. Accepting help felt a lot like charity. She said as much to the pair doing their best to persuade her.

"Now isn't the time to let your pride get in the way," Colt told her. "And if you're worried about Ace being in prison, it might help to know that the killing he was accused of back when he was younger was accidental. He got in a fistfight and the other guy's head hit a rock when he fell. But because Ace was an Indian, they took the word of the bystanders. He spent two years at hard labor for something men do all the time.

"When Elton was caught and sent to prison for robbing Gabe, Sarah and the others, and word was that his partner was an Indian, he said it was Ace to protect his friend, and the judge sent Ace back to jail for the second time. Elton was lying."

Meg wrung her hands together and looked at him with a furrowed brow. "How can you know that for sure?"

"Because I followed some leads and found out Joseph Jones was the guilty party. Ace was set free. He's a good man. Will you be uncomfortable around him because of Elton?"

"No, not really," Meg told them. Everyone in town knew Elton's death was a result of his own actions.

"Look, Meg," Rachel said, "I know you've had a lot to deal with, but you need to let us help however we can. We care about you. At least give some thought to letting Ace and his mother help."

"He learned to do about everything while he was locked up," Colt added. "He's a jack-of-all-trades if ever there was one, and Nita will be a big help, too."

"Don't worry about payment. We'll figure out something," Rachel added, her brown eyes smiling. "And it will not be charity."

"But I already owe you a small fortune."

"And you'll pay what you can, when you can. You have two children who need you, and you can't take care of them alone just yet." She gave a wry lift of her eyebrows. "You can't even fully take care of yourself yet. Doesn't it make sense that if you want them to come home you need to get better as fast as possible?"

Of course it did.

"Fine, then," Meg had told them at last, and Colt and Rachel had promised to take care of everything.

They'd done just that, even making certain her children were taken to her aunt Serena's place. Now she was home, and Ace Allen and his mother were here, as well.

Slipping on her worn shoes, Meg wandered into the larger space that served as both kitchen and parlor. She stood in the center of the room, hugging herself against a sudden chill despite the warmth of the morning.

Why had she ever thought she could come back here to live when memories of Elton were everywhere? She looked at the door and imagined him lounging against the door frame, three sheets to the wind, that arrogant, cocky grin on his handsome face before he…

No! No! Don't think about it.

Malignant memories bombarded her from every direction, and she couldn't think for the raw terror rising inside her. She turned in a circle, rubbing her upper arms, confused and unsure what to do next.

Stay calm and breathe. Remember that Elton can't hurt you anymore. If things seem overwhelming, think them through. First things first.

Rachel's voice, so soothing and sensible, played through Meg's mind. She drew in several deep breaths and felt the anxiety begin to recede.

First things first. Coffee. She wanted coffee. Needed coffee. Was there any here? She couldn't remember. She recalled Gabe Gentry saying that he'd brought a few staples from the general store, but she had no idea what. She knew she should eat something, even though she had no appetite. Was there water in the bucket?

She pressed her fingertips to her temples to try to still the pounding in her head.

"Breathe."

She drew in another deep, cleansing breath. Her ribs throbbed in objection. Bit by bit, her alarm began to ease and her composure returned.

Coffee. There were plenty of logs lying next to the fireplace, along with a bucket filled with slivers of resin-rich pine knot that would flame in an instant. Her heart sank. She could handle the kindling, but there was no way she could lift the logs with one arm. Doc Rachel was right. She wasn't able to do this alone just yet.

A loud rapping at the door sent her spinning around, the fire forgotten.

"Come in," she called and was surprised at how hoarse and unused her voice sounded.

The knob turned, and Ace Allen, former inmate, the man who had killed her husband, stepped inside. The small room seemed even smaller when filled with his powerful presence.

As if he sensed her sudden discomfort, he left the door open and made no effort to move closer.

"Hello, Mrs. Thomerson. Do you remember me? Asa—Ace Allen? I've seen you in town a few times."

His voice was deep and as dark as his hair, but smooth-dark, like the black velvet dress Mrs. Van-Sickle sometimes wore to church in the wintertime.

His eyes were compelling, perhaps because their crystalline blue was so unexpected in someone who, for the most part, had received his mother's looks and coloring. There were lines fanning out at the corners of those incredible eyes. Faint furrows scored his forehead and his cheeks were lean and held grooves that might be attractive if he were not so stern-looking. There were scars, too, around his eyes and on his cheekbones. It was a face on a first-name basis with grief and pain. For the briefest second, her heart throbbed with empathy.

"Why?"

He seemed as surprised by the question as she was to hear it break the stillness of the room.

"Why?" he asked, frowning.

"Why do they call you Ace?"

His gaze never faltered. He seemed to relax the

slightest bit. The subtle shift in his demeanor and stance eased Meg's own distress somewhat.

"When I finished at the mission school in Oklahoma, I went to Texas and became a tracker for the Texas Rangers. They all said I was an ace tracker, so they shortened my name to Ace."

He—an Indian—had finished school. Meg had no schooling past the fifth grade. As usual, she felt lessened by the knowledge. "So…hunting men down is something you know how to do."

It was a statement, not a question. From the expression in his eyes, he took it as an accusation, even though she hadn't meant it that way.

"I shot him in the thigh, Mrs. Thomerson." Instead of exhibiting the evasiveness she expected, he confronted the specter standing between them head-on.

"He'd taken a shot at Colt that only missed by inches. I yelled and he turned and took a shot at me, just as I pulled the trigger. His bullet grazed the fleshy part of my arm, and I flinched. The plan was to disable him, not take his life."

He stated his side of things with simple directness and no attempt to color his actions one way or the other. She heard sincerity in his voice. Her instincts told her it was real, but she'd learned the hard way that her intuition was often wrong. Making a lie sound like the truth had been a hallmark of Elton's. After a while she'd learned not to believe anything he said. Ace Allen wasn't Elton, but those lessons had been hard-learned and not easily forgotten.

"I didn't know Elton shot at you, too."

It was the first she'd heard of that. Or maybe, like so many other things, she'd heard but didn't remember. Though she had no doubt that Elton had brought about his own demise, she now understood more fully why Ace Allen had taken aim.

"I know I can't expect you to forgive me, but—"

"Please," she said, cutting him off with a raised hand. Hearing and accepting his apology, feeling as she did about Elton's death, would be the height of hypocrisy. "No more. Please."

He gave a sharp nod.

Meg focused on his face. "I can't pay you."

He shrugged in a surprisingly graceful lift of wide shoulders. "It doesn't matter. The way I see it, I owe you."

No. She owed him a debt of gratitude for releasing her from her prison of pain and degradation. Meg lowered her gaze so he wouldn't see the truth in her eyes. He wanted to make amends for leaving her without a husband, though he, more than most, would know that Elton hadn't been worth much in that regard. Her husband's contribution to the marriage had been two babies too fast and the occasional promise when he was filled with drunken self-pity to do better. Of course, when he drank even more and she did something to irritate him, that promise, like all his vows, went by the wayside.

"Sheriff Garrett says you can do laundry."

"I can do a lot of things," he said with a solemn nod. "I won't let you lose your business. It's the least my mother and I can do. Maybe you can take up your mending again now that you're home and the ironing as you get your strength back."

Thinking of her future, she moved toward the fireplace and rubbed her hands up and down her upper arms. Taking up her mending would be a step toward standing on her own two feet again, and it would give her something to do, keep her from feeling so helpless. Give her an inkling of hope that she could make a good life for herself and her babies.

"I'll make a fire and start some coffee, if you'd like."

Meg whirled at the sound of his voice. She'd been so caught up in her thoughts that she'd forgotten that the stranger was still there.

Within arm's reach.

Her heart stumbled and she pressed her palm against the sudden tightening in her chest. How had he moved so silently? So quickly?

As if he knew she was uneasy with his nearness, he went to the fireplace and squatted in front of the hearth, removing himself to a more comfortable distance.

Her nerves quieted. How silly of her to feel frightened by him, she thought. Just because he looked dangerous didn't mean he was. After all, he'd helped her before, and two of the most respected people in Wolf Creek had vouched for him.

Meg had no solution for feelings she knew were irrational, but at the moment it hurt her brain too much to try to figure things out. She decided to fetch a shawl to ward off the chill that gripped her despite the warm morning. As she neared the door to her room she found herself drawn to the other bedroom, the one she'd avoided the previous night.

The door swung wide on creaking hinges and she stepped inside. The room was musty-smelling after being empty so long. She reached for the tin of talcum powder that sat atop the chest of drawers next to a stack of diapers. Doctor Rachel had given it to her when Lucy was born.

Twisting the top, she sprinkled a little onto the inside of her forearm and smoothed it in. She'd used the precious gift sparingly, but still, it was almost gone. She raised her arm and breathed in the pleasant lavender aroma. The scent triggered a vision of her now-nine-and-a-half-month-old daughter, Lucy. Lucy of the sweet smile, chubby cheeks and dimpled knees.

She was filled with the sharp pain of loss, and at the same time her body ached in memory of nursing her baby. But that was finished. Her milk had dried up weeks ago. Meg closed the top of the canister and blinked her burning eyes. What was done was done. There was no changing it. All she could do was move forward. Somehow.

Holding the oval-shaped tin against her chest, she let her gaze roam the room. Some of the church ladies had come out and tidied up for her return. Teddy's cot, with his ragged, patchwork rabbit sitting atop the pillow, was neatly made, as was Lucy's little bed. Meg's heart twisted in sudden longing.

"You must miss them terribly."

She whirled at the sound of the unfamiliar feminine voice. Though middle-aged, the Indian woman who stood there was lovely. Her slender body was attired in a patterned skirt and blouse. A leather thong with a black stone hung around her neck. Her oval face boasted nicely shaped eyebrows, a bold nose and a pretty mouth. Ace Allen's mother stood before her, a soft, understanding look in her dark eyes.

Meg tried to rein in her emotions and gave a short nod. "I'm afraid—" she swallowed "—they'll forget me."

"Then we should bring them home."

The first hope she'd felt since the day that had changed her life stirred in her heart. "But I… There's no way I can take care of them yet."

"I'm here to help for as long as you need me."

Rachel Gentry was right. There were good people in Wolf Creek. "I can't pay you," Meg whispered.

"I'm not looking for money," Nita said. "Christians help each other out. And please accept my condolences on the loss of your husband. I understand how you're feeling right now."

Nita and her son were Christians? Meg hoped her surprise didn't show on her face. That thought fled in the face of another. How could Nita know how Meg felt about Elton? Had she said something while under the influence of the laudanum?

"I lost my Yancy when Ace was eighteen." A wistful smile curved the older woman's lips. "A logging accident. It was hard, even though Ace was grown and away at school. Maybe harder since he wasn't around to share my grief."

Meg wondered what Nita Allen would say if she

knew Meg felt no grief, only joy. This gentle woman who'd had a good husband wouldn't understand that.

"I think it was the quiet that was the most disturbing," Nita confessed.

The blessed, blessed quiet... No cursing. No yelling. No foul name-calling...

"Yancy was so big and blustery and fun-loving, he kept everyone laughing so hard they could hardly breathe when he was around, especially when he'd get to singing those Irish ditties."

Elton had kept everyone on pins and needles. Afraid to breathe. Afraid to do or say anything for fear of it being wrong. And no one felt like singing in his presence.

"Your husband was Irish?" Meg asked, clinging to the single fact that jumped out at her.

"He was," Nita said with a reminiscing smile. "And as handsome as could be. Ace got his blue eyes from his father, though Yancy's were not so light as Ace's."

Meg found the notion of two people marrying from such disparate upbringings an intriguing notion. "Was it difficult, the two of you having such different backgrounds?"

"I won't say it was always easy, but we had enough love and joy to make up for the bad. My Yancy was not a boring man." Memories softened her smile. "He loved life and he was filled with Celtic songs and stories and romantic dreams and notions."

"How on earth did you meet?" Meg asked, her problems forgotten as Nita Allen talked of her love for her Yancy.

Another smile curved the older woman's lips. "He'd come to America and was just roaming around, looking over his new country, he said. We were drawn to each other from the very first and married, despite my parents' fears of the worst."

"And the worst never happened?"

"People can be very judgmental," she said cautiously. "A white man married to an Indian woman...well, it isn't always accepted. Yancy and I were able to look past it in most cases, and more often than not, people were standoffish rather than mean."

Meg, whose own background wasn't something she liked to remember, had often found that to be true with her, as well. With her mother's lifestyle often the talk of the town, most people just avoided her as if she had the plague.

"Acc is the one who suffered the most. He grew up not really belonging anywhere. He lived with us until he convinced us to let him go live with his grandmother on the reservation, but he didn't fit in there, either. He was neither white nor Indian. He was a half-breed. Believe me, it's much more than a name people call you. It took him years to figure out who he is and what his place is in this world."

Meg looked through the open door into the other room, where the man they were discussing had a small fire burning in the hearth. He still squatted, placing logs just so. It was strange to think of him as vulnerable in any way.

"And as for repayment," Nita said, "someday you can return the favor."

"What?" Meg said, as the words brought her thoughts back to their conversation.

"Someday I may need help from you, or someone else will. Then you'll do what you can for them."

Yes, she would. Somehow she would find a way to pay back the woman with the kind eyes and gentle manner who had taken her mind off her guilt and hopelessness for a few precious minutes. She would pay her back somehow, if it were the last thing she ever did.

Ace heard the murmur of the feminine voices coming from the other room. Maybe he should have listened to his mother. Maybe Meg Thomerson would have been a bit more receptive to his apology after some time spent with his mother and a good breakfast, but he had overridden her wishes and insisted on speaking to Meg first. At the time it had seemed imperative that he tell her what was on his mind and in his heart, to try to make her understand, at least as much as he did, about what had happened that day.

Elton's widow hadn't wanted to hear what had happened or know how terrible he felt for robbing her of her life's partner. As rotten as Ace knew Elton Thomerson was, he'd still been a husband and a father, and Meg must have seen something in him to love or she would never have married him.

He brushed his palms on his thighs and stood, planting his hands on his hips and staring into the flickering flames. He wanted to do the right thing, but he could already see that it would be much harder than he'd expected.

Chapter Two

The breakfast Nita fixed might have been sawdust for all the enjoyment Meg seemed to take from it. Ace and his mother made desultory conversation while trying not to watch the way Meg pushed the eggs and bacon around on her plate, partially covering them with buttery grits when she thought no one was looking so that they would think she'd eaten at least a few bites.

"Do you think we can go get the children today?" she asked as Ace mopped up some yolk with a piece of biscuit.

"You can't go anywhere," Nita said. "Doctor Rachel made that very clear to us. She said the wagon trip out here about did you in, and she doesn't want anything setting back your recovery."

"I'll be better when I can hold them," Meg insisted.

Ace thought he heard a bit of steel in that voice, the first emotion he'd seen besides her very real fear of him and that disturbing melancholy. He shot his mother a questioning glance, and she answered with a slight lift of her eyebrows and an almost imperceptible shrug of her shoulders.

"I was going to cut down a couple more trees this morning," he told her, pushing back his chair and carrying his plate to the waiting dishpan of hot sudsy water. "Winter will be here before we know it, and I don't want you running short of wood."

He didn't tell her that if her husband had been taking care of his family instead of robbing people, the wood would have been cut and stacked long ago, making starting a fire a lot easier.

If you hadn't killed him, he could be here right now, doing just that.

The voice inside his head that reminded him of his sin several times a day put a stop to his mental criticism of Elton Thomerson. Meg had grown up a country girl; Ace figured she knew you needed a mix of seasoned and green logs to keep things going.

He also knew there was no way the fragile woman sitting across from him could have done the work herself. How would she have kept warm when she'd burned the scant supply of wood in the lean-to? Despite his attempt to not think ill of the dead, a muscle in his jaw knotted in anger at a man he'd known only by reputation.

He turned to face her, leaning against the narrow table that sat against the wall. "Would you like for me to go and see about bringing them home instead of chopping more wood?"

"Would you?" she breathed, a glimmer of hope in her eyes.

"I'd be glad to."

It wasn't a lie. Though it was fitting that he step up and do the right thing for the woman whose husband he'd shot, Ace hadn't realized how hard it would be. Not the work—he was no stranger to backbreaking labor—but seeing how badly she was scarred from the whole experience, and how deep her wounds were, left him feeling angry and helpless. He just wanted to fix things for her.

A sharp gasp caught his attention. His gaze flew to Meg's. The pure terror on her face took him aback. What had happened? Why was she so afraid? Seeing no cause for her alarm, he shot his mother a questioning glance and saw reproach in her eyes.

Understanding slammed into him. His loathing for the way Elton Thomerson had treated his family, especially his wife, had somehow slipped past his usual outward show of stoicism. Seeing his feelings stamped on his face had terrified her.

It was time to go, time to get away from this woman who had somehow gotten beneath his skin the first time he'd seen her sunny smile and worked her way into his heart. For all the good it would do him. Whether or not Elton was corrupt and no good, Meg had no doubt loved the man she'd married. Ace would do well to remember that.

They finished the meal in silence.

"I'll go to town and talk to Rachel," he said when they were done. "If she says it's okay to bring the children home, I'll make the arrangements."

"Thank you," Meg said, without looking up. He

gave his mother a brief hug goodbye and left, thinking that winter would be a long time coming.

Feeling guilty and with nothing to do, Meg sat on a stump in the shade of an oak tree and watched Nita finish stacking the wood Ace had split earlier.

Overcome with guilt, Meg waited until Nita stopped to rest a moment and said, "I feel terrible, sitting here watching you work. I'm not used to being so lazy."

"It isn't called laziness, child. It's called healing. There's a difference. All you need to do is sit there and soak up God's sunlight." She gave Meg a teasing smile. "But if you feel you *must* do something, you can help me shell the last of the beans that dried on the vine. I thought I'd fix them for supper. It would give you something to do and be a great help to me."

"Yes, thank you," Meg said, excited to be doing something worthwhile after being inactive for so long. "Where are they?"

"In the basket next to the front door."

Meg went through the back door and crossed the room. The basket was sitting right where it was supposed to be. Meg bent over to pick it up with her un-injured arm. As light as it was, the effort still brought an ache to her chest.

She was about to carry it out when she realized she'd seen the basket before. It, or one very like it, had shown up on the porch with predictable regularity while Elton was in prison. More often than not, it contained vegetables, though sometimes there was coffee or a little meal or flour. When she'd emptied the basket of its bounty, she'd put it back on the porch, only to find it gone the next morning. Then it would show up again in a week or so.

Sometimes, she'd find a skinned and gutted squirrel or rabbit hanging on a nail, always fresh, as if someone were aware of her habits and knew just when she'd be there to find them. It never entered her mind that she should be concerned about someone watching her comings and goings, since she wasn't the only person who had benefited from the mysterious benefactor. Ace and his mother were rumored to be responsible, but no one had ever proved it one way or the other. Recognizing the basket was as close as anyone was likely to come to solving the mystery.

Readying herself for the task at hand, Meg tied a faded apron around her waist. She'd lost weight since the day of the shoot-out, and Rachel said she was far too thin. Well, maybe her newfound freedom would relieve her of some of her worry, and her appetite would come back. Most likely, she'd just find a new anxiety, like how she was going to provide for her kids. She couldn't rely on the good folks of Wolf Creek forever.

She was almost to the door when she realized she was thirsty. No doubt Nita was, too. The water bucket sat on the tall table she used for preparing meals, beneath the dishpan that hung on a nail and two shelves that held her few dishes and bowls. The long narrow stand, the same one Ace had leaned against that morning, was pushed against the wall, and the breakfast dishes she'd insisted on washing were draining on a flour-sack towel.

After filling two spatterware mugs with the fresh water Nita had carried in, Meg looped the basket over her right arm and took the drinks outside. It felt good to be useful, even in a small way.

Nita, who was just finishing with the wood, smiled when she saw Meg with the mugs. "Thank you," she said, taking one. "I was getting pretty parched."

Automatically, the two women headed toward the shade of the small back porch, where two unpainted, worse-for-wear ladder-back chairs sat. Meg took the one with the sagging woven seat, leaving the better one for Nita, then went back inside to fetch a couple of thick pottery crocks. Nestling them in their laps, the two women began to shell the beans into the bowls, letting their aprons catch the hulls. They worked in companionable silence for a while before Meg said, "I want you to know that I appreciate your help, Mrs. Allen. Your son's, too. There's no way I could have come home if you weren't here. And I certainly couldn't have brought the children back."

"We're glad to do it. And please call me Nita." She ran her thumb along the seam of a shell. Beans popped out into her bowl. "Tell me about your babies. I've seen them around town with you, but don't know much about them except that they're beautiful."

"Thank you." Meg beamed with pride. "Teddy is nearly three, and Lucy is going on ten months. I've missed them."

"Haven't you seen them these past weeks?"

"Yes, but not nearly enough. My aunt and uncle are

taking care of them, and with the way they work, it's impossible for them to get off the farm very often."

"Farming is a challenging occupation," Nita agreed. "You have good ground here. It doesn't seem as rocky as some places."

"It's a pretty nice ten acres," Meg said. "I always wanted to plant some corn and things to help out during the winter, but my husband...he wasn't much for farming."

He was more for robbing and cheating and womanizing.

"I couldn't seem to find time since I stayed so busy with my laundry and mending."

"Plus the care of two little ones."

Yes. Her little ones.

She loved Teddy and Lucy more than anyone on earth, but sometimes...there were worries that lay heavily on her heart, and there wasn't a single soul to talk to about her concerns. She and her mother, Georgina Ferris, whose well-known escapades with the opposite sex were a frequent topic of gossip in town, had been at odds for years, which left her Aunt Serena and Uncle Dave.

Elton hadn't wanted her having any friends, hadn't wanted her to have frequent contact with anyone. He'd seen to it that they lived far enough from Serena for visits to be almost impossible, and they'd drifted apart since her marriage. Still, it was her aunt and uncle who had stepped up to take the children while she recuperated.

"Is something bothering you, child?"

Meg looked up and found Nita's keen gaze fixed on her. There were a lot of things bothering Meg. It was so tempting to let out her doubts and fears.

Tell her, Meg. Tell her that your greatest fears are that you will turn out like your mother and that your children will turn out like their father.

The little voice inside her head appealed to the lonely, needy part of her she kept hidden from the world. She wasn't sure why she felt so compelled to confess her worries to this stranger, but as strong as the urge was, Meg knew she couldn't do that.

One of her mama's favorite sayings was that no one wanted to hear another's problems, that you shouldn't air your dirty laundry to the world. Of course, Georgina Ferris's laundry was dirtier than most.

"I was just wondering if you have other children?" she asked, knowing by the look in the older woman's eyes that she recognized the lie for what it was.

Nita shook her head. "Even though Yancy waited on me hand and foot, I lost two babies early in my pregnancies and two to illness when they were little more than babies. Ace is my only living child."

As a mother herself, Meg was keenly in tune to the older woman's pain, even though the words were delivered with little emotion. Though Elton had still tried to maintain his image of caring and decency during her pregnancy with Teddy, he had slapped her a time or two. There had been another baby before Lucy that had not survived, maybe because Meg had been so worn down and distraught and Elton had been so furious that it had happened so soon. She would never know.

By the time Lucy came along, he had abandoned or lost any good that had ever been in him, though Meg suspected that what little decency she'd seen was nothing but a show he put on for the world. It was a wonder that she'd carried Lucy to term.

Meg and Nita worked silently for several moments, the kind silence that usually came with long acquaintance and deep trust. The soft rattle of dried beans falling into the bowls and the sweet song of a robin wove seamlessly into the tranquillity of the late September day. Simple, everyday sounds. The sounds of life and peace.

Peace. Would God give her peace once she put enough distance between herself and her memories, or was she destined to be forever lost in this numbing emptiness?

Be still and know that I am God. The favorite passage stole quietly into her mind. She took a deep breath and looked around her at the familiar barnyard scene and realized at that moment she was at peace, that there were no memories tormenting her. Could she dare to hope that her joy in living would return to her this way? In small moments of contentment and little snippets of the day that were filled with something as simple as the soothing sameness that was in itself a sort of peace? Could she trust that God would help her healing by blessing her in tiny ways throughout the coming days? After what she'd suffered at Elton's hands, it would be hard.

But what about Nita? Though she'd been blessed with a husband who cherished her, her life had been filled with problems and grief, too. She'd lived close to God and yet she'd lost four children and her son had gone to prison—not once, but twice. She and her family had been ridiculed and persecuted because she was Indian. How did she reconcile that with her love and trust of God? How had she stayed so optimistic and encouraging?

Meg wanted to ask, but thought she'd spilled enough of her guts for one day. Besides, it wouldn't be a good idea to become too dependent on Nita or to like her too much, because she would be gone before year's end, taking Meg's secrets and fears with her.

The trip to Wolf Creek and back gave Ace plenty of time to think about things. He'd needed to escape from the fear he saw in Meg Thomerson's eyes that his nearness seemed to generate. His guilt was bad enough without adding to her distress. He never wanted her to be afraid of him for any reason.

Meg had caught his eye the first time he'd seen her. About a year ago, he'd come back to Wolf Creek after spending a few years in Oklahoma, where he'd tried to put himself back together again after his two-year stint in prison. Tiny, blonde and green-eyed, she'd captured his interest with her bright smile and shy but sweet disposition.

It hadn't taken long for him to find out she was married. It had taken even less time to learn that she had one child with another on the way and that her husband was pretty much good for nothing. At best Elton was handsome and shiftless; at worst, he was a drunk, guilty of ill treatment. Whenever Meg was a victim of Elton's anger, the news spread around town, but she always seemed to put it behind her. She never lost her smile or gave in to her circumstances. He admired her for that and even for sticking to the no-account man she was married to. She was one of the strongest women he'd ever known, and Ace figured she and her kids deserved better, but then, that wasn't for him to say.

He recalled the day he and Colt and big Dan Mercer had surrounded the Thomerson house. Every minute of that day was etched into his mind in vivid detail— from getting word that Elton and his cohort had escaped from prison to the moment he'd felt for a pulse in Elton's neck.

What he remembered most was cradling a battered Meg in his arms on the way back to Wolf Creek, trying his best not to jar her lest he do her even more harm than Elton had. In retrospect, he should have hitched up her old wagon and made her a pallet in the back to transport her to Rachel's, but he hadn't wanted to take the time. Besides, he knew it might be the only time he ever got to hold her.

Especially since you robbed her of a husband and her children of a father. The cruel reminder slipped into his mind as it was wont to do when he least expected it.

There was no making amends for something like that. To say he was sorry and ask for her forgiveness would be a waste of breath. He hadn't yet found the courage to tell God he was sorry for shooting Elton and ask for His forgiveness. Ace figured that until he could go through a day and not feel glad that Elton was dead, asking for the Lord's forgiveness would be futile. He didn't want to add to his other transgressions.

He was miserable without the Lord to lean on, weighed down by guilt and disgust. He'd been through a lot in his life. Clinging to a deep spiritual belief system and parents who demanded his best, he'd managed to come through all his trials with minimal emotional scarring. He wondered if that would be the case this time or if this second accidental killing would be his undoing...one way or the other.

He wasn't sure how he could get to the point of true sorrow for what he'd done, since sly memories had a habit of slipping into his mind at unexpected times. Like Elton's taunting voice saying that he wondered how Meg was paying Ace for the food he left on her doorstep.

Ace ground his teeth at the remembrance, and his horse danced sideways, the reins a conduit for his anger. Until he could forgive Elton for his treatment of Meg and himself for his lack of sorrow, the best he could do was help Meg get through the next few weeks.

He returned to Meg's house just after noon and saw her leaning against the trunk of one of the big oaks in the front, staring up into the leafy branches that shaded her. Though her hair still straggled around her thin face, and purple shadows beneath her eyes proclaimed her sleepless nights, she was still beautiful.

When she heard his horse, she looked at him, an expectant expression on her face instead of the alarm he halfway expected. Relieved, he nodded at her in acknowledgment and shifted his gaze to the front porch, where his mother was busy scrubbing the graying pine boards with a broom and a bucket of soapy water.

He couldn't help noticing the chunk of wood missing from a board a few feet from the edge. He'd put that mark there, a warning to Elton, who'd grabbed his wife by the arm he'd already broken. Just thinking about it brought back the fury that had overwhelmed him at the other man's callous disregard for the woman he'd promised to love and cherish.

Ace closed his eyes and drew on the strength that had seen him through the dark days of his incarceration. When he opened his eyes, he was calmer, at least on the outside. Meg was following him toward the house.

His mother glanced up from her scrubbing, and he experienced a surge of love he never failed to feel whenever he looked at her. Like Meg, life had given her many hardships, yet both women had overcome their struggles with enviable serenity and a quiet dignity.

Nita Allen suffered no fools but had often been deemed foolish by her husband for her willingness to give of herself and her means, even to those the world labeled as takers and users. She was often hurt, yet she never changed, nor would she ever.

So here she was, lending a hand to yet another lost and needy soul. He hadn't been the least surprised when she volunteered to help. He smiled at the busy image she made. From years of living with her, he knew that the water had already been used inside the house to clean something or other. When she was done with the porch, she'd water some plant or another with what was left. Nita Allen wasn't one to see anything die or go to waste, especially a life.

He could smell the beans she'd brought. They were simmering in a cast-iron Dutch oven hanging on a metal tripod that straddled a small fire she'd built outside. It smelled as though she'd added some salt pork from the smokehouse. There would be johnnycakes and wild green onion and perhaps some potatoes fried in the bacon grease left over from breakfast.

Neither woman spoke, but they both watched as he rode closer and slid from the gelding's back. It struck him how very different his mother was from the small blonde woman, yet how very alike their expressions were. He suspected that they had other traits in common, too.

"Well?" Nita asked with her customary bluntness.

Ace looped the reins over the hitching post. "Rachel says she thinks we should wait to bring the children home."

The anticipation in Meg's eyes faded. Something inside him stirred in response—the innate need born in a man to protect, to shield loved ones from any more pain.

"But she told me they could come home." Meg's voice was laced with distress.

"Rachel says she knows mothers and she knows you, and she's afraid you'll overdo it with them around. She doesn't want you picking one of them up without thinking or chasing after them yet. She said you need at least another week or so to heal before taking up their care again. I'm sorry."

Instead of answering, Meg turned and walked away. Her back was ramrod-straight, and her chin was high. She placed her feet carefully, as if she were so fragile she might shatter if she took a wrong step. And perhaps she would. Automatically wanting to comfort her, Ace started to follow.

"Let her go." Nita's voice was low but firm. "You, of all people, should know that she has to work through this in her own way, in her own time."

They watched as she entered the edge of the woods at the side of the house, the same area where Dan Mercer had wounded Joseph Jones.

Ace thought of all the time he'd spent in the forest through the years. It was the place he'd often gone as a boy to try to sort out his mixed heritage. He'd learned of his Celtic past from his father, who'd filled his mind with stories of bards and fanciful tales and a strangely melodic language he'd tried so hard to learn.

From his mother he absorbed tales of the Keetoowah, the spiritual core of the Cherokee people, who stressed the importance of maintaining the old ways. The mission school he'd attended taught him the tenets of Christianity.

Vastly different, yet with fascinating similarities. All sought solitude for meditation and prayer. Both cultures thought nature was sacred. God had created a place of nature for Adam and had walked with him in the garden; God spoke to Adam there.

The woods were Ace's garden. His refuge. A place

to listen for the voice of God that whispered in the wind and murmured through the leaves of the trees and the rustle of creatures going about their day-to-day lives: finding nourishment, caring for their young, being wounded or hunted. Dying. Becoming part of the earth again, continuing the cycle put into place before the earth was spoken into existence. Ace believed that the voice of God could still be heard in the world around you, if you chose to hear it.

He watched Meg disappear into the woods and wondered if she would hear God's voice. According to those who knew her, she had a strong will and a stronger faith. This time, though, her injuries were worse, the pain deeper.

He wished he could follow her, but he had trees to fell and wood to chop. He would be here when she returned. Deep in his heart, he knew that he would always be there for Meg.

Chapter Three

It was late afternoon when the noisy clatter of the dinner bell roused Meg from a light sleep. Nita must have supper ready. Meg felt a pang of guilt for leaving the older woman to do her work, but she'd been crushed by the news that she would not be snuggling with Teddy and Lucy just yet. Knowing Rachel was right didn't lessen her disappointment. Holding her babies would have been a sweet balm to her spirit.

As she'd done so often in the past when things threatened her peace of mind, Meg had wandered into the woods, making her way to her favorite spot, where she'd always sought the healing quiet of the solitude. Soon after Elton had moved her away from her family, she'd found this place that had become her sanctuary, a place set apart from the reality of her life.

She'd often brought the children there and found comfort in the whisper of the breeze and the pleasing chuckling of the water that meandered along the rocky bottom of the creek, running to some faraway place she could only imagine. She'd often wished she could follow it.

A bed of moss beneath a giant oak made a cool spot for a nap when she needed a place to rest. In the early spring, she'd brought a broom to sweep away the leaves that had fallen throughout the winter. By chance or God's design, a wild rose of vibrant pink had sprawled and clambered up and over the branches of a nearby dogwood in early summer, reaching for what sunlight it could find in the mostly shaded area and sending its sweet fragrance adrift on the whispers of the vagrant breezes.

Even now, in the heat of September, hurting and wondering if she would ever feel whole again, she found the place beautiful. The rose and bleeding hearts had long since bloomed and the resurrection fern had dried up and curled into brown patches that clung tenaciously to the sturdy limbs of the tree, yet the sweet blessing of one good rain would return them to vibrant life.

Secure in the hope that that same vibrancy of life would be hers again someday, she'd closed her eyes and waited to see if the peacefulness of her surroundings would work its healing powers as it had in the past. In time, it did. She'd let her thoughts wander at will, from wondering where the creek emptied to how much Lucy and Teddy had probably grown since she'd seen them and how she would give them a better life. They might not have a lot of extras, but she would make up for it by giving them a life filled with love, not fear.

Throughout the afternoon, she'd heard the measured

whack of an ax against wood. Ace cutting down more trees. She must have dozed off while thinking about him and his mother and their willingness to help a woman who was more or less a stranger.

Awake now, Meg sat up and looked around, hardly able to believe that she'd slept so long and without any frightening dreams. She wondered if finding a few hours of peace was a good start for putting the pieces of her life back together and knew that Rachel would say it was.

This had always been a perfect spot for dreams and plans. Dreams. Like all young girls, she'd had dreams once, daydreams about a life free of the shame of her mother's life. Visions of finding a way out. Then she'd met Elton, with his good looks and his own extravagant fantasies of big houses and fancy clothes and trips to San Francisco and St. Louis, and she felt that her yearnings had come true at last.

Those dreams had begun to flee one after the other, shortly after marrying him almost four years ago. Now her mind was filled with plans, but the dreams were as dead as her husband and the resurrection ferns that had turned brown from the heat of summer.

When she'd first awakened at Rachel's and was coherent enough to make sense of the things she was told, she'd thought—even dared to hope—that with Elton out of the picture her life would change for the better. Would it?

She gave her head a shake to dislodge the brief moment of melancholy and doubt. She could not let gloomy thoughts take hold. She had no idea how to move ahead with her life, but she knew that if she dwelled on her mistakes and her past, Elton would win, and she refused to let him rule her life from the grave. She would get past this, just as she'd always done.

Could she, all alone?

One day at a time.

Rachel's gentle reminder. In the early days, when Meg had been racked by unbearable pain, Rachel had told her to take it hour by hour, one day at a time. She also told her that to find her way back she should look for joy in small things, telling Meg that God sprinkled dozens of blessings throughout our days if we only took time to look for them.

Well, there was this place, she thought, looking around. It was surely a blessing, since she had slept without interruption or bad dreams. And, she thought wryly, as the dinner bell rang a second time, it was a blessing that she didn't have to cook supper.

She stood and stretched her arms and shoulders with care to get out the kinks. Giving her faded skirt a shake, she started back to the house, using the much-traveled deer path. She was a few feet from the clearing when she stopped dead still. Like a wild creature sensing danger, her head came up. A sharp gasp escaped her.

Ace stood on the path, blocking the way to the house just as the breadth of his shoulders obstructed the clearing behind him. He loomed over her. The lacy pattern of sunlight and shadows gave his lean cheeks the impression of wearing war paint, like the pictures she'd once seen in a book. He looked untamed and dangerous. His sheer size and raw maleness were overpowering, making her feel weak and defenseless.

"What are you doing here?" The breathless question sounded accusatory even to her ears.

His troubled blue eyes seemed to take in every inch of her in a single glance. "Mother was worried that you'd gone too far or got turned around. She was afraid you didn't hear the bell, so she sent me to find you." His voice was deep and low, mesmerizing. The frightened fluttering of her heart slowed.

"I was down by the creek. I'm fine. I'm here." The explanation came out in a flurry of words that tumbled over one another.

"So you are."

Did she imagine the flicker of gentleness that came and went in his eyes? Without warning, he reached out toward her. With a little yelp, Meg cringed and brought up both arms to cover her head in an instinctive gesture of self-preservation. The action was both instant and involuntary as he took her wrists gently.

Breathing hard, eyes shut tight and little whimpers of fear escaping her, she waited for the blow to come, but instead she heard words murmured in a language she didn't understand. Soft words. Soothing words.

"Meg." His deep voice persuaded, compelled. "Look at me."

Bit by bit, as if she were expecting it to be a trick, she did as he commanded and saw the remorse clouding his crystalline eyes.

"I'm sorry," he told her. "I didn't mean to frighten you. I was only going to get a twig out of your hair."

Trembling, Meg stood stock-still. She'd seen regret before. She'd heard all the ways to say *I'm sorry*. She'd learned not to believe them. Still, something held her immovable. What was it she saw or felt in him that told her she could trust him, despite his fierceness?

"No!" she heard herself saying. "I…I'm s-sorry."

Moving at a snail's pace so as not to alarm her further, he let go of her wrists. Then he held one palm up in a *stop* gesture and reached out with the other to pluck the twig from her tangled hair. Without a word, he held it out to show her.

She felt like a fool for overreacting. "Th-thank you," she whispered, daring to let her gaze make contact with the disturbing intensity of his. She saw nothing there but the same tenderness she heard in his voice.

He nodded. "I know you don't have many reasons to believe anything a man says, but I want you to know that I have never raised my hand against a woman, and I never will. You have no reason to be frightened of me. Ever."

Then, without waiting for her to answer, he held out his arm as if he were a well-heeled gentleman from the city and she an elegant lady going to some fancy social event. She looked from his arm to his face in confusion. She was no lady. He was no gentleman.

When she made no move to take his proffered elbow, he stepped aside for her to precede him to the house. She brushed against him on the narrow path and caught a whiff of leather and pine. She stumbled and glanced up at him, even as he reached out to steady her. Once again her heart began to beat faster, but not because she felt threatened. Disturbingly aware of his nearness, she cast an occasional glance over her shoulder just to be sure he was keeping his distance.

She didn't want him too close. The question that tumbled through her mind was *Why?*

Nita Allen had been busy while Meg hid out in the woods. Her little house fairly sparkled. Ace's mother had taken the cleaning begun by the church ladies a step further. She'd scrubbed the windows, polished the beat-up buffet table Elton had found dumped somewhere and brought home to her in the wagon, and washed the dust from her scant collection of mismatched plates and glassware. Even the globes of her kerosene lamps glistened. The scents of fried potatoes and pinto beans mingled with the sharp, clean odor of the lemon balm and beeswax used on the furniture.

A crockery bowl with a blue rim was filled with crisp fried potatoes. The pot of beans with a dipper in it sat on a folded dish towel, as if the table were a piece of fine furniture that the heat might ruin. A plate of corn bread baked in a small iron skillet had already been sliced into wedges. A bowl of fresh butter sat next to a jar of pickled beets, and a small plate held wild green onions.

It was like walking into a fairy tale. Thanks to two strangers, her tired little house felt like a home, but not because it was clean and tidy. Even though she worked hard and had little, Meg had always kept a clean house. Elton demanded that.

The difference was in the *feel* of the house. She'd experienced no dread or fear when she'd walked through the door. No need to walk on eggshells to keep whatever tentative peace might be found on any given day. No need to guard her tongue lest she set Elton off with some innocent comment. No dread of when he might come back and shatter the temporary respite she found during his absences. No despair.

The house felt warm. Welcoming.

As she stood letting the differences register on her mind, her stomach growled. Nita smiled. Embarrassed, Meg turned away, but for the first time in weeks, she thought she might be able to eat more than a few bites.

When they were seated and thanks had been given for the food, Ace began to pass the bowls. Feeling she should show her appreciation in some way, Meg scooped a few potatoes onto her plate and said, "The house looks so nice, Mrs. Allen. Thank you. And supper looks delicious."

"It was nothing. Things were already in order. It just needed the dust washed off. Did you have a good rest this afternoon?"

The question surprised Meg as much as the answer that came to mind. She realized with something of a start that she had rested, and not just during the time she slept. There had always been something about her special spot that brought her at least passing peace. Today had been no different.

"Actually, I did."

"That's good." Nita finished filling her plate and turned to her son. "Did you let everyone know Meg is back in business?"

"I did," he said, slathering some fresh-churned butter onto a piece of corn bread. "Hattie is really excited. So is Ellie." He glanced at Meg. "Keeping up with the wash has been hard for them since you've been out of commission."

Though she did weekly laundry for a few of the more affluent people in town, Hattie's Hotel and Boardinghouse and Ellie's Café were Meg's biggest customers.

"I'll take the wagon in and pick up what they have early in the morning," Ace told her. "If you ladies will have the kettles boiling when I get back, we ought to be done by evening."

It was good to know that her services had been missed, but she hated relying on someone else to do her work, even though she needed the money.

"I think I'll be able to help with the ironing," she said, looking from Ace to Nita, knowing Ellie and Hattie would have several tablecloths to do up with starch.

"I don't think it will hurt you, either," Nita said, "as long as you don't overdo things. I'll bring my ironing board and iron in the morning. Together, we should be able to get it done in no time."

It sounded like a good plan, Meg thought. She would iron until she got tired, do any mending and gradually work back into her regular routine. A step toward taking control of her life once again.

Meg had forgotten that the Allens would be leaving soon, probably as soon as the supper dishes were done. After all, they had their own chores to do. It occurred to her with something of a start just how much of a sacrifice they were making to help her. Their log cabin that sat on a small parcel of land must be at least four miles from her placc.

Though she hadn't wanted to spend any more time with them than necessary, now that she knew they were about to go, she wondered how she would pass the long hours of the night that stretched out before her, empty and lonely.

She'd spent more nights than she could number here alone except for her kids, and she'd stayed by herself last night, but she had been so numb, so exhausted from the ride from town, that sheer weariness and a dream-filled, restless sleep had claimed her early in the evening.

Now that she was a bit more herself, the thought of being alone was a little troubling. Except for the kids, she'd been here alone when Elton and Joseph Jones had barged in after their prison escape. Without warning, her heart began to race. As Rachel had taught her, Meg forced her breathing to a slow rhythm and reminded herself that she no longer had to worry about either of them.

"I hope it's all right, but I picked up some mending for you while I was in town."

She was grateful for the sound of Ace's voice that brought her wandering thoughts back to the present.

"Just a few things Ellie needed repaired and a tear on the sleeve of one of Daniel's shirts that Rachel hasn't had time to get to."

"Oh, yes!" Meg heard the relief and eagerness in her voice. "That's fine. It will give me something to do when you go."

"Would you like for me to stay with you tonight?" Nita asked. "I don't mind. Ace can take care of things at home."

Longing to take her new companion up on her offer, Meg stiffened her spine and her resolve. She'd stood on her own two feet all her life, and just because things were…different now was no reason to become a namby-pamby. She couldn't lean on others forever. She raised her chin a fraction and met Nita's troubled gaze. "Thank you, but I'll be fine."

She gave her attention back to her plate, almost missing the look that passed between mother and son. When the meal was over, Meg was surprised to see that she'd eaten almost all the food she'd dished up.

"Being outside did you a lot of good," Nita said, rising and gathering the plates.

"I guess it did."

"You'll be surprised at how much better you feel the more you're able to be up and around. No one has much appetite when they're lying around all day."

Meg hoped it was true. She was tired of being an invalid.

By the time they finished the supper dishes, dusk was settling in. Ace came in from outside and put a couple of eggs into the wire basket sitting on the scarred buffet.

As she watched, he rolled his shoulders and arched his back. "I gave the horse some oats and penned up the chickens and the pig for the night. I think things are fine until morning."

"The question is, are you?" There was a teasing note in his mother's voice.

Something that might have been a smile crossed his face. "I'm getting a little stiff," he admitted. "I haven't chopped this much wood in a long while, and I'm not as young as I used to be." He leveled a teasing look at his mother. "Which means you aren't, either."

Meg watched the loving interaction between the two. How long had it been since she'd heard that kind of lighthearted banter? Her second thought was to wonder how old he was. Older than she was, for certain, yet he looked to be in his prime, and he was certainly strong.

A wisp of memory floated across her mind, drifting in and out of her consciousness. She was hearing the sound of hoofbeats in rhythm with the steady heartbeat that throbbed beneath her ear, feeling powerful arms around her and knowing without a doubt she was safe.

Her thoughtful gaze found the man who had suddenly come to play such a huge role in her life. She recalled being told he had taken her to Rachel's. It had been Ace's arms that held her. Ace's strength that made her feel safe. Ace's heart that beat against her ear. Common sense told her that a man who would hold her so gently would not hurt her, but putting aside the wariness her past had instilled in her would not come overnight.

"Well, if there's nothing else we can do, we'll go," Nita said, scattering Meg's thoughts. The older woman crossed the room and enveloped Meg in a tender embrace. Unaccustomed to displays of affection, she stiffened. Her mother had seldom hugged her—Elton, never—and it had been a long time since she'd seen her aunt Serena.

Nita drew back at once, sensing that she'd overstepped some invisible boundary. "I'm sorry," she said. "I'm afraid I'm a hugger. I forget not everyone is."

Without waiting for Meg to reply, she gave a little wave and slipped through the door. Ace followed, leaving Meg alone with her memories, her sorrow and an aching loneliness. She wished Nita would come back. Wished she could let the older woman hold her in her arms while she cried out all her fears and worries.

Wished she could cry.

Nita and Ace climbed onto their horses and turned them toward home. "She's worse than I expected," Nita said as they rode side by side.

"She's been through a lot."

"I know."

"When I went to fetch her for supper, I saw a twig in her hair and reached out to get it." His tormented gaze met his mother's, and his jaw knotted in a familiar way. "She covered her head and shrank away from me."

"It's what she knows," Nita said after a moment. "It's what she's come to expect from men."

"It isn't right," he said in a low, savage voice. "It isn't fair."

"Oh, my son," Nita soothed, tipping her head back to look up at the first star of the evening. "You, of all people, should know that much of what happens in our lives is neither right nor fair."

Yes. He should know. Did.

"Rachel told me today that she's never seen Meg cry a single tear."

He never stopped to think that neither had he, though he'd been imprisoned wrongly twice, beaten and even left for dead on one occasion. He considered tears a weakness, something men didn't indulge in. He was Cherokee, from a people who had suffered more than he ever would. And he was Irish, able to put on a smile when it was called for.

"Some wounds are so great that the only way to survive is to lock them up in a little box and put them somewhere deep inside," Nita said.

"Do you think she'll get better?" Ace would rather rely on his mother's knowledge than that of any other healer.

"Rachel says the mind is a strange thing," Nita told him. "I pray that she will, in time. We can't lose heart or patience."

She looked at Ace with a solemn expression. "I'm proud of you, my son. Though it has taken time, I can say that the things you've been through have not destroyed you. They've made you the man you are. That's something we need to try to get through to Meg. And it's something you need to keep in mind, too, when you think about your role in all this."

"Killing Elton, you mean?"

"Yes. You've come too far to let that destroy your faith and your peace."

He sucked in a harsh lungful of air and met her tender gaze with one of defiance. "I hate that it happened, but God help me, I'm glad he's dead."

Instead of chastising him for the un-Christian thought, his mother asked, "Why?"

"I'd think that's pretty obvious. He was a terrible human being who mistreated his wife."

"And you care for her."

Ace was appalled by her suggestion. Or perhaps he was appalled that his mother had discovered his secret.

"I think you care for Meg Thomerson. I think you've cared for her for a while. And I think that's why you're happy Elton is dead."

"Are you saying that you think I did it on purpose?" he asked with a scowl.

"Of course not!" his mother scoffed. "You're experiencing remorse for having feelings for another man's wife. Those feelings only increase your guilt for taking his life, even though there is no doubt in anyone's mind that it was warranted.

"You are not a killer, Ace Allen, and despite your past, you are an honorable man. I think that is why you are having such a hard time making peace with yourself," she said.

"How can I ask God to forgive me when I'm sorry for shooting him but not sorry he's dead?"

"Maybe it's time you stopped trying to figure out things on your own and have a serious talk with God."

Chapter Four

Meg was awakened by the rooster before sunrise the next morning. Groggy with sleep, it took her a moment to realize where she was. A rash of memories assaulted her. Expecting to find Elton passed out in a drunken stupor next to her, she whipped her head to the side. She was alone in her feather-tick bed. There was no snoring Elton, no reason to be afraid ever again.

A soft September breeze blew through the screen tacked to the outside of the window frame. The days were already growing shorter and the mornings would soon become crisp and cool. She'd always liked autumn, though she couldn't say the same about winter.

Thinking of winter brought a new problem to mind. How would she manage to get the laundry back and forth with two children in tow? Arkansas winters were known for their fickleness. The weather might be as warm as spring one day and rainy and cold or snowy a few days later. The previous winter, Meg had dropped the children off at Widow Hankins's house on the way to town and picked them up again on her way home. The widow had watched them while Meg did the laundry. According to Rachel, Mrs. Hankins wasn't doing so well, and Meg figured the last thing the older woman needed was to chase after two little ones.

One more problem to work out, she thought, getting to her feet. Well, at least she had plenty of time to do so. What else could a person do while they were mending and ironing but think?

As she was stripping off the worn cotton gown she'd donned soon after the Allens left, she caught a glimpse of her reflection in the wavy, splotched mirror leaning against the wall. Even in the room's dim light, she gasped at what she saw. There were no visible scars on her body; they were all inside, but the ordeal had taken its toll, nonetheless.

Never one to carry any extra pounds, she'd lost so much weight that she looked as if she were recovering from a long illness, which she supposed she was. There were dark smudges beneath her eyes as well as tiny lines at their corners, and her mouth tilted downward at the sides. Her tangled hair looked as dull and lifeless as she felt.

It was enough to bring her to tears. Almost. But she'd learned the hard way that crying changed nothing, except to sometimes make things worse. No, she would shed no tears over how she looked, just as she'd shed no tears since Elton's last assault. Things were what they were and all the crying in the world would not change them. Aunt Serena would tell Meg that she was still pretty and that inner beauty was the important thing—not that she was doing too well in that department, either. Rachel would tell her that the weight would return and that her body would soon regain its glow of health. She would tell Meg to be thankful she'd been spared to bring up her children.

Done with self-pity, Meg drew in a shallow breath and donned the clothes she'd worn the previous day. When she and Nita finished the laundry, she'd heat some water for a bath and make herself presentable. A good scrub always made her feel better.

She thought of Ace plucking the twig from her hair and wondered in dismay what he'd thought about her appearance. Her body flooded with sudden shame. For all her faults, maybe *because* of her excess vanity, her mother would be the first to tell her that there was no excuse for not taking care of your appearance. Aunt Serena would second that, but for entirely different reasons.

Filled with a new purpose, Meg went into the kitchen, coaxed the coals into a small fire and put on some coffee. Oh, how she'd love to have one of those pretty white granite stoves Gabe Gentry sold at the mercantile!

She'd no more than thought it when she pushed the ridiculous notion from her mind. In the scheme of things, a new stove was the last thing she should be thinking about. She went back to her room, picked up her brush and began to work the tangles from her hair. By the time she'd finished and plaited it into a long braid, the coffee was ready and the early-morning sun was streaming through the clean windows.

After a breakfast of coffee and leftover corn bread

fried in a little butter and drizzled with sorghum molasses, Meg took the remainder of the mending and a second cup of coffee to the front porch. She sat in the warmth of the morning sun while she plied her needle. She was finishing her third cup when she saw Nita coming down the lane on her horse. She was alone.

"Good morning!" the older woman called as she neared the house.

"Morning," Meg replied, wondering why Ace wasn't with Nita.

"Ace went on into town to pick up the laundry in our rig," she explained without Meg asking. "He thought it would save a little time. He has my ironing board with him."

Meg nodded. She still found it hard to believe that a man as blatantly masculine as Ace Allen would willingly do wash. "So we should have the water hot enough to start by ten or so," Meg said, calculating how much time the trip both ways would take.

"I'd say that's about right," Nita agreed, sliding from the gelding's back and hitching him to the post.

"I was wondering if we could heat some water for a bath when we finish," Meg asked in a hesitant voice. "I...I'm a mess."

"Of course we can," Nita said readily. "I should have thought of that yesterday. Why don't we heat your bathwater along with the laundry water and have that behind us before Ace gets back? That way we can throw in your clothes at the end. We have plenty of time."

"That sounds wonderful. Thank you."

"Have you had breakfast?"

Meg nodded. "I fried up some corn bread and had it with butter and molasses."

"One of my favorites," Nita said with a smile. "I see you're working on the mending Ace brought yesterday."

"Yes. I didn't quite get finished last night." She blushed. "I fell asleep in the rocker."

"Well," Nita said, "that's not so surprising. You've had a busy couple of days, and you're still recovering. You'll be back to your old self soon."

Her old self. Meg didn't think she wanted to be her old self. That woman was spineless and took what was dished out to her, whether she deserved it or not.

"Why on earth not?"

"What?" Meg looked at Nita sharply. What had she asked?

"I was asking why you said you weren't sure you wanted to be your old self," Nita explained.

Meg couldn't believe she'd spoken her thoughts aloud, but since she must have, she felt obligated to provide an answer. "The old me put up with a lot of things I shouldn't have."

"Did you have a choice?"

"Not much of one," she conceded.

"I suppose I'm being nosy, but I've been wondering if you knew how your husband was when you married him."

Meg's burst of bitter laughter had no place in the sweet tranquillity of the morning. She gave a negative shake of her head and kept her eyes glued to the shirt in her hands. "I didn't have a clue. All I knew was that he was handsome, and he told me I was beautiful and

I believed him. He bought me presents and said he'd love me forever."

Seeing the sympathy on Nita's face, Meg gave a helpless shrug. "I knew he drank a little, but before we married I never once saw him lose his temper. He was always so sweet and gentle."

"So you fell in love with him."

"Love?" A sigh trickled from Meg's lips. "I'm not even sure what love is. I thought what I felt was love. Maybe it was. Or maybe I just liked the notion of loving someone. Whatever I felt, it didn't last long after we said our 'I dos.'" She shot Nita a quick embarrassed look. "I'm sure you've heard around town that I was expecting Teddy when Elton and I married."

"There are always those who like to gossip," Nita said. "I don't pay much attention to it."

"In this case it was true."

Nita offered her another of those kind smiles. "At least he had the decency to do the right thing and give the child his name."

"Yes, well, we'd all have been better off if he hadn't," Meg said in an acerbic tone.

Nita Allen might be shocked by the bold confession, but Meg didn't care, and she made no offer to explain. How could she tell this giving woman who'd come through so many trials herself about her fears for her children? How could she explain that she was afraid that her sweet Teddy would grow up to be like his father, or that somehow the inability to see a man's true colors had been passed down from Georgie to her and on to her precious Lucy at the moment of her conception?

She couldn't. Nita Allen might be easy to talk to, and she might be as good as gold, but there was no way Meg could share her deepest fears with someone who was little more than a stranger.

Fearful that Nita would comment on the rash statement, Meg took a final stitch in Danny Gentry's shirt, bit off the thread and scooped up her sewing basket. "We'd better see to those fires."

By the time Ace returned with a wagonload of dirty linen, fires were burning hotly beneath both of Meg's cast-iron kettles. She'd shaved a cake of lye soap into the boiling water while Nita carried more from the well to fill two galvanized rinse tubs.

As if they'd worked together before, the two women set about sorting the clothes as Ace brought the baskets to them. Nita allowed Meg to help as they rubbed the cake of soap into the stains and scrubbed them on the washboard before punching them down into the boiling, sudsy water.

Overriding Nita's protests, Meg insisted on tending one of the kettles. It didn't take but a few moments to realize that though her ribs had more or less healed, she was not up to the work. Weeks of inactivity had left her as weak as a kitten. She might not like relying on strangers, but there was no doubt that she couldn't do things on her own just yet.

Catching the look of concern in his mother's eyes, Ace made fast work of adding more wood to the fires. Then he went to take Meg's place. Their gazes clashed, headstrong green to cool, determined blue. He held out his hand for the stick she was using to transfer the clean tablecloths from the hot water to the rinse tubs. To his surprise, she relinquished the cut-off broom handle with no argument.

"Go sit on the porch," he said. "Your clean hair will get all smoky if you stay out here. Mother and I have this."

Self-consciously, she raised a hand to her hair with a look of surprise. "Oh, I hadn't thought about that."

The first thing he'd noticed when he pulled into the yard was that Meg was wearing a different skirt and blouse. She'd obviously bathed and washed her hair. The straight blond mass was still damp and hung more than halfway down her back, glistening like spun gold in the sunlight. Ace couldn't help wondering what it would be like to bury his face in the silken strands and breathe in its clean scent. Would it smell like lavender? Jessamine? Some other sweet-smelling flower?

"I suppose I could go and make the starch."

"That would be good," he said, pleased that she hadn't cringed away from him. "We'll need a lot."

"I know."

Mesmerized by the slight sway of her hips, Ace watched her walk toward the back of the house. He blew out a frustrated breath and glanced over at his mother. Nita's face wore an expression of contemplation.

He suppressed a sigh. Like most mothers, his didn't miss much. As always, she was in tune to every nuance of his emotions, and from what she'd said the evening before, she knew exactly how he felt about Elton Thomerson's young widow.

Meg went inside and mixed up the flour and cool water that would be used for starch. When she was reasonably certain it was lump-free, she added boiling water to thin and smooth the mixture.

She was about to go and tell Ace that she was ready for him to carry it outside when she felt a prickling of awareness on her neck. Placing a hand over her heart and whirling around, she saw him standing in the doorway, a hand braced on either side of the aperture.

It was a pose often adopted by Elton, one where he regarded her coolly or mockingly...even appreciatively, depending on his mood. For a few painful heartbeats, it was Elton who stood there. Her eyes closed to shut out the sight. The room dipped and her knees gave way. Strangely, her only thought was that when she hit the floor she would reinjure her newly healed ribs.

It never happened. One second she was falling like a one-egg pudding; the next she was being held against something hard and warm and realized that she hadn't fallen after all. She was in a safe place. Then she seemed to be floating through space, perhaps through time. Something soft gave beneath her, and the warmth and safety started to move away. With a cry of protest, she reached out blindly, pulling it close once more. The scent of pine and wood smoke enveloped her.

Something rough brushed her cheek. The harsh abrasiveness had no place in the velvety shadows and security of her shelter. With a murmur of denial, she forced her heavy eyelids upward. She didn't expect to see a bronze face shadowed with a day's growth of beard so near hers. She could see the slightly darker blue that fanned out in a starburst shape from the pupils of his eyes and smell the sweetness of mint-scented breath against her face.

She realized that her arms were looped around his neck. A flash of unease flickered through her, triggering the instinct to shove him aside and flee his overwhelming maleness. The feeling vanished as quickly as it appeared. This man meant her no harm. Instead, she heard herself say, "You smell like peppermint."

Tiny lines appeared at the corners of his light blue eyes. Their customary coolness was warmed by the same smile that claimed his mouth for the space of a heartbeat. The brief upward curve did miraculous things to his austere features. He looked less threatening. More approachable. Handsome in a severe sort of way. Another flutter of alarm scampered through her, but this was different somehow and frightening for reasons that had nothing to do with the fact that he was a big, powerful man.

"And you smell like sunshine," he told her before she could make sense of her emotions.

The oddly poetic words sounded strange coming from a man who looked as if he'd been hewn from a bold outcropping of Arkansas rock. It wasn't the sort of thing she expected to hear from a man like Ace Allen.

And why not? What do you really know about him?

Nothing but what she'd heard around Wolf Creek, and that wasn't much. She'd been too busy keeping body and soul together to pay much attention to talk—good or bad.

She wasn't aware that her hands still rested on his shoulders until he circled her wrists with his fingers as he had the day before. Lowering her hands, he stood. She realized then that he'd been sitting on the side of the bed.

"You rest. You must have done too much this morning, or you wouldn't have fainted."

Meg sat up quickly and regretted the hasty action. "It wasn't the work." She didn't want Ace and his mother thinking she was overdoing things. "It was you."

Shock molded his features and he leaned toward her. "Me? What did I do?"

Too late, she realized that once again, she'd done or said the wrong thing. Hadn't Elton told her time after time that she was the one who made him crazy and caused him to do the things he did?

"I'm sorry!" she cried, holding up her hands in a futile attempt to keep him away. To her surprise, Ace mimicked her action and took two steps backward, away from her. The simple, nonthreatening action slowed her racing heart.

She swallowed and forced herself to look up at him. "I'm sorry. It's just that when I…when I saw you standing there with your hands on the door frame just… looking at me, I just… I saw…"

Ace didn't say anything for several seconds. Then, to her surprise, he went to the doorway and stood in the same pose that had caused her such alarm.

"Look at me, Meg," he said in that deep voice. "Who do you see?"

"What?" She frowned, unsure of what he was doing and wondering at the sorrow reflected in his eyes.

"Who do you see standing here?"

What did he want from her? she wondered in confusion. "I see you," she said at last. "Ace Allen."

"Exactly. You see the mixed-breed ex-convict who killed two men. I'll always be sorry for that, but if you never believe anything else about me, you can believe that I would never deliberately harm a hair on your head."

His statement was much the same as what he'd said the day before in the woods. It seemed he was determined that she knew he was no threat to her.

"You're wrong," she told him.

His dark eyebrows snapped together in a frown. "What?"

"What you said. I didn't see th-that at all." She hurried to explain. "Elton used to stand in the doorway like that a lot. For just a moment when I looked up I saw him, not you. I...I'm s-sorry."

"I'm not Elton, Meg."

His voice held an urgency she didn't understand. "I know that."

"Do you?" he persisted. "Look at me. Do I look like Elton?"

"No," she murmured. Elton hadn't been nearly as tall, and unlike Ace he'd been almost too good-looking to be masculine. She'd once heard him called pretty.

No one would ever think of Ace Allen as pretty. Striking, surely. Magnificent, maybe. Pretty, never.

"No, and I don't act like him. Can you see that? Do you believe it?"

Still confused, but knowing somehow that her answer was of utmost importance, she whispered, "Yes."

He nodded, and the torment in his eyes faded. "You have nothing to be sorry for, Meg Thomerson. That's something else you can be certain of, so never think it again." With that, he turned and left her alone with her thoughts and a lot of questions.

After a lunch of cheese-and-tomato sandwiches that Meg fixed while Ace and Nita finished the laundry, they took up the sheets and tablecloths that had been drying on nearby bushes and replaced them with those they'd just starched. The tea towels were spread on the grass to dry, and the tablecloths and sheets were sprinkled with water and rolled up until it was time for them to be ironed.

With three people, they finished the laundry in less than half the time it would have taken Meg working alone. Ace used the soapy water to scrub the back porch, watered the thirsty plants with the rinse water and turned the tubs upside down until they were needed again.

As she dampened and rolled up the starched linens, Meg sneaked glances of him through the open window. He worked with an economy of movement and an easy grace that was unexpected in a man his size. She tried to imagine Elton offering to do the wash while she recuperated from an illness and almost laughed aloud.

When he finished, Ace took his rifle and ax and went to chop down a few more trees. Nita and Meg set up both ironing boards and started the ironing, even though they knew there was no way they would finish until the following day. Still, it felt good to do something productive, to know that she'd taken another step toward healing herself both physically and mentally. A rush of hope suffused her.

She'd never minded ironing. It had always been a time for her to think through her problems and make plans for the future. Nita, too, worked mostly in quiet, but with the older woman standing just a few feet from her, Meg felt compelled to make some conversation. At the same time, she was at a loss for something to say.

She wasn't really shy, but Elton's daily activities hadn't been the sort a man wanted to discuss with his wife when he came home at day's end, and talking to two small children made conversations a bit one-sided and not very stimulating. The only time she had an opportunity to talk to fellow grown-ups was when she went to town, and those exchanges were usually confined to questions about how she and the kids were doing or to discuss when she would return with the clean laundry.

Her world was so confined and her learning so limited that she felt incapable of holding up her side of a conversation. Everyone she knew, including Ace, was more knowledgeable than she would ever be on any range of topics.

"Ace says you need a real clothesline for the amount of washing you're doing."

The statement pulled Meg from the web of her thoughts. She glanced up from the tablecloth she was ironing. A clothesline? Now, wouldn't that be wonderful? It was something she'd often dreamed of having, but never supposed she would.

"Maybe someday when I get some of my doctor bills caught up," she said.

Nita nodded. "What else should he do to get you ready for the winter?"

Winter. How she dreaded its arrival! It was miserable working over the boiling kettles in the summertime and keeping the inside fire going for the irons, but at least the clothes dried in a hurry.

Though the southwest Arkansas winters were usually milder and shorter in duration than many places, winter often brought a whole new set of problems and its own share of misery. Cold rain. Sometimes sleet and ice, and even the occasional snowfall. No matter how hot the fires, it was still frigid work, and often days passed when it was so nasty and wet she couldn't possibly do any laundry.

"I'm sure there are a lot of things that need doing, but I hadn't given it much thought," she said after a moment.

"And no wonder," Nita said with a gentle smile. "You've been through a lot. Thank goodness there's still time to get things when he finishes getting the wood put by."

"Shouldn't he be...working somewhere else or doing

things for you?" Meg asked, frowning at her companion.

"Ace is real smart and got a good education, but he doesn't do well working for other people. Says it stifles him. Nate Haversham offered him a job at the bank, but Ace says he's not cut out for suits and ties or being in a cage all day."

Meg was amazed. Ace had turned down a good-paying job at the bank so he could hunt and trap? Why would anyone do something like that, especially when he had an education? Before she could bridle her tongue, she'd asked Nita that very question.

"It is strange, I know, but he says he's happier outside hunting and trapping and such. He tans the hides to sell."

"Is there enough money in that to take care of things?"

"Depending on the hide, they'll bring from twenty-five cents to a dollar each." Nita shrugged. "He's a grown man and it's none of my business, and Ace has always made his way doing this and that and gotten by just fine. Of course, he does other things that help me, too."

Meg looked at her expectantly.

"We always have a big garden and I have an orchard," Nita told her. "What I don't can or dry for winter, we sell to Gabe at the mercantile. Some of the people in town who don't garden depend on us for fresh fruit and vegetables. A while back, he traded out some work with Caleb Gentry for a hog, and we'll slaughter it when it turns cold. With our other smoked meat, we're pretty much set for winter."

Meg couldn't imagine being so well prepared.

"Ace keeps a lot of needy folks in food, too," Nita added, almost as an afterthought.

That bit of news was not surprising. Meg offered the older woman a wan smile. "I know. When I saw the basket with the dried beans yesterday, I figured out that I'm one of them. Thank you."

Nita laughed. "Several people suspect he's the one, but no one knows for sure. He never brags on what he does. I know I sound like a boastful mother, but he's a good man, and he's been through a lot, like you."

Meg supposed Nita was talking about Ace's two prison stints. Meg had never thought about the two of them having anything in common, but now that it had been pointed out, she could see similarities in their pasts. She wondered what prison was like and what sort of things he had suffered there. More important, she wondered how he'd come away from the experience with his faith, peace and decency intact.

"Tell you what," Nita said. "When we finish the ironing tomorrow, maybe you and Ace can take a look around and see what else needs doing. He won't mind taking care of anything."

"That sounds like a good idea," Meg said, though she had no idea how to tell if something needed doing or not. Elton hadn't spent much time here, and he'd pretty much let things run down since they'd bought the property. As long as the shed was standing and he had a place for his horse and a pillow for his head, he couldn't have cared less if the rest fell down around him.

Meg knew what she'd like to do, but had no way of knowing if her ideas were practical or not. She had little if any money to have things done, and besides, most of her longings were nothing but pipe dreams, like the clothesline and a new stove.

After more than an hour of ironing tablecloths and sheets, Meg was exhausted and figured her new friend was, too. Nita was strong, and though she wasn't old by any means and didn't look her age, she was no longer young, either, and she'd already done a hard day's work.

"I think it's time for a break. My back is getting tired," Nita said, almost as if she'd read Meg's thoughts. "Why don't we sit and have a glass of cold water on the back porch?"

Meg suspected that even though the older woman probably was fatigued, it was likely she'd seen the weariness on Meg's face and was blaming the halt on herself to persuade Meg to take a break. She admitted to herself that she was tired enough for them both. As the day had progressed, she'd begun to see that the doctor and her new caretakers were right. She wasn't ready to be on her own just yet. She might not like being beholden to anyone, but she was a long way from being well enough or strong enough to get back to her regular routine. She certainly didn't want to overdo it and have a setback.

"That sounds good," she said with a weary smile. "We can warm up the breakfast coffee and have some of those leftover biscuits from breakfast with a little of that peach jam I made."

Nita nodded and smiled. "I do like a little something sweet in the afternoon."

Ace felled a couple more trees and chopped off the limbs. Tomorrow he would bring Meg's gray mare to snake the timbers out of the woods and then he could cut them into proper lengths and split what was too big to burn easily.

He'd worked all afternoon with memories of Meg Thomerson filling his mind: the way the sunshine glistened in her freshly washed hair, the remarkable green of her eyes, the delicate wing of her eyebrows and the shape of her wide mouth. He also thought of the way it felt to have her arms around his neck. Knowing it was pure foolishness, he couldn't help imagining coming home to her every evening and having her throw her arms around him in pure happiness that he was there.

He must be getting daft in his old age. There was no way a pretty woman like Meg would have any interest in him. Not with his background. Why, she couldn't be much more than twenty or so, and he was approaching his thirty-first birthday.

It had been a rough thirty years. But for the grace of God, he'd have never come through it as well as he had. From the time he was young and had begun to wonder where he belonged in the world, he'd struggled to reconcile the quick, hot temper that often got him into trouble with an inborn sense of right and wrong. Even though he'd sown his share of wild oats as a young man, he'd always been tormented with a powerful guilt afterward.

The two years he'd spent in prison for getting into a brawl and unintentionally killing a man had gone a long way toward improving his control over his temper and forcing him to take a good look at his life. Seeing how quickly and unexpectedly everything could be snatched from you, he'd started taking stock of where he was and where he could go from there.

Looking for something to help ease his inner disquiet, he'd done a lot of Bible reading. To his surprise, he'd found peace in the pages of the worn leather Bible a visiting preacher had given him. He learned about forgiveness and the grace of God, and over time, he realized the only way a man could be truly happy was to live a life for Him.

Faced with the reality that in one way or another, he'd been running from the differing cultures of his heritage, he spent the remainder of his time in jail mulling over the various aspects of his mixed birthright and considering the ways they had shaped him. This time, instead of dwelling on the discrepancies in his background, he began to appreciate and reflect on the similarities.

While still in prison, the preacher who'd given him the Bible had baptized him in a nearby river while a small army of guards stood watching, just in case he tried to make a break for it. His act of obedience had been cause for a lot of jeering and laughter, but he hadn't cared. He'd begun to treat things he'd once con-

sidered burdens as opportunities to change his thinking and to grow in faith and trust in God.

More important, he began thanking God for the
things that caused him grief and pain or disappointment. That was no easy thing to do, and he often failed
miserably. Even so, his newly found faith made the
long days of tending the prison garden, shoeing the
guards' horses and doing mountains of laundry bear-
able.

When he was released, he'd chosen to go to the reservation in Oklahoma. He'd needed time to put things
into perspective, to heal inside and out. After a few
years, he'd decided to come back and help care for
his mother.

One of his deepest desires was to build a life that
would make him acceptable to the people in Wolf
Creek. It wasn't that he was often mistreated or in-
sulted, but neither was he welcomed into the small
town's social circle, which made finding a suitable
wife next to impossible. There was no Indian popula-
tion from which to choose a bride, and even if any of
the available ladies had appealed to him, he doubted
his suit would have been acceptable.

Then he'd seen Meg Thomerson coming out of Ellie's
Café, and as improbable as it seemed, he had known in
an instant that she was the one he'd been waiting for.
When he'd discovered she was already taken, he'd let
a new kind of bitterness eat at him. Eventually, common sense returned and he realized that as much as he
didn't like the situation, it was time to practice what he
professed to believe.

Did he trust that God had his best interest at heart, no matter what happened? Did he truly believe that if he lived for the Lord, that everything that happened to him had a purpose and would work out the way it was supposed to? As hard as it was, with much prayer, he did his best to accept that he'd come to care for a woman he could never have.

It was plain to see that Elton was often away doing whatever it was that he did, leaving his wife and two children to fend for themselves. Ace saw how hard Meg worked and heard through the Wolf Creek grapevine how she struggled. He'd seen her lifting heavy baskets of laundry into and out of her rickety wagon. A couple of times he'd approached with offers to help, and she'd always accepted with a sunny smile of thanks that brightened his day and cheered him until the next time he saw her.

He was careful to not make a habit of helping her too often, or people would talk. He discovered that there were other opportunities to relieve a little of her burden as well as those of others in need, so that no one could fault him.

He'd started leaving food of some kind for Meg and several others who struggled to make ends meet every now and then. The grapevine provided the information that she was appreciative and, like the others he helped, she wondered who her benefactor might be. Ace had been secure in his secret until the day of the showdown on the Thomersons' front porch.

Elton had known, or at least guessed, what Ace was doing, or he wouldn't have made the crude comment about wondering how Meg was paying for the things he left for her and the kids when he'd dragged her out onto the porch to taunt the posse.

Ace's anger had flared upon hearing the insult and witnessing Elton's treatment of her when she was already in pain, and he had foolishly taken a shot near Elton's feet. For the space of a single breath Ace had wished he could put a bullet through Thomerson's black heart. But the bullet that killed Elton wasn't fired until later, and it hadn't been meant to kill.

Still, it was that brief moment when he'd lost control and shot into the wood of the porch that he thought about when, hours later, Elton had sneaked through the woods and taken a shot at Colt. Wanting nothing but to save his friend, Ace had returned fire and his bullet had gone awry and hit a major vessel. He'd gone over those few seconds a million times, and each and every instance his common sense told him that he had done nothing wrong. He'd saved his friend and perhaps himself.

Contrarily, it was that moment when he'd wished Elton dead that came to mind every time he told Meg that the killing was an accident.

Ace didn't know how he could go on day after day, caring for her, wanting to help her. Being with her was pure torture.

Winter couldn't come soon enough.

Chapter Five

It had been a good but hard day. As Meg watched her self-appointed helpers' wagon disappear down the road, she knew she would rest well. As weary as she was, it felt good to be doing something worthwhile. Idleness did not suit her.

Closing the door, she turned and looked around the small room. Her kitchen was clean and the mending was done. There was nothing to do until the following morning. A wave of loneliness swept through her.

She imagined what her evening might have been like before the incident. Elton was often gone, so it would have been just her, Teddy and Lucy. Once they'd had their supper, she would get them washed up and ready for bed. They would cuddle in Teddy's little bed, and Meg would tell them a story, read them a fairy tale or nursery rhyme from the books that had been given to her by the ladies at church. Sometimes she sang songs like "Froggie Went a-Courtin'" or "The Fox."

Then they would say their prayers and she would tuck Teddy in and rock Lucy to sleep.

When they were down for the night, she would be alone, just as she was now. The difference was that she'd always had things to do to fill the hours until her own bedtime. Mending. Ironing. Cleaning. But all that was done.

She looked around the room again, thinking that it was too bad that she had nothing to read besides the children's books. Even though she wasn't the best reader, she'd always loved books and the stories captured within their pages. Unfortunately, she'd never had the time to pursue that love. She was always too busy trying to get by, and there was no pay for spending time in such a frivolous pursuit.

Through Ace, Rachel had told her to use the next week or so as a time to pamper herself. Meg wasn't sure what that meant, but it sounded as though she was supposed to spoil herself. How on earth was a grown woman supposed to do that? She recalled the times she did special little things for Teddy or with him, things that were not part of their everyday activities. Was that pampering?

She thought of her bath earlier in the day. Nita had insisted that Meg take her time. Even in the cramped washtub, it had been nice to sit in the water until it grew cool with no one calling for her and no one waiting for her to do something for them. It had been special to lather her hair with the small remaining piece of sweet-smelling soap Elton had bought her once when he was trying to worm his way back into her good graces. As Nita poured warm rinse water over her hair, Meg *had* felt special…spoiled, even. If that was pampering, it was nice.

On impulse, she stirred up the fire and put the kettle back on. Taking down one of the blue speckled cups and the plain brown teapot her aunt had given her, she measured out a couple of spoonfuls of the tea that Gabe and Rachel had left for her.

It occurred to her that she could make some cold tea for Nita and Ace the next day. The water from the deep well was good and cold, and the sugary sweetness would make a nice treat for them all.

While the kettle boiled, she pulled the long swath of her hair over her shoulder and buried her face in it. Thank goodness it still smelled sweet and clean, she thought as she began to braid it. She could thank Ace for reminding her that the smoke would mask the smell of her clean hair.

Abruptly, she paused in the midst of her nightly ritual. What kind of man thought about keeping a woman's hair smelling clean? It was certainly not the kind of thing that would ever enter Elton's mind.

Ace Allen was nothing like any man she'd ever known. How had he even known her hair was clean? How had he become so sensitive to the things that were important to a woman? It certainly wasn't the sort of thing you learned in prison. Had Nita somehow made him aware? Meg doubted she'd ever know, but just recognizing that one small thing about him changed her perception of him the tiniest bit.

After braiding her hair, she changed into her gown

and grabbed a light shawl. When her tea had steeped, she poured herself a cup and added a generous amount of honey. Then, fetching Teddy's book of fairy tales, Meg padded barefoot onto the porch, settled into the old rocking chair and set the spatterware mug on the wooden box she used as a table.

Even though the evening was still warm, October would soon arrive. To someone who watched the changing of the seasons as closely as she did, it was easy to see that the shadows were changing position as the year wound down.

With a sigh she wasn't even aware of, Meg tucked her feet under her and thumbed through the book, looking for a story world to fill her mind and enable her to escape reality for a few moments.

She chose "Cinderella," one of Teddy's least favorites but one she suspected Lucy would love as she grew older. Wasn't the idea of being rescued and loved by a handsome prince every young woman's dream? It had been her own dream once, and she'd believed Elton was her prince.

Forget Elton! Forget dreams. There is no Prince Charming to rescue you, take you to his castle and give you everything your heart desires.

What did her heart desire?

The question sprang from somewhere deep inside her. She didn't want riches or fancy things. She didn't want to sit around all day and do nothing. She liked being busy, though she admitted that it might be nice if she didn't have to work quite so hard. She wanted a place that offered peace and happiness where she and the kids could go at the end of the day. It didn't seem like too much to want or to ask for, but God hadn't seen fit to give it to her.

Enough! Blaming God was not only futile, but also wrong. She'd made the choices that shaped her life, and some of them had been bad choices. She could blame only herself for her circumstances.

Her expression set in grim determination, Meg forced herself to focus on the story. In a matter of moments, she was caught up in the words of the story, imagining each scene. As she sipped at her tea, she did manage to slip into that world of make-believe. Two cups later, it grew too dark to see the words and, with a regretful sigh, she rose, gathered up her things and went inside.

Moments later, she lay in her bed, thinking about the story. If that tale—and the others in the book— were to be believed, there was a man out there somewhere, just waiting to come to the aid of a woman who needed him. The problem was that that kind of man was in short supply in Wolf Creek.

Ace came to your aid. The random thought caught her off guard. He had. She suspected he was motivated at least in part by guilt, but he was still here, helping her. As she drifted off to sleep, she saw again the quiet dignity and the pain in his eyes as he'd told her that there was no reason for her to ever be frightened of him. And, drifting in that state between sleep and wakefulness, she believed him.

Once Ace drove the wagon out of sight of Meg's little house, he'd handed the reins over to his mother and slipped back through the woods so that he could watch over Meg during the night. At Rachel's suggestion, he'd been standing guard ever since the night Meg had first come home. They hadn't told her because Rachel knew Meg would refuse the offer, and under the circumstances, the doctor was afraid that knowing a man was on the premises might do Meg more harm than good.

She was one stubborn woman. Too stubborn, maybe.

As he'd made his way through the woods to his makeshift bed, he'd seen her come out onto the front porch with a book and a cup of something to drink. His first thought was that she'd changed into her gown. His second was to wonder what she was reading. He hadn't seen any books lying around except a Bible, and he had a strong suspicion that she hadn't opened it since she'd been home.

Knowing she was safe on the front porch, he'd sunk down onto the pile of dusty straw he'd covered with a blanket from his bedroll. As he shifted around, trying to find a comfortable position for his aching muscles, he wondered if Meg did much reading and decided it was unlikely. Would she like other books? He couldn't ask. She was still as gun-shy as a skittish hunting dog, and if she suspected he was hanging around at night, she'd most likely get the wrong idea. Instead of seeing his presence as the help he intended it to be, he was afraid she'd become hysterical—or worse, retreat into the remoteness that seemed to be loosening its grip on her inch by small inch.

After a long while, he saw the lamplight go out

as Meg settled in for the night. Now he could do the same, though he knew his sleep would be light—as it had been since his prison days—and probably filled with impossible imaginings of him and Meg together.

Meg and Nita finished the ironing by noon the following day. Smiling, the older woman set her iron on the stove, collapsed her board and leaned it against the wall.

"I'll fix us some sandwiches if you'll go tell Ace it's time to eat. I imagine he could use a break about now. Maybe you could show him what other things need doing before winter. Then he can load the laundry and take it back to town."

"Of course."

Meg said the words because they were expected. She didn't want to fetch Ace, and she didn't want to spend time alone with him. Even though she believed what he said when he'd told her she had nothing to fear from him, he still made her nervous. He moved so quietly that he could sneak up on a person without them being aware he was anywhere close. After she'd jumped a time or two, he made sure to let her know he was nearby before speaking to her.

Today was worse than usual. She didn't recall dreaming about him, but she'd awakened with an image of him leaning over her the way he'd done when she fainted. That early-morning memory made her even more aware of him.

Meg rounded the corner of the house and stopped in her tracks. Ace was splitting wood. His shirtsleeves were rolled up to the elbow and sweat glistened on the bare skin of his forearms. Perspiration dampened his shirt in a line down his spine, and the soft blue chambray clung to his wide shoulders. She was gripped by a series of conflicting emotions she was hard-pressed to identify, though she recognized one as bewilderment.

After everything Elton had put her through, how could she possibly be spellbound by the masculine picture of perfection that stood before her? He'd traded his usual denim pants for buckskin, and with his hair held back by the ever-present bandanna, his Indian heritage was even more obvious.

Barely able to move or breathe, she watched as he hefted the ax over his head and brought it down on a chunk of wood, splitting it with a single impressive blow.

She must have made some sound, because he turned and saw her standing there. Without a word, he sank the head of the ax into the stump. He used the tail of his shirt to wipe the sweat from his face and started toward her.

"It must be time to eat."

The sound of his voice brought her back to the present.

"What?"

His gaze was as sharp as his tone. "Food?"

Meg realized with a feeling of dismay that she'd been staring, and she'd been taught from an early age that it was impolite to do so. "Oh. Yes. Your mother is fixing lunch. She thought you'd be ready for a break."

He gave a single nod. He passed her in two long-legged strides, heading toward the back porch and putting lots of space between them.

"I was staring. I'm sorry."

He stopped so fast that she careened into him and made a grab for him to regain her balance. Neither of them moved. Ace was so still, she wondered if he were breathing. She could feel the warmth radiating from his broad back and the slight dampness of his shirt.

Instead of turning, he looked at her over his shoulder. She looked into those distant ice-blue eyes. It was a long way up.

"You have nothing to be sorry for," he said, turning and forcing her to let go of him. "I understand why you're afraid of me."

"I'm not afraid of you," she told him with a shake of her head. She couldn't tell him that she was afraid of herself and the unacceptable admiration she felt for him.

He regarded her with a lift of one black eyebrow. "No?"

"It isn't you...exactly," she confessed.

"I killed your husband. Freak accident or not, I understand how hard it must be for you to be around me." The tone of his voice was as distant as the expression in his eyes. Without a word, he started for the house again.

Meg clasped her hands together to still their trembling. He'd misunderstood the look on her face, but now was as good a time as any to try to clear the air. "Ace, wait!"

Again, he stopped. This time he turned a frowning look toward her.

She hesitated, not knowing how to make him understand something she didn't understand herself. "I know that Elton was…was an accident. I do. It's not that. But he…"

She stopped, searching for the words to express how the fear of her husband had colored her view of all men.

"I know what he did to you, Meg," he told her in a soft voice. "I'm the one who found you."

She sucked in a sharp breath.

"Elton Thomerson was a wicked man, and I have no doubt that your existence was a miserable one, but that part of your life is over. It's up to you to pick up the pieces and move forward—for your sake and for your children."

The pitiless statement sparked a flash of anger she hadn't felt in ages. Knowing more than most what she'd been through, how did he dare be so offhand about how she should live the rest of her life? He seemed to think that she should just go on and pretend nothing had happened.

"How do I do that?" she snapped, grabbing his arm to stop him. "How did you pick up and go on after… after prison?"

He blew out a harsh breath. "I can't tell you how to do it, Meg. Our situations are different. Prison was…a living hell."

The expression in his eyes was distant—he was clearly haunted by memories of a time and things he'd rather forget. "I grew up fighting for every ounce of respect I ever got, and while I was in jail I wanted nothing more than to fight everything and everyone inside those walls, but I didn't, for my mother's sake."

For a moment she was taken aback by his honesty. Being a man, he would have taken his inability to respond to his punishment as a blow to that manhood. But they weren't talking about him. They were talking about her—her future and how she was supposed to get through the rest of her life without going crazy or crawling into a hole to escape the whispers and the pitying looks.

"I can't tell you what to do or how to do it," he told her again. "All I know is what I did. When I'd served my time, I knew that how I chose to live the rest of my life was my decision. Mine. Your feelings can't be changed overnight. I can tell you that it helps to talk about your feelings with someone you know and trust to give you good advice."

A bitter laugh slipped from her lips. "No one cares about my problems," she said, repeating one of Georgina Ferris's favorite tenets.

"You're wrong. A lot of people care, and a lot of them will listen, including me and my mother."

"I hardly know you."

"Sometimes that's easier," he told her cryptically.

No. There was no way she could talk to him about the things she'd suffered at Elton's hands. Nita, maybe. Someday.

"There's always God."

Her mouth twisted into a humorless smile. "I tried talking to God, but He must have been taking care of someone else." She plunged her hands into the pockets of her faded blue skirt. "He didn't listen, and even if He did, He didn't answer. Just look where I am."

"He always answers, Meg, one way or another. Sometimes His answer is 'not right now.' And as for where you are, I know where you are, and believe it or not, you're in a far better place than a lot of people. Stop wallowing in your pity and count your blessings."

"Blessings? Like what?" she snapped. "Broken ribs, a broken arm and…and memories of things so terrible I can barely stand to think of them, much less put them into words?"

For the first time, she saw the expression in his blue eyes soften. "You're alive, Meg!" he said in a low, fervent voice. "Your children are alive and healthy and being well taken care of. You have concerned friends, a roof over your head, food to eat and an income. You have plenty to be thankful for. Elton took your dignity and your self-worth. Don't let him take away your faith."

Deep in her heart, she knew he was right, but fury that he would dare criticize her after everything else she'd been through left her speechless. Afraid she would say something she would regret, she made no reply. Instead, she stalked past him to the house.

Chapter Six

The noon meal was a strained affair, yet contrarily, it was over far too fast for Meg. It was clear that Nita knew something had happened during the short time Meg had been away from the house.

Meg sat silent, letting the faltering conversation flow around her, trying to corral her thoughts that jumped from the mortifying fact that Ace had been the one to find her, to anger over his audacity in telling her she should let go of the past. How *dare* he presume to tell her she should be thankful for her circumstances? What did he know about it? He was a man, and men didn't have to put up with the things women did.

He'd said he wanted to fight back against the violence done to him in prison, but hadn't because of his mother. The problem, Meg thought, was that it did women little good to fight back. If she'd dared to return a blow to Elton, she would no doubt have been found dead, and then what would have happened to her babies?

She sneaked a peek at Ace. He didn't seem the least bit upset by their argument. In fact, he seemed in better spirits than ever. He ate two deer-steak sandwiches and drank two glasses of the tea Meg had made, clearly enjoying the sweet, cold beverage.

When he went to get his second glass, Meg found herself regretting her impulsive gesture to make something special for him. Then she realized that she and Nita were both enjoying it, too, and felt like the most wretched person alive for being so petty. Still, her shame didn't dull her anger at him.

She cast him another sideways glance. The last thing she wanted to do was walk around the farm with him and pretend interest in getting things up to snuff. She'd rather he just took the laundry on to town, got her money and disappeared for the day while she wandered through the woods and tried to soak up what peace she could.

To her dismay, Nita was determined to keep to the agenda, despite the tension between Meg and Ace. Like her son, Nita Allen was single-minded beneath that mild, helpful exterior. Unwilling to disappoint her, Meg had no choice but to bow to the inevitable.

When the kitchen was clean, she went out to join Ace, who was stacking an armload of split logs beneath the shelter of the lean-to. He'd made a considerable dent in the pile of wood he'd split earlier. Exhausted from standing in a hot kitchen wielding an iron all morning, she found his tirelessness annoying.

No emotion showed on his face when he turned and saw her watching. "Ready?"

"Yes," she said, but she stopped and looked around as if she had no idea where to start. The truth was she didn't.

"I've noticed some things that could stand some repair," he said, "but I'm sure you have a better understanding of what needs doing than I do."

Gritting her teeth, Meg forced herself to ignore the man sauntering along at her side and focus on the task at hand. She would get through this and she would get through it without losing her temper.

To be fair, she appreciated his and his mother's willingness to help, and she knew that there was much that needed doing, but the fact was that she couldn't afford to do much. With a frustrated sigh, she planted her hands on her hips and scanned the area, determined to get through the next half hour and keep the peace. Her gaze landed on the rusty roof of the small structure they called a barn. "Some of the tin on the barn roof is loose."

"I saw that. I think I can nail it back into place. I may have to pick up one new piece of tin."

"I can't afford to buy tin."

He slanted a bland look at her. "Then I'll do the best I can with some nails." He gestured toward the rickety corral. "What about the fence? It looks like a couple of posts and some boards need replacing."

She didn't answer. Was he listening? she wondered, as she felt her control slipping.

"I can cut a couple of small trees down for posts," he was saying as he scanned the area, totally unaware that all the color had leached from her face. "I'll figure out something for the rest. I think we have a partial roll of chicken wire to replace that one side of the chicken pen. It looks like easy pickings if a fox comes along, and I've been seeing a few tracks around."

Meg listened to the litany of repairs. It seemed endless. Her head began to pound and whirl in confusion and futility. Roofs. Fences. Foxes after her chickens. How could she deal with all these things when it was a chore to just get out of bed and get dressed every morning?

"Meg?" She felt, rather than saw, gentle hands reach out to grasp her shoulders. "Meg."

She looked toward the sound of the voice. Ace was frowning down at her.

"Are you okay?" His fingertips combed through the side of her hair, tucking back a stray strand that had escaped her braid.

She drew a shaky breath and blew it out slowly. "I'm just... It's so... I'm sorry."

"Stop saying you're sorry," he chided. His fingertips brushed over the line of her jaw with feather lightness.

She barely dared to breathe. Was it anxiety that held her so still or the tenderness of his touch?

"I'm the one who should apologize, and Mother will be upset with herself for all this disturbing you."

"It's all right," she said. The last thing she wanted to do was make Nita feel bad.

"Sometimes we forget that even though our intentions are good, you're at a far different place than we are. We're rushing you—"

"No!" she interrupted. "I want to work. I need to do something to keep from thinking too much, to keep from remembering..."

"I understand, but I imagine after everything you've been through, just coming back here has been pretty overwhelming."

She nodded, and Ace let his arms fall to his sides. "Come with me."

"What?" *Where? Why?*

He held out his hand. "I want to show you something."

As if she were in a daze, Meg placed her hand in his and allowed him to pull her along behind him. She almost had to run to keep up. To her surprise, he led her into the woods, along the path he took to the place he'd been cutting trees.

As they approached the spot, he slowed his pace, stopping several yards away from the clearing, where one of the trees he'd felled the day before still lay. She had no idea why they were there, and after a few moments of watching him examine the area, she opened her mouth to ask.

Immediately, he reached out and silenced her with a finger against her lips. His touch was warm; his finger was calloused. He gave his chin a sharp jerk and pointed upward.

Meg looked but didn't see anything except a squirrel with a mouthful of leaves sitting on the branch of a pine tree across the small clearing. She frowned at Ace, who whispered, "Watch."

After a moment, the squirrel looked around, seemed to decide there was no immediate danger, scampered up to a higher branch and stopped. Once more, it sat stone-still except for its twitching tail, then looked around and darted higher. The squirrel repeated this strange activity until it reached the top branches of the tree, where it fussed and tucked until the materials were exactly right.

Building a nest.

Then it started back down the pine, stopping at the same branches along the way. In a flash, it was headed back up with another mouthful of leaves, pausing at exactly the same spots and going through the same routine once again. After they'd watched the ritual twice more, Ace turned her and indicated that she should precede him back to the house.

When they'd gone several yards down the path, she asked, "Isn't it a bit late to be building a nest?"

"It is. It's my fault." There was genuine regret in his voice. "I was distracted yesterday and didn't look closely enough when I picked a tree to cut down. Her nest was a casualty, so she's rebuilding."

"Why did you want me to see it?"

Something that might have been a teasing smile appeared briefly on his finely shaped lips. "I'm going to let you think about that awhile. Let's get back. I still have to take the laundry to town."

It was only when the wagon had disappeared down the road to Wolf Creek that Meg realized she wasn't angry with him anymore. There had been nothing but gentleness in his voice and his touch. She hadn't been afraid, either.

Ace returned near suppertime with more wash. Thankfully this batch was smaller. After he'd unloaded the baskets and carried them into the house, he handed Meg the money she'd received from Hattie and Ellie.

"You and Nita keep part of this," she said, holding out some of the cash. "There's no way I could have done it without you."

Nita shook her head. "You'll need it for those babies. Ace and I are fine. We're glad to help out."

"It's very sweet of you, Nita," Meg said. "But coming here every day must be getting old, and I know you have things at your place that need doing."

"There's always something to do on a farm," she said with a smile. "Even one as small as ours. I know you're worried about us, but don't ever think that we don't understand that our presence here every day is an intrusion on you, even though it's necessary right now."

Before Meg could reply, Nita asked. "How often do you usually go into town for laundry?"

"Usually on Mondays and Saturdays. I deliver the clean things when I pick up another dirty load. It saves two trips. Why?"

"Well, we agreed to help out at least until the cold sets in, and we will, but it won't be long before we have things more or less caught up around here. What if I come on laundry and ironing days? That will give me some time at my place. If you need help with the children once they get home, Ace can help see to them, or I'll be more than happy to come over. How does that sound?"

"Fine," Meg said. She looked askance at Ace. "Except that I'm sure Ace didn't have taking care of babies in mind when he agreed to help me."

"I don't mind," he said, a rare, crooked grin lifting

one corner of his mouth. "In fact, it's high time I got a little experience, since she keeps nagging me to find a wife and give her grandchildren."

Meg's breath hung in her throat. Ace as a father. She couldn't picture it, yet at the same time, she had no doubt he would do it with as much steadiness and grace as he did everything else.

"Well, that's settled, then," Nita said, pouring the last of the buttered potatoes into a bowl. She smiled. "Let's say the blessing and eat. I need to do a little weeding before dark."

An hour later, Nita and Ace left Meg standing on the porch, her hands stuffed into the pockets of her skirt. As soon as they were out of earshot, Nita asked, "So what happened out there before lunch? She looked fit to be tied."

He flashed his mother one of his infrequent grins. "That's what happened."

"I don't follow you," Nita said.

"I made her mad today."

"Oh, Ace! We're supposed to be helping," Nita chided. "She's in a very delicate frame of mind and should be treated with gentleness."

"I disagree. I think she needs to start feeling again," he argued. "I just shook her out of that little shell she's been hiding under. I think it's a step toward coming back to join the living."

"She is pretty unemotional for the most part," Nita said.

"It's like she's holding the world at arm's length.

Like she thinks that if she doesn't get involved she won't be hurt anymore."

"I agree, but I also get the feeling that she's having a hard time just adjusting to life without Elton."

"That doesn't make a lot of sense. Elton was no good."

"I know that, and so does she," Nita told him. "She may not realize it, but the dread she must have felt whenever he came around had to be paralyzing, and it will take her time to recognize the fact that she doesn't have to look over her shoulder at every loud noise."

As usual, his mother was right. Being a woman gave her an insight into Meg's thinking that he didn't have. "It will be a long road back," he agreed. "Today, when I tried to talk to her about things that needed doing, she couldn't seem to take it all in or deal with it."

"We need to stop rushing her," Nita said thoughtfully. "She must be more than a little overwhelmed right now."

"She let me take her to the woods." Seeing the question in his mother's eyes, he said, "I wanted her to see a squirrel that was rebuilding her nest—her life—and to think about it."

"She's taking baby steps."

"I'm going to keep encouraging her to take those little steps until memories of her past don't hurt anymore and she starts feeling again."

"That's quite a goal, son."

"I know, but I also know that she has to let go of all the bad before she can replace it with good." He met his mother's troubled gaze. "I won't be happy until she cries."

* * *

Meg watched them go. As usual, she experienced mixed feelings as the wagon pulled down the lane. It was a relief to see the back of Ace. Hopefully, once he was out of sight and out of mind, she could think about the things he'd said without growing angry all over again…or remembering the gentleness of his touch as he'd tucked a lock of hair behind her ear and stroked her cheek.

She managed to keep thoughts of him at bay while she sat on the porch with her cup of tea and listened to the sounds of the countryside readying itself for sleep. The songs of the crickets and frogs and even the lone call of a coyote filled her with a calm that had too often been lacking in her life.

She watched the evening star appear and sat with her cooling drink in her hand until the heavens were littered with other sparkling gems. The vastness of the ebony sky filled her with an overwhelming sense of awe. When was the last time she'd even looked up? She was struck anew with the knowledge that God had spoken everything around her into being.

There was a huge world out there filled with people. It all belonged to Him. She belonged to Him. At least she claimed to. That thought made her uncomfortable, and with a jerky movement, she stood and went inside to her solitary bed.

Then, with the sound of the crickets and bullfrogs filtering through the screen at the windows, she let her mind roam back over the events of the day. To her annoyance, most of those events centered on Ace Allen.

His calmness. His gentleness. And the way he seemed so in tune to the world around him.

Remembering his statement about how she should proceed with her life and all the things she should be thankful for rekindled the anger that her quiet time outside had calmed. What did he know about what she was going through?

Plenty.

The word seemed to come from nowhere, slipping into her thoughts and demanding that she take a closer look. Though their circumstances were far different, there was no doubt that his time in prison had given him a clear understanding of injustice and pain, just as her marriage to Elton had to her.

She realized that in her own way, she'd been in captivity. She'd been Elton's prisoner, he her guard and elected punisher whenever she did something to displease him. She never knew what that something might be, and it didn't matter how sorry she was for whatever she had done.

You have nothing to be sorry for.

Ace's words slipped softly into her mind. He was right, she thought. Deep inside, she knew she had nothing to regret, just as she knew she had done nothing wrong those times Elton had taken out his wrath on her. Any wrongdoing she'd been accused of, any unacceptable attitudes he may have claimed she'd had, were all products of his twisted thinking or his drunken fancies.

More than that, and perhaps worse, his treatment of her had been his carefully calculated way of keeping her under his thumb. She suspected it had been a way of making him feel more important, more like a man.

And she'd allowed it.

She knew from sermons at church and studying her Bible how men were supposed to treat their wives, and she knew that a real man didn't have to be cruel or make a woman feel small and insignificant to bolster his own manhood.

Gabe Gentry didn't do that with Rachel. Caleb treated Abby like a queen. Dan Mercer and Sheriff Garrett both seemed besotted with their new fiancées, and Ace...

An image of him flashed through Meg's mind and she sucked in a startled breath. His sheer size and the intensity that radiated from him made him look the part of an Elton; instead, he was the perfect example of force held carefully in check.

There was softness in him, too.

Strange, that contradiction. She'd seen it when he'd trailed his fingertips along her jaw. His touch had been gentle and his voice filled with concern as he'd coaxed her away from the edge of the dark void that called to her and back to the light. She realized with a bit of wonder that she hadn't pulled away from him. She'd felt no suffocating alarm, no overwhelming desire to escape.

No fear.

The knowledge filled her with something that almost felt like a sense of accomplishment. A step in the right direction. She thought about that while crickets sang outside her window, and her mind whirled with questions and possibilities. Gently, the arms of Morpheus closed around her, and just as she felt herself sink into the welcome embrace of slumber, she heard again the claims her friends had made about Ace.

He's a good man.

A noisy commotion shattered Meg's sleep and drove away a dream she didn't remember. She bolted upright, her eyes wide and her hands clutching the sheet in fright. Her heart pounded in her chest and her mouth was dry with fear. The last time a ruckus had awakened her at night was when Elton and Joseph Jones had broken out of jail and come back to get the loot they'd hidden in the barn.

The loud sound of squawking snapped her out of the memory. Something was after the chickens! Probably the fox Ace had mentioned. Knowing she couldn't afford to lose any of her precious laying hens, Meg threw back the sheet and raced barefoot into the kitchen, where the double-barrel shotgun rested in a rack above the fireplace. The soft glow from a waning moon gave her enough light to see her way.

Without taking time to light a lantern, she snatched the twelve-gauge down with shaking hands and ran to the shelf where she kept a box of shells. Accompanied by the strident squawking and flapping wings of scared chickens, she loaded the shotgun and flung the back door wide.

The outbuildings stood in stark relief against the darkness of the woods. Uncertain what to do, she decided that her best course of action was to shoot into the air to see if the noise would deter the furry thief.

Aiming the shotgun heavenward, she gave a scream loud enough to raise the dead and pulled the trigger.

She heard an exclamation of surprise from the vicinity of the chicken coop. Almost simultaneously, she saw the silhouette of a man separate itself from the shadows and hit the ground while a small critter raced from beneath the coop and slipped under the fence.

Meg's heart thudded in her chest. Someone was out there! Had Joseph Jones managed to escape again and come back for some of the hidden loot? Determined to stand her ground, she aimed in the general direction of the chicken house and pulled the other trigger.

"Stop shooting!"

The man's voice was hoarse with fright. He didn't sound threatening at all. Meg stood rooted to the spot at the bottom of the steps, her bare toes digging into the damp ground, her thoughts tumbling round and round like Teddy turning somersaults down the hill. Why hadn't she aimed better on that last shot? Did she have time to reload? Could she really shoot him if he meant her harm?

Finally, a sense of self-preservation kicked in. She would not be a victim again. Determined to stand and fight, she turned and ran up the steps, gripping the shotgun with both hands.

"Meg!"

The low command stopped her halfway to the door. Recognizing the voice, she turned slowly, new questions bubbling up inside her. Ace was striding across the yard. What on earth was he doing here in the middle of the night? He stopped at the bottom of the steps.

"Wh-what are you doing here?"

"Trying to protect the chickens and not doing a very good job of it," he said.

"You stayed to protect the chickens?" she asked in disbelief. He was there to guard the chickens without telling her? What on earth was he thinking after everything she'd been through?

I shot at him. I could have killed him.

A new kind of anxiety filled her. "Well, that's a silly thing to do." Her voice gained strength with every angry word she flung at him.

"Why?" he asked. "I know you need the chickens, and it may be a day or two before I get around to fixing the fence and that little hole in the house I saw today."

"You almost scared me to death!" she yelled, losing all semblance of control. "I thought Jones had broken out of jail again and come...come back for me."

The break in her voice was like throwing kerosene on her fury. She was tired of being the prey. She held the gun tightly. She wouldn't let a man make a fool of her again. Any man. Not even one who claimed he was only helping.

"If you planned on staying, why didn't you say something?" she demanded. "Do you realize I might have killed you?"

"Believe me, I'm well aware of that fact."

He moved up another step. Meg stood at the edge of the porch. They were almost eye to eye. He reached out to take the weapon from her, and though uncertainty raced through her, she made no move to stop him. She let him pull the shotgun from her grasp and unload it and then watched him prop it against a nearby post.

There was a glint in his eyes that looked very much like enjoyment. "Are you *laughing* at me?" she cried.

"No," he was quick to reply. "I'd never, ever laugh at you, Meg."

Oddly enough, she believed him. He was a man who'd been teased and ridiculed and laughed at all his life. He understood too well the pain it could cause.

"I thought that if you'd stop being mad and recognized the humor of this little escapade, you might laugh with me," he added as her gaze searched his.

What a strange man. What did that mean?

"I have a confession to make," he told her, but he didn't really look too contrite.

Her eyes widened.

"I wasn't really here to watch out for the chickens. Not exactly."

Something in her chest tightened. She didn't want any more secrets, couldn't stand any more surprises. She'd had enough of that to last a lifetime. *What? What are you keeping from me?*

"I've been staying here every night since you came home. Gabe and Rachel wanted to make sure you were all right."

"Why would I not be?" she asked, even though she knew the answer to that was pretty obvious.

"Rachel was afraid that if you spent too much time alone, especially at night, you might start thinking about things and it might be too much. She wanted someone close by in case you needed…reassurance."

That sounded like Rachel.

"So you've been leaving every night and then coming back when you finish the chores at your place?" she asked with a frown.

"Usually. Sometimes I just hop off the wagon and come back through the woods."

"Where on earth have you been sleeping?"

"In the lean-to or the barn, depending on the weather."

Meg was having a hard time grasping everything he'd told her and was humbled by the realization that she had better friends in town than she'd realized. Rachel, who was willing to wait for her money. Gabe, who had given her staples to get by on for a while. Ellie and Hattie, who provided a way to make a living. Colt, who had led the party that had come to her rescue. And of course, Ace and Nita.

The comment that had made her so angry earlier in the day took on new meaning. Ace was right. Though she had been deeply wronged, she did have much to be thankful for.

"You don't have to do this."

"You're wrong. I do."

She wanted to ask him why and then saw the self-reproach in his eyes. How had she ever thought those eyes were cold and expressionless? There were all sorts of emotions reflected in those cool depths for anyone who took the time to really look. The problem was that few could meet that proud gaze for long without feeling intimidated.

As she was now. Here she stood, being protected by a man who had killed her husband, a man who was suffering true remorse for doing so. What would Ace think of her if he knew how glad she was to be free of Elton? Would the tenderness in his eyes change to disgust?

Seeing the sudden slump of her shoulders, Ace said, "Go to bed, Meg. I'll be here."

Without a word, she obeyed. She fell asleep, truly secure in the knowledge that nothing would harm her as long as Ace was watching over her.

Chapter Seven

Despite being awake during most of the night, Meg woke before sunrise at the insistence of the rooster, who was already announcing the start of a new day. She got up, dressed and made the morning coffee, which she carried to the east-facing back porch that looked over the outbuildings.

Whatever the season or weather, except maybe during the bitterest part of winter, it had been part of her morning ritual to bring her coffee out here and watch the sun creep over the treetops as the day awakened. Barefoot as she was now, or wrapped in the warmth of a quilt, those few stolen moments of reading her Bible and praying before the children and Elton woke up helped prepare her for the day.

During that brief time, she'd felt truly connected to God. It was when she gave Him her fears and her worries, and He gave her peace and a certainty that she would be fine, no matter what the day held.

She hadn't opened her Bible since coming home.

Hadn't prayed in… She couldn't remember when. Her last encounter with Elton had left her feeling as if God had abandoned her. The bitter thought was quickly followed by guilt and shame. She knew better.

Pushing aside the uncomfortable feelings, Meg sank into one of the straight-back chairs and sipped at her coffee while watching the eastern sky begin to lighten. Aware that someone was stirring, the gray mare whickered softly, ready for her morning grain allotment. From inside the coop, Meg heard rustling from the chickens waiting to be freed into the yard.

With a resigned sigh, she rose and made her way across the rocky ground, being careful not to step in anything unsavory along the way, though heaven knew she'd done that often enough through the years. She wondered who had been letting out the chickens. Ace or Nita?

She lifted the latch to the chicken house and stepped back as the white birds straggled out, led by the rooster, who promptly flapped his way to a fence post and let loose another gruff wake-up call. One hen looked a little bedraggled, and another was missing, which meant the fox had done some damage after all. She wondered if Ace had taken care of the problem as he'd said he would and then chided herself for the moment's uncertainty. Ace wasn't like Elton, who'd put off unpleasant chores as long as possible.

Thinking of Ace, she looked around the rapidly lightening area, wondering where he'd spent what was left of the night. As difficult as it was to admit, she was glad to know he was nearby if she needed him.

On impulse, she decided to hike her way across the pasture up the hill to the plateau that was hidden behind a grove of trees. The morning views there were breathtaking, and she seldom got to see them because she couldn't leave the children. This might possibly be one of her last chances to see a sunrise from that view before they came home or the mornings grew too cold.

Wincing when the rocks gouged her tender feet, Meg started up the steep path, enjoying the patches of wild sunflowers scattered along the way. The going was slow, and she sent a small shower of pebbles tumbling with almost every step she took. Once she entered the stand of trees, the path became somewhat easier to tread, with pine needles and fallen leaves underfoot.

She shivered, wishing she'd brought a shawl. It was much darker and still cool in the shadowy woods, since the sun had not yet risen enough to offer any warmth. The closer she got to the plateau, the more she realized someone was singing, but the words and melody were like none she'd ever heard. Frowning, she stepped out of the shadows and into the brilliance of the sunlight just breaking over the tops of the trees on the far hills.

She stopped, overwhelmed by the sight that greeted her. Her first whimsical thought was that God must be having a wonderful morning. The sky was awash in pinks and salmons and lilacs. Wisps of golden-edged, amethyst-hued clouds floated across the heavens like wood smoke on a listless wind with no particular place to go.

A lone man stood near a huge boulder, silhouetted against the startling backdrop. Ace. What was he doing? His face was turned upward and his arms were outstretched, as if in welcome. The strange words and lilting melody she'd heard came from him. Though she looked, there was no one and nothing on the hilltop but Ace and a Bible that lay open on the large rock.

In the instant that it took her to realize what the book was, she knew he was doing what she once had—preparing for the day by spending time with God. She wondered what the words he was singing meant. Were they in Gaelic or Cherokee? It really didn't matter. What mattered was that they were words of praise and probably thankfulness. What mattered was that he was the kind of man who spent time with his Creator.

The song ended, and she took a step backward, hoping to escape into the trees before he realized she was there. As she retreated again, he turned and reached for his Bible. He must have seen her move from the corner of his eye, because he looked up and noticed her, poised to flee.

She was too far away to read the expression in his eyes, but instinct told her to turn and run.

"Meg, wait!" His voice followed her as the trees and vines swallowed her up.

She kept going, hiking up her gown and ignoring the sticks and rocks digging into her feet. How could she explain interrupting his special time? What excuse could she offer so that he wouldn't think she was spying on him? Fear lent wings to her feet, and she burst out of the other side of the trees and onto the path that led down the hill as if a pack of wild hogs chased her.

She might have made it to the safety of the house if her foot hadn't skated on some loose pebbles. It happened so fast she didn't even try to catch herself, since all she could think of was that she absolutely could *not* reinjure her left arm and she couldn't afford to break her good one.

The only alternative was to land hard on her backside, which jarred her to her very soul and sent her ribs into an explosion of agony. Breathing hard, she sat there, trying to ignore the pain and doing her best to assess any new injuries. Her bottom. Her foot. No, both feet. One elbow. How had that happened? None of the new damage felt severe, but the combined pain, coupled with the fear that something worse might have happened, left her feeling light-headed.

From a distance, she heard the crunching of boots on rocks. Before she could put a name to the sound, Ace was there, squatting down and slipping an arm around her.

"Are you all right? What happened? Why did you run from me?" He spat out the questions one after the other, and if she didn't know how unflappable he was, she might have mistaken the tone of his voice as one of concern.

She looked up at him, wondering which question to answer first, and realized that she'd forgotten what they were. The harsh planes of his face seemed to waver like ripples on the water. She clutched at his arm. "Hold still."

His dark eyebrows snapped together. "What?"

"Your face is floating around. Maybe it's my head. Is my head floating?"

She heard him mumble something she didn't understand before he shoved his Bible into her hands and gathered her into his arms. When he stood, Meg moaned and Ace turned white beneath the bronze of his skin. "I'm sorry."

"Shh."

She reached up and touched her finger to his finely shaped lips. Even as she watched herself doing it, she knew it was inappropriate, but it was something she'd wanted to do ever since she'd first seen him standing outside her bedroom window. She'd longed to see if he really was warm flesh and blood or as cold as the rock from which he looked as if he'd been carved.

He was warm.

So very warm.

The arms holding her tightened.

"You have nothing to be sorry for," she said, letting her eyes drift shut and her head fall against his shoulder. She'd heard the words somewhere and knew they were very important for some reason. She also knew she was behaving very foolishly, but for the life of her she didn't know why. Furthermore, she didn't care.

Meg had no recollection of the trip down the hill and into the house. She was content to lie boneless in Ace's arms, clutching his Bible and knowing that he would take care of everything. When he placed her on her bed, a sigh of relief trickled from her.

"Did I faint?" she asked without opening her eyes.

"Maybe for just a minute." His nimble fingers probed gently at her ribs. "Does that hurt?"

"No. Not really," she murmured. "I think I just hit the ground so hard it jarred my teeth loose."

"Let me see."

Her eyes flew open and she looked up at him. His mouth was curved into a smile and there was laughter in his eyes. Fine lines fanned out from their corners. The change was startling. He became magnificently attractive in a rugged, masculine way.

"I was just teasing," she said.

"I realize that. I think you may have been playing possum, too," he told her, as he picked up each of her hands to check for injuries.

"What?"

"Maybe you didn't faint at all. Maybe you just didn't want to talk about what happened."

"I fell."

He nodded. "Because you ran from me. Why?"

Meg weighed her choices. Years of playing it safe told her not to admit the truth, but from the way he was treating her, she didn't think he meant her any harm. Besides, she was so weary of walking on eggshells just to keep the peace.

"I didn't know you were up there," she told him. "I didn't want you thinking I was looking for you or spying on you. And when I realized what you were doing, I didn't want to interrupt."

"So you ran. I still don't understand why."

She frowned, trying to find the words to make him

understand. "Elton would have been furious. He would have accused me of following him to check up on him."

"Why do you think that was?" Ace asked, lifting one arm to check her elbow.

Meg frowned. She'd never given it any thought. Just knowing it was forbidden was enough to deter her. Now she considered the reasons. Grasping the truth, her eyes widened. "Because he was usually somewhere he shouldn't have been or doing something he shouldn't've been doing."

"That would be my guess."

He went to the washstand and poured some water from the plain white pitcher into the matching basin. Dipping a soft cloth into it, he squeezed out the excess moisture and brought the rag to the bed. He sat down next to her and began to sponge off her face. Meg was too shocked to do anything but let him. When he began to wash her arms and hands, she tried to pull away.

"You don't have to do that. I'm fine."

"Looks like you skinned one elbow a little," he observed, dabbing at the abrasion.

"It's my backside that hurts," she admitted without thinking and then could have bitten out her tongue. The condition of her bottom was not a proper topic of conversation between a man and woman.

Instead of making an unseemly remark the way Elton would have, Ace said, "Did you hurt your tailbone? That can be painful."

Rattled, she closed her eyes. "I don't think so."

When he finished with her hands and arms, he rewet the cloth and started on her foot. Embarrassed that a man was not only seeing her bare feet and ankles, but was also washing them, Meg curled her toes and tried to pull away, but he held her in a firm but gentle grip.

"You have some cuts on your feet," he told her. "But I think I got all the grit out. Do you have something to put on them?"

"Peroxide," she said.

That smile flashed again, briefly. "Ah, yes. Peroxide. My mother thinks it will raise the dead."

For just an instant, Meg forgot the circumstances and smiled back. "My aunt, too."

"I wish you'd do that more," he told her in a wistful voice.

"What?"

"Smile. You used to smile a lot."

"How do you know?"

"When I saw you in town, you were never without your smile."

"Maybe I had something to smile about then."

"I keep telling you that there's still plenty to smile about."

Vexed, Meg pressed her lips together.

"What makes this time different, Meg?" he asked in a concerned voice. "What makes this time worse than before? Maybe if you can put it into words, you can get past it."

He was good at getting to the heart of a matter, she thought. What *was* the difference? Nothing. Absolutely nothing. Elton had beaten her before, had broken bones before. Had abused his husbandly rights before.

"Maybe this was the last straw. Maybe I'm tired of fighting for everything. Maybe I'm just tired."

"All that is over," Ace told her. "You never have to go through that again."

Except in my mind, almost every time I close my eyes.

"How can I be sure it won't happen again?" she demanded.

"By letting your heart heal and being careful not to rush into anything. By finding a man who will treat you with the love and respect you deserve."

The idea of deserving love and respect had never entered her mind. "In case you don't know it, I'm a Ferris," she told him. "I've been talked about all my life, even though I've done my best not to be like my mama. How do I merit those things?"

"Everyone deserves them, but before you can expect to receive it from others, you have to learn to love and respect yourself."

When she only looked at him with a question in her eyes, he said, "It seems to me you've let your past mold your present. You've allowed your mother's reputation to impact everything—your decisions, your friends, maybe even the men you socialized with. Why did you choose Elton?"

Meg gave a harsh laugh. "He was very good-looking, and he made me feel special. He bought me things. He made me believe that he really cared and that he would take good care of me." She laughed again, a bitter sound. "Boy, was I wrong."

"You may have been wrong about Elton, but you

are special, and when you grow up fighting your way through life, it's easy to be misled. I've been there."

"You have?"

"When I was young, I ran with a pretty rough bunch. Only by the grace of God did I come out of it without turning bad to the bone. Prison gives you three choices. You can let it crush your spirit or harden you until you don't care what anyone thinks about you. Or you can use it to learn and change."

"That's what you chose."

"Because of my parents. Even during my worst times there, I never forgot what my father always said about rough times. 'When something bad happens to you, lad, it seems to me you've three choices.'" To Meg's surprise, Ace had adopted a perfect Irish brogue. "'You can let it define you, destroy you or make you strong.'"

He smiled at her. "Until now, you haven't let circumstances crush you or harden you. You've always come through with your smile and your faith intact. There are few people who could weather what you have and stay close to the Lord."

Meg thought about that for a few moments. "Your mother told me that you went through a lot growing up because of your mixed heritage. Is that how you got through it? God?"

"My mother talks too much," he said, but there was tenderness in his eyes as he said it. "I didn't start accepting who I was until I went to prison. Until then, I spent my life running back and forth between two worlds because I didn't know where I belonged.

"A man has a lot of time to think in prison, and a lot

of time to read the Bible. When I realized how much God loved me and how special I am to Him, I started thinking that I wasn't just half-white and half-Indian. I was the product of two very different, yet very special, cultures."

Meg hung on to his every word, fascinated by his thinking.

"I'm the son of Yancy and Nita Allen, but more importantly, I'm a child of God. I realized that none of the rest of it was that important. Most days, that's enough. Sometimes I still fall into that trap of feeling sorry for myself, but it doesn't last long."

Meg recalled feeling the same way. Always before, she'd bounced back.

"I think the most important thing I did was to start dwelling on the similarities of my different backgrounds instead of the differences."

"Like what?"

"People are people, Meg, no matter what their skin color is or how much money they have or what country they come from. We all breathe and feel joy and pain. We all hate and love and laugh and cry and bleed. And no matter how different we may be on the outside, God loves us all and never leaves us. If there's any leaving done, we walk away from Him."

"Didn't you ever feel like He'd deserted you?"

"Often."

He glanced away for a moment. "When I was younger I was pretty hostile toward authority. Then I realized how my actions were affecting my parents. They didn't bring me up to be a brawler and a convict, and I don't imagine Elton's parents did, either."

"Probably not."

"It's all about choices, Meg. We make hundreds of choices every day, some of them more important than others. Are we going to be happy or let life get us down? Will we buy that new dress material or wait? Are we going to forgive or hold a grudge for some wrong done to us? It's up to us."

"You make it sound so easy," she said. "Anyone who can do that all the time would have to be perfect."

Ace smiled. "You're right, and we aren't. We all make bad choices, but God wants us to keep trying. I'm not saying it's easy. I'm saying it's worth it. One of the hardest things for me is to thank God for the bad things that come my way."

"How can anyone do that?" she asked, wide-eyed.

"Believe me, it isn't easy," he said in a wry tone, "but I truly believe that things, good and bad, happen for a reason, and I know God sifts us, gives us trials, little tests to see how loyal we really are."

"You're saying that I chose Elton, and everything he did was to see if my faith was strong enough?"

"I'm saying it's a possibility. You have to decide what your lessons are."

"And I'm to forgive the things Elton did to me."

"You know you are," he told her. "And you will, in time. The forgiveness is more for you than for him. And I hope that you'll forgive me for what I did one day, too."

"I already have," she said without hesitation and

realized as she said it that it was true. "I know that if you hadn't taken that shot that not only might Colt be dead, but the kids and I. You, too. I know that the bullet going astray was an accident."

"Thank you for that," he said. They stared at each other for several awkward seconds. "I should go find that peroxide," he said, getting to his feet.

"What were you singing?"

"What?" he asked, turning back to her.

"When I saw you on the plateau. What were you singing?"

"It's the Cherokee morning song. I try to spend time every morning alone with my prayers and my Bible, and I always try to sing something. Sometimes I sing Christian hymns. Sometimes they're in Irish, sometimes Cherokee. I doubt He cares what language it's in, as long as it's praise to Him."

"No." Actually, she was impressed with his knowledge, which made her feel only more inadequate. "You're very smart. With such different backgrounds, how did you become a Christian?"

"Believe it or not, a lot of things overlap."

"Like what?"

"The Celts and Indians believe that God was a continual presence and that He could be found in nature. They both feel a special closeness with the earth. I think most Christians would agree with that. My father's people believed that spiritual and creative renewal was obtained through a simulated death and rebirth experience. When the Cherokee celebrate the Great New Moon Ceremony in October on the day they believe the earth was created, they cleanse themselves by immersing in water seven times. They call it 'going to water.'"

Meg thought of baptism.

He offered her a wry smile. "You probably think I'm crazy."

"No."

"I like to study about things that interest me, so I read a lot," he told her with a shrug. "Once I thought it all through, Christianity seemed the sum total of all those things."

Meg couldn't think of anything to say to that.

He started for the door again and turned in the aperture. "Will you do something for me?" he asked.

Her eyes widened. "What?"

"I believe that you were spared and Elton was taken for a reason. Promise me you won't waste this second chance."

Ace finished doctoring Meg's scrapes and went back outside to take care of the morning chores. His heart was heavy. He had no way of knowing if the things he'd said had any impact on her or not. She hadn't agreed to think about what he'd said, and she hadn't commented when he'd asked her not to throw away her chance at a new life. Well, he'd planted the seeds. All he could do now was pray and hope that her heart was still tender enough that they took root.

He was bone-tired. Carrying the hen that had no doubt died of a heart attack during the fox raid, he'd gone through the woods in the dead of night to take the chicken to his mother, who had promised she'd bring dumplings with it the next morning. By the time he'd gotten back to Meg's, he'd managed to get only a couple hours' sleep before waking at his usual time.

When Meg had come upon him on the hilltop, he'd just finished praying for them both, something he did every day, several times a day. He prayed for Meg to come out of this latest ordeal healthy and happy and stronger than before. He asked God for help in ridding himself of his inability to get past feeling glad that Elton was dead, and that the Lord would forgive him for taking another life.

Despite the depth of her wounds, Meg was gaining strength each day, not just physically, but emotionally and mentally. It looked as if she had put on a bit of weight now that she was up and about and doing something to whet her appetite, and she'd lost the sickly pallor that spoke of far too much time inside. The empty look in her eyes appeared less and less often as he did everything in his power to goad her into displaying some sentiment.

Anger had been the first reaction he'd sparked, and that was fine. Anything was better than numbness. Unfortunately, today the emotion he'd triggered when he called out to her had been fear. Fright had sent her flying down the steep, crooked hillside, but when he'd carried her to the house, she'd trusted him enough to relax against him. That simple act had triggered a longing inside Ace to hold her close and tell her that he would never let anyone hurt her again.

Forget thinking anything can ever come of what you feel for her.

Even if she did learn to care for him, Ace knew that after all she'd suffered as Elton's wife, he could never ask her to be his. Despite her mother's background, Meg was good and kind and decent. From all he knew of her, she was a hard worker, a good friend and a good mother. He didn't doubt she'd been a good wife. She deserved to be looked up to and respected, and Teddy and Lucy deserved a father who was respected. That wasn't likely to happen if she married him. He didn't want her called "the half-breed's woman" or his children labeled "the Indian's brats." Worse, he couldn't bear to think of her labeled as "the ex-con's wife."

The sad truth was that he feared he would never marry and have a family of his own. Meg was the only woman since his wild youth that made his blood sing. She was the only woman who made him want to be better, stronger. She was the only woman whose spirit cried out to him. For her sake, no matter how much he suffered, he had to ignore the call.

Meg found comfort and a measure of peace in the sameness of her days, each one passing much as the one before. She no longer had to worry about anyone coming along to spoil the little joys she was once again beginning to see along the way, or to wait in fearful trembling for Elton to come home and take out his frustrations and temper on her. There was no more worrying that he'd lose control and hurt one of her babies.

She mended clothes, and she and Ace and Nita did laundry. Then he took it back to town and brought Meg her money. To her surprise, he'd also brought some books for her to read from the new library in town that Caleb and Gabe's mother, Libby Granville, had opened with the books she'd brought with her from Boston when she'd moved back to town recently.

At first Meg wondered how he knew she needed something to read, but soon realized that since he was keeping an eye out for her, he must have known about her time on the porch in the evenings.

Though she was glad for new reading material, the books he brought home were of a style that held little interest for her. She read them anyway, knowing she needed the practice, but found no real enjoyment in Jules Verne's *Journey to the Center of the Earth* or *Tales of the Grotesque and Arabesque* by Mr. Poe.

Though she had no idea what kind of books Ace might like, she imagined those he brought for her were ones he might enjoy, a suspicion that was confirmed when she caught him reading them at odd free moments.

Once he decided she had enough wood for the winter, he began to work on the many repairs that were needed around the small farm, while she and Nita shared the cooking and cleaning and pieced together a new quilt for Lucy's bed.

On the days there was no washing or ironing to do, Nita stayed home and Meg helped Ace with some chore or other. Ace cut dead and broken limbs, and Meg used her good arm to help him drag them to the burn pile.

Together they set some new posts in the corral and re-placed boards. The chicken coop was fox-proofed, and Ace even replaced several cedar shingles.

When they worked together, he explained what he was doing and why, so that she could learn. In re-sponse, Meg tried to anticipate what tool he would need next. He never failed to thank her. He was polite, she thought, a word that hadn't even been in Elton's vocabulary. She felt more in control for the knowl-edge Ace was imparting and more confident know-ing that he found worth in her contributions, no matter how small.

They often went for an hour or more without speak-ing. When Elton had grown quiet, it was like the calm before a storm. With Ace, it was a pleasing quiet. There were times when the only sounds were the birdsong, the rustling of the changing leaves and the rapping of the hammer.

Surprisingly, the hours they spent together were not uncomfortable as she'd expected them to be. She began to think of them as a team. They tackled painting the house together. Even before Elton's death, Meg had been saving up for some whitewash, hoping to spruce up her tired-looking little dwelling. She painted the lower portion of the house, and Ace climbed the lad-der to reach the high places. They worked together for several days, and when they stepped back to examine their handiwork, Meg was amazed at the difference.

When she wasn't helping Ace, she spent as much time as possible at her favorite place. October had brought a fair amount of rain and a cold snap that lasted a couple of days. It was a common occurrence, just as it was equally common for them to be swatting mosquitoes into November.

As Meg sat beneath her favorite tree and watched the leaves and the seasons changing, it was inevitable that her thoughts turned to God. Weakened faith or not, He was too ingrained in her past for her to dismiss Him out of hand. She tried to see His plan in the events of the past few months and tried being thankful toward Him for the very things that had brought her to this point in her life, as Ace suggested, but her guilt always kept her from finding a rationale that worked in her mind. She still could make no sense in the things that had happened.

Not surprisingly, thoughts of the past led to thoughts of the future. What would it bring to her and her children? Would she ever have the courage to trust another man with her heart and body? Was there a man out there who was willing to live the words she read in the Bible?

Time would tell. Until then, she vowed to work to regain her strength so that her babies could come home. She would keep trying to find her peace in the world God had created and forgiveness in her heart. And, as Ace suggested, she would try to think of each new day as a second chance.

Meg sat on the back porch, waiting for Nita to return with their tea. After finishing their other chores, they'd watered the small garden plot Ace insisted on planting in hopes that the turnips and other fall crops would produce before it got too cold.

She and Nita had decided to call it a day while they waited for him to return from town with the laundry they would start the next morning. After they'd washed up at the creek and tidied their hair, laughing and gasping at the coldness of the water, Nita had volunteered to go make a pitcher of the cold tea of which she'd become so fond.

After counting back, Meg was surprised that she'd been home more than two weeks. She was feeling better in every way, except that she wanted Lucy and Teddy home. She'd mentioned it to Nita earlier in the day and she'd given Ace instructions to ask Rachel when the children could return.

Meg hoped he gave the doctor a good report on how well she was behaving and that he brought the news she wanted to hear, yet at the same time she was a little anxious about seeing Teddy and Lucy again. Teddy was old enough to know who she was, but it might take time to get back to their former relationship. Meg feared that Lucy might not remember her at all. It would absolutely break her heart if her baby girl wanted nothing to do with her.

Almost as if she'd summoned up Ace with her thoughts, Meg heard the clank and rattle of the wagon nearing the house.

Nita walked through the back screen door, carrying two glasses of tea. "It's a good thing I made this," she said, her eyes dancing with pleasure. "It looks like we have company."

Meg jumped to her feet. "Company? Who?"

"Looks like Doc Gentry's rig up ahead of Ace."

"Lucy? Teddy?" Meg cried, hardly able to believe what she was hearing.

"I can't tell," Nita told her, but she was speaking to Meg's back. Meg was already down the steps and halfway to the lane.

Chapter Eight

Even through the dust blowing back from Rachel's rig, Ace saw Meg running toward the lane as soon as he rounded the curve in the road. The joy on her face was inexpressible. His heart, the heart that longed for a woman to love him with that same depth, constricted in sudden pain when he realized hers would be broken when she realized Rachel had not brought Teddy and Lucy.

He knew the exact moment she recognized there was no one with Rachel but her mother-in-law, Libby Granville. The joyous expectation on Meg's face vanished like a dandelion puff in the wind, and like the puff, she seemed to fall apart before his eyes.

As he pulled toward the back of the house, he saw Rachel alight from the wagon and take both of Meg's hands in hers. He had no idea what she was saying, but he could imagine. Before he rounded the corner of the house, he saw Meg straighten and urge something that resembled a smile to her lips as she gestured toward the porch. Then she welcomed Libby, who swept her into a warm embrace. Still holding her hand, Mrs. Granville and Meg followed Rachel up the steps.

Having no desire to interrupt the ladies' visit, Ace unloaded the baskets onto the back porch. He could hear the feminine chatter through the screen and tried hard not to eavesdrop. He was almost finished with his chore when the back door opened and Rachel stepped out onto the porch.

The first thing he noticed was that her pregnancy was beginning to show. Always a beautiful woman, Rachel Gentry positively glowed with health and happiness.

"You're looking well, Doc."

"I'm feeling well," she said with a contented smile. "There's nothing like love to make things right in the world. You should try it."

Ace swung the last basket down from the wagon bed and set it on the porch. "I don't see that in the cards for me."

"And why not?" she said, planting her capable hands on her hips.

He did the same. "Half-breed. Ex-con. Killer." He cocked a dark eyebrow at her. "Shall I continue?"

She mimicked his expression. "How about good Christian? Devoted son. Dependable deputy. Shall I go on?"

"Let it rest, Rachel."

She sighed. "I thought having you help her would give you a chance to…" Her voice trailed away.

"To what?"

"I don't know," she said with a shrug. "We all know how you feel about her, and Gabe and I thought it would be a chance to show her that there are good men, and that she doesn't have to be alone or afraid forever."

One corner of Ace's mouth lifted in a crooked smile. "Even if I thought there was any future for us, and I don't, it's a little hard to make any kind of impression when the object of your affections cringes if you get too close."

Rachel frowned. "What do you mean?"

"She's scared to death of me."

"Surely it isn't that bad."

He offered her a mocking smile. "Actually, it isn't, and I don't think it's just me. I suspect she'd do the same if any man got too close. On the other hand, I have seen some improvement." He gave a negligible lift of his wide shoulders. "I like to think she's getting better bit by bit, day by day."

"I'm sure she is. She'll be a lot better when the kids come home."

Ace lifted one booted foot to the porch and rested his arm on his knee. "When's that likely to happen?"

"I thought I'd come and see how she's doing to make sure she can handle them. Maybe in a couple of days."

"She was really disappointed when she realized you didn't bring them with you."

"I know. I almost burst into tears myself when I saw her face fall, but I wanted to check on her first, and I'll have to make arrangements with Serena and Dave."

She flashed Ace a quick smile. "I'd better get back inside before she suspects we're talking about her. Do you mind carrying in those things from the buggy? We brought supper, and Pip brought some books she thought Meg might like."

Pip. Ace smiled. He didn't think he'd ever get used to the nickname Gabe's elegant mother, Libby, insisted her grandkids call her. "I'd be glad to."

Rachel went back inside, and Ace went to unload the buggy. He entered the front door, carrying a cast-iron Dutch oven in one hand and a pie plate in the other.

Rachel turned to Meg. "We brought supper. I fixed a pot roast, Allison sent a loaf of bread and Ellie baked you one of her peach pies."

"Abby sent you some things her girls had outgrown for Lucy, and I brought you some books and a couple of magazines," Libby added. She cast an oblique glance at Ace. "Somehow, I didn't think Mr. Verne or Mr. Poe were your kind of reading material. I suspected they were for someone else."

Ace, who was replacing the lid to the iron kettle after sneaking a peek, caught the look and smiled. "Guilty as charged."

"I've been reading them," Meg said, avoiding eye contact with him, "but you're right. They aren't the kind of thing I normally would enjoy. Actually, I'm not sure what I might like."

"I'm certain you'll much prefer *Undine* or *Jane Eyre*."

"Romances?" Ace said with raised eyebrows.

"Yes, romances!" Libby's face was flushed with indignation. "*Undine* even has an enchanted forest, sort of like a grown-up fairy tale. I know that romances are considered dangerous." She adopted a scandalized look and placed a hand over her heart in a dramatic gesture. "Why, they might even cause a woman to dream about a life where two people love each other madly. Can you imagine?"

When everyone laughed, she dropped the pretense and said, "I beg to differ. Romances aren't at all dangerous. Why, I lived a romance. My marriage to Sam was a beautiful love story, even though it had a miserable beginning."

Ace knew people seldom spoke of Libby's first marriage to Lucas Gentry, Gabe and Caleb Gentry's father. Her marriage to him had been very similar to Meg's marriage to Elton, but as she said, things had turned out well in the end, when Lucas divorced her and she married Sam, Blythe and Win's father, who gave her the love she deserved.

Lifting her chin, Libby looked from Meg and Rachel to Ace and Nita. "I also believe with all my heart that no matter what our circumstances, sometimes God gives us a second chance."

She offered the group an uncomfortable smile. Rachel was smiling fondly at her mother-in-law, and Meg was regarding her with a thoughtful expression.

Good, Ace thought. Libby had mentioned second chances, too. He wondered if Meg noticed.

"I'm sorry," Libby was saying. "I'm afraid it's a subject I'm quite passionate about. I see romance novels as reminders that there is the hope of happiness for us all out there, if we'll only find the courage to trust."

She threw her hands into the air. "Well, good heavens! What would we do without hope?"

Exactly, Ace thought. That was exactly what Meg needed. Hope and the courage to trust. Without commenting, he headed outside to bring in the last of the gifts. As he loped down the steps and out to the buggy, he hoped that Libby was right and that Meg did find renewed faith in love in the pages of the books she'd brought. If she weren't so broken, she could find it in her Bible, but just now she didn't seem much interested in anything God had to say. He prayed that would change soon, but for now, he'd settle for Meg finding hope anywhere.

After carrying in the books and the bread, Ace disappeared, leaving the ladies to their visit. Nita fixed them all some tea and sliced the pie while Meg visited with her callers.

Don't get used to it, Meg. Things will go back to the way they were once you're up and about. They always did. No one came to visit unless she was recuperating from one of her encounters with Elton. Still, manners demanded that she show her appreciation.

"Thank you so much for everything," she said, overwhelmed by the display of kindness, however brief it might be. "You didn't have to do that."

"Of course we didn't have to do it. That implies it was a duty. We wanted to," Rachel said. "Allison and Ellie have both wanted to come and visit, but they knew you didn't need any company at first."

"Miss Grainger and Miss Ellie want to come and

just…visit?" Despite her background, all the ladies had been kind to her in the past, and they did go to the same church, but they were far above her economically and socially. Why, Rachel was a medical doctor, for goodness' sake. Abby was married to the wealthiest man in Pike County, and Allison was an educated woman, a teacher.

Rachel must have seen Meg's uncertainty and disbelief. "Meg, all of us have tremendous respect for the way you've handled your life. We wanted to be your friend, but Serena told us how Elton didn't want you getting too close to anyone, and we didn't want to cause you any grief by pressing the matter."

Friends. The sad truth was that she didn't have any. She could thank Elton for that.

"We're all hoping that maybe now that—" Realizing that she was about to overstep the bounds of correctness, Rachel paused. "We're all hoping we can be your friends now." Before Meg could comment, she added, "When I let them know you're doing so much better, I'm sure they'll have Colt drive them out some evening."

"Colt?"

"Mmm-hmm," Rachel said. "I guess with everything that's happened, you haven't heard that the sheriff and Allison are a twosome. In fact, they're planning a January wedding."

Everyone in Wolf Creek knew that Allison Grainger was the town's spinster schoolteacher, but Sheriff Garrett's headstrong children had come between him and every woman he'd tried to court since moving to town.

"What about his children?" Nita asked.

"Believe it or not, they're ecstatic," Rachel said incredulously. "Once Colt had a showdown with them and they realized he was serious about wanting to complete their family, they helped orchestrate the whole thing."

"That's unbelievable."

"That's what everyone says," Libby added. "The whole town is waiting for the other shoe to drop, but the children really seem to like her, and it's obvious that Allison and Colt are crazy about each other."

Satisfaction glowed warmly inside Meg. Thank goodness happiness was in the cards for someone. Though she knew Allison Grainger only from church, she'd heard lots of good things about her, and of course her sister Ellie, whose laundry she did weekly, was a sweetheart.

"Are you settling in here, Mrs. Granville?" Nita asked Libby when Meg grew silent.

"Oh, yes. The library is open, and everyone is very supportive. It makes me feel good to know that the books are doing something besides sitting on the shelves gathering dust."

"And your son and daughter who came with you… are they still in town?"

Libby offered a bittersweet smile. "No, they left last week. Win plans on returning soon, though. He's been talking with Nate Haversham about buying the bank."

"Nate's wife's health has gotten progressively worse the past few months," Rachel offered, "and he'd like to spend more time with her."

"Win has also talked to Will Slade about buying part of his sawmill business. It seems it's been going downhill since that, uh, incident with his wife," Libby added with an apologetic look at Nita and Meg. "Ex-wife now, I suppose."

Meg had heard about the incident. Martha, the pretty, dark-haired wife Will had brought home from one of his trips to Little Rock a few years back, had run off with a bigwig who'd come down from Springfield, Missouri. Will had been like a bear with a sore paw ever since. No one, least of all Will, expected her to divorce him, but he'd been served papers a year ago, and he was rumored to hit the corn pretty hard from time to time. That couldn't be good for business.

"Does Win think Will will take him up on the offer?" Meg asked.

"It's too soon to say."

"And what about your daughter?" Nita asked.

"Blythe doesn't think a small town is right for her. When Win moves here, she'll stay in Boston. Her dream is to open a boutique and design clothing for wealthy ladies."

"That sounds exciting," Meg said. "I know you'll miss her."

"I will," Libby agreed with a rueful nod, "but she's a grown woman of twenty-two, and she's been well educated and brought up to know her own mind, even though she's far too shy to speak it very often. Neither Sam nor I wanted her to be at the mercy of any man the way I—"

Libby paused a moment before continuing. "Though

it is not at all acceptable in certain social circles, Sam and I wanted Blythe to be independent, though neither of us feel she has an enterprising nature the way her brothers do. She's actually more of a caretaker." A resigned breath trickled from her. "She'll have to find her own way, just as we all have."

"Whatever she chooses, at least she has a way to support herself if the need arises. That must be a comfort to you," Rachel said.

"Yes," Meg agreed, thinking that even though she and Blythe Granville were the same age, they had far different opportunities for the future. "Having an education is bound to give her more options than I've had." She offered her guests a wan smile. "It's too bad I don't live in Boston. I could sew for her."

"You're going to be fine, Meg," Libby said. The belief that what she said was true shone in her eyes. "You just need to trust that God has a plan for you. My own past has taught me that He can turn even the ugliest of experiences into good things."

Meg glanced away toward Nita, who was looking at her with compassion in her dark eyes. Meg didn't want pity. She didn't know what she wanted. Even though she didn't doubt Libby's sincerity, Meg couldn't see anything good coming from the treatment she'd suffered at the hand of her husband, except that it was over at last.

"We should go," Rachel said. "We're tiring you."

Meg glanced up, aware that she'd drifted off to that dark place in her mind where she tried to keep all the bad things locked away. "Oh, no! Stay a bit. It's nice to have company. I was just woolgathering." She forced a smile. "Ellie's pie is really good, isn't it?"

"It definitely is. I'll tell her you said so," Libby replied.

The conversation drifted off to other, less painful topics, and all too soon, Rachel was telling Meg that she'd like to examine her before leaving. When they exited the bedroom several moments later, Nita held out the Dutch oven to Rachel.

"I swapped pots, so you could take yours back with you," she said.

"Thank you, Nita."

Nita placed her hands on her slender hips. Her gaze moved from Meg to the doctor. "In my opinion, she's doing too much. What do you say?"

Rachel laughed. "I haven't seen what she's doing, but knowing her as I do, I suspect you're right. Actually, she's coming along very well. Being at home and getting back to her life seems to be good for her, and I think if she does overdo it, her body will let her know." She gave Meg a pointed look. "What happened to your elbow?"

"I slipped coming down from the plateau. I'm fine. Really."

"I just don't want those ribs reinjured," Rachel said.

"Am I well enough for Teddy and Lucy to come home?" Meg asked hopefully, ignoring the comment about her ribs.

"Yes, but I'm not sure what day. Soon, though, I promise. Okay?"

Meg beamed. "Yes."

* * *

Later that evening, as Ace went down to the creek to bathe away the grit of the day, he thought about the change the doctor's visit had brought about in Meg. It was slight, but he'd made a life of studying details—of behavior, appearances and changes in the world surrounding him. Whether he was in prison and on the lookout for someone planning to waylay him, or if he were tracking a man or a deer, it was those subtle variations that often made the difference between success and failure.

For the first time, he'd seen a full-blown, genuine smile on Meg's face and a hint of optimism in her green eyes, all because she had something to look forward to. All because she had hope.

After they enjoyed the wonderful supper the ladies had brought, Nita insisted on doing the dishes so that Meg could take a walk before dark. Like her son, she saw the glimmer of optimism in Meg's eyes, and just for this one day, Nita wanted to give Meg an opportunity to savor the knowledge that she would soon hold her babies in her arms and to dream about what she would say to them.

Nita Allen knew that the sweet dreams of future happiness could hide the bitter taste of the past and the present, at least for a while. She watched Meg disappear into the shadow of the forest with a feeling of satisfaction in her heart. It seemed that God was answering her prayers for Meg to once again be whole in body, mind and spirit.

* * *

Meg followed the path through the woods to her favorite spot near the creek. It was cooler in the deepening shadows, and she was glad for the shawl Nita had insisted she drape over her shoulders. Nita Allen was a kind woman, and more and more, Meg realized that despite his past, Ace was a good man.

There were a lot of wonderful people in her world, she thought, recalling the generosity of the women who had visited her earlier. Her thoughts turned to Libby Granville's encouraging words. She knew the older woman meant well, but even though their pasts had many parallels, Libby's story was far different from Meg's. Libby might have had an abusive husband, but she had married very well the second time. Meg didn't see any wealthy or kind man in her future to make her life easier.

As soon as the thoughts crossed her mind, shame pushed them aside. It was unlike her to begrudge another person happiness or good turn of events. Despite the hurt Elton had done to her, she was up and walking around. Lucas Gentry had beaten Sam Granville so badly he'd been left an invalid, confined to a wheelchair. He could easily have become hateful and cynical, but by all accounts, he hadn't.

Don't forget that you still have your babies, Meg. Something else to be thankful for. Libby had gained her freedom from Lucas, but only at the expense of losing her two boys to Lucas, who had more power and money. That cold, hard truth brought Meg's comparisons to a halt. Libby Gentry Granville had been forced to leave her sons with a man who had shown them no love. But for the grace of God and the love of two amazing women, both Caleb and Gabe might have grown up as embittered and mean-spirited as their father.

Meg shuddered and pulled the shawl more closely around her. She was thankful that Lucy and Teddy had escaped physical harm. Hopefully, with loving care and prayer, they would forget the bad things they'd seen and heard during their short lives. That couldn't be said for Caleb and Gabe or even Libby and Sam. They would never forget, yet they had chosen to pick up the fragments of their broken lives and piece together new ones.

And so, here she was. She had been given a second chance. She could wallow in the past and let Elton win by hiding away from life and love, or she could take a page from the Gentry family's book and look for the potential good that might spring up from the trials she'd suffered.

It was up to her.

Chapter Nine

Meg smelled the wood smoke before she rounded the head-high stand of sumac, whose crimson leaves rivaled the red of her knitted wrap. She stopped at the sight before her.

Ace had built a small fire and was sitting with his forearms draped over his upraised knees. He must have sensed her presence because he glanced over his shoulder with a sharp jerk of his head. In profile, he was the image of hidden power and fierce beauty. She realized that he must have bathed in the chilly waters of the creek, because his wet hair clung to his bare shoulders and back.

He reached for the shirt lying next to him, stood, raised it and drew it over his head, but not before she'd seen the scars covering his back. She was hardly aware that he'd turned to face her.

He's been beaten in prison, she thought. How many times had they whipped him? How often? How many lashes had they inflicted? Had anyone tended his bleeding back, or had they just let him suffer?

Long-suppressed emotions surged through her, mercilessly dragging out the memories of her last encounter with Elton. Fresh insights and raw feelings burst through the barrier of numbness she'd erected, filling her with anguish.

The aching sorrow she felt was not for her own suffering, but for a young man who'd grown up in two worlds and felt he belonged to neither. She felt regret for the time he'd spent behind bars and joy and thankfulness that he'd overcome it all.

The painful prickles of emotion were not unlike those she felt when feeling returned to a hand or foot that had fallen asleep. She was so caught up in the surge of emotions that she was unaware of the sob that escaped her throat and the tears running down her cheeks.

For long seconds, he stood there just looking at her, and then he came nearer, stopping mere inches from her. Without a word, he tipped her face upward. To her astonishment, she saw that his cheeks were wet with tears, too. Why was he crying?

"Shh."

He cupped her face in his big hands, and his thumbs brushed the tears from her cheeks with a gentleness she'd never before experienced. She mimicked him, reaching up to take his face between her hands and brushing aside the moisture on his cheeks.

Slowly, so slowly that she wasn't sure he was moving at all, he lowered his head. He was going to kiss her. A renegade memory of Elton's brutal kisses sneaked into her mind. Ace must have felt her stiffen, because he stopped and started to draw away.

You have no reason to be frightened of me. Ever.

The memory of those words and the tenderness she saw in his eyes quieted her fear. She had grown to dread her husband's touch and despise his kisses, but this man was not Elton, and he was nothing *like* Elton.

With that realization, the threat and fear vanished, and the only thing she felt was inevitability and anticipation. A quiver of pleasure she'd never expected to experience again shivered through her. Still holding his face in her palms, she raised herself on tiptoe to meet him halfway and felt the sweetness of his breath against her lips.

Then, to her surprise, Ace stepped back, dropping his hands to his sides and leaving her feeling abandoned. Brazen. Embarrassed.

She lowered her arms and for a moment they stood staring at each other, both breathing heavily. Why had he stopped? It was impossible to know; he'd spent too many years perfecting that expression of cool stoicism.

"I'm sorry. That was totally inappropriate under the circumstances. I hope you'll forgive me."

Disappointment washed through her, and the breath she'd been holding lodged in her throat. The stilted apology sounded like something Win Granville might say. She stifled a sudden fit of nervous, ill-timed giggles and looked up at Ace, wondering what she was supposed to forgive. Nothing had happened, and even if it had, she'd have been as much to blame as he.

"There's nothing to forgive," she said, humiliation making her voice a mere thread of sound.

Swiping at the lingering moisture on her cheeks, then dabbing her fingers on her skirt, Meg squared her shoulders, turned and retraced her steps down the path toward the house. She was halfway back to the cabin when she realized that the tears had started all over again.

He had what he'd wanted. Meg had cried, though she hadn't wept for herself or the things she'd suffered at Elton's hands. Instead, she'd spilled tears for a man she hardly knew. Besides his parents, Ace didn't think anyone had cried for him before.

When he'd seen the moisture streaming down her cheeks and realized the tears were for him, he'd been both humbled and overjoyed. He prayed that the protective walls she'd built around her heart had finally crumbled and she was feeling once more. If so, the healing would inevitably follow.

As happy as that made him, Ace was furious with himself for almost kissing her. But she'd looked so beautiful as she'd stood staring up at him with her heart laid bare and tears flooding her eyes.

Fortunately, he'd realized at the last possible moment that his timing was all wrong. She was a recent widow. She was not in a position to welcome the advances of any man. He was surprised that she wasn't angry at him for taking advantage of her, and even more surprised that she hadn't run back to the house screaming. Instead, she was cool and controlled, a side of her he'd never seen before.

He sighed. Now what? Would she revert back to her old ways and shut herself off from him? He hoped not. He'd worked too hard to gain her trust.

He prayed. For her and him, and for God to provide a path of forgiveness and peace for them both. As hopeless as his loving her was, Ace knew that whatever happened between them in the future, Meg Thomerson was forever imprinted in his mind, his heart and his soul.

When Meg woke the next morning, she heard Nita bustling around in the kitchen. Wide-eyed, she sat bolt upright in bed, knowing she'd overslept after lying awake for hours. She'd been braiding her hair for the night when she thought of Ace telling her that he was sorry, that the kiss had been "totally inappropriate under the circumstances."

Womanlike, she had latched on to the words. Had he been trying to tell her that he was sorry because it was too soon after Elton's death, or had he drawn away out of disgust that she could even think of kissing another man so soon after losing her husband? Was he thinking that she was indeed Georgie Ferris's daughter, or could he possibly be feeling guilt for almost kissing her so soon after her husband's death, a death he was responsible for?

Meg knew that if anyone should feel guilty about that near kiss with Elton barely cold in the ground, it was she. In truth, she didn't feel one iota of remorse.

Any feelings she'd once had for him had been over long before a stray bullet took his life.

For the first time since it happened, she took out her memories of that terrible day and looked at them with an objective eye, trying to imagine how it had impacted not just her, but everyone involved.

She thought long and hard about how the sheriff and his deputy had changed because of it. Colt had been jolted from his doubts and realized that he needed to make his peace with God for blaming Him for his wife's death so many years ago. Dan Mercer had come out of the ordeal and devoted himself to becoming the best man he could be.

And how had it affected Ace, the main player in the tragedy? Until recently, she'd thought of him as the man who'd shot her husband. She didn't blame him, not when there was no doubt that what he'd done was necessary to save lives. The fact was that God had chosen to spare Colt, as well as her and her children, through Ace. Nevertheless, she realized that the burden he carried on his broad shoulders was a heavy one to bear, even though the true cause of Elton's death was the violent life he'd chosen.

For the very first time since that day, Meg felt sorry for him. Not for her loss, but because it finally hit her that Elton was separated from God by the sins he committed. He'd never expressed regret or any desire to repent and change the course of his life, which he'd proved right up to the last moments of his life, when he had tried to kill both Colt and Ace.

On the other hand, she'd learned enough about Ace to know that day was a burden on his heart. Not only did he feel guilt, but he also felt responsible for the situation in which Meg now found herself, which was one reason he'd come to help during her recuperation.

What he didn't know was that his aid had not only saved her business, but his actions the past weeks had also helped banish her fears and gone a long way toward teaching her to trust. His work ethic and respectful manner, his patience and the peace that seemed to radiate from him like the warm rays of the sun, had shown her that not all men were like her late husband. Some men were good and kind and worthy of a woman's love.

She drew in a sharp breath.

Love. Was it possible? No! Though she'd wanted him to kiss her and was disappointed when he hadn't didn't mean that she loved him. She'd been treated too badly to consider falling in love with another man so soon after Elton's death. Ace was right. It was totally inappropriate.

You don't consider falling in love, Meg. It just happens. She drew a shallow breath and tried to convince herself that those few moments were out of time. They were both hurting and needed the emotional warmth and closeness of another person. Surely that wasn't love.

She'd fallen asleep near dawn with no answers, Now, in the light of day, she was still afraid to look too closely at what had happened and what it could possibly mean. Meg readied herself for the day and went to see if she could help Nita with the morning meal.

"Good morning," the older woman said, pouring a cup of fresh coffee into a mug and handing it to Meg. "Did you sleep well?"

Meg felt a blush creep up over her face. "After I finally went to sleep, yes. You should have awakened me."

"For what?" Nita smiled. "You and Ace already have this little farm looking like a showplace."

Ace. Where was he? She wanted to ask but held her tongue. "Hardly that."

Nita looked at her with raised eyebrows. "Have you really stopped and looked at what the two of you have done, or have you been so busy working that you haven't noticed the results?"

"The latter, I guess," Meg confessed, taking a sip of the fragrant brew.

"Well, sometime today, walk up the lane a ways and look back. When I came this morning, I thought I'd made a wrong turn. Everything looked so nice I wondered if I was at the right house!"

The notion that things looked *that* good was so outlandish that Meg laughed. She sobered suddenly. When had she last found anything to laugh about? Heaven knew there'd been little enough to find funny in the past.

All that is over now.

Yes. Over. Teddy and Lucy would soon be home and she promised herself that she would see to it that their lives were filled with fun and laughter, even if the joy was built around simple things.

Almost as if she could read her mind, Nita said, "I know you must be excited about the children coming home soon."

"Yes," Meg said, another smile blooming on her face. "I can hardly wait. I've missed them so."

"I know you have," Nita said in a gentle voice. "It will take time, Meg, but things will work out, and you and your children will be just fine."

Would they? Or would there just be more talk and speculation? Did she know and trust Nita Allen well enough to share those fears? Nita would not judge her, she knew. Just as she knew that any advice she gave would be rock-solid.

Meg took a breath to work up her nerve and plunged. "I'm worried, Mrs. Allen."

"About what?"

"The gossip. I imagine everyone in town is talking about me and saying I should have left Elton long ago and maybe this wouldn't have happened, but things are more complicated than just packing up and leaving."

Nita waited, giving Meg a chance to speak what was in her heart.

"Elton wasn't a very nice man," she offered, confirming what was common knowledge. "I'm sure everyone in town knew that, and I'm sure they talked about him and me, even though I tried not to give them any reason to."

Nita only nodded.

"Even though we had to marry, Aunt Serena taught

me well about the sanctity of marriage, and I took my vows seriously. For a long time, even after things got bad, I tried to love him as best I could, and then one day that love was just gone. I prayed for him and me, but nothing changed. He blamed me for every bad thing that ever happened to him and for every wrong thing he'd ever done."

Nita looked as if she wanted to say something, but Meg held up a restraining hand as the words seemed to spew from her very soul.

"He said I shouldn't be so mouthy. Maybe I was. I don't know, but I never gave anyone in town a reason to speak ill of me."

"I know that."

"He told me I should be a better wife and that I needed to stretch the little dab of money he gave me further than I did, but it was never enough."

She shuddered at the vivid rush of memories and swiped at the tears burning her eyes. "I tried to take care of what I had, and even though my kids' clothes were hand-me-downs or made from feed sacks, they were always starched and ironed and mended, and we never went to town unless they were bathed and their hair was combed."

She heaved a deep sigh. "I thought that if I did something to help make ends meet, he'd be glad. So I started the laundry business. You know what hard work it is. Elton started complaining that I'd let myself go and looked twice my age. He'd ask me how I expected him to care for me when it was plain that I didn't care about myself."

She met Nita's concerned gaze boldly, as if daring her to comment on what she was about to say.

"I prayed that I could find the courage to pack up my babies and leave him, but when I threatened it, he said he'd track me down and drag me back, so I stayed. I went to church services when I could, but after a while, he just wore down my hope and my faith like water dripping on a stone."

Nita regarded her with a solemn expression.

"When I became a Christian, Brother McAdams assured me that God had forgiven all of my sins, but sometimes—" she gulped back a huge sob "—sometimes I wonder if He might still be holding the things I did with Elton before our marriage against me."

"No, Meg," Nita assured her in a soft voice. "I can promise you He doesn't."

"Then I don't understand!" she cried. "I've tried living right, and I've tried prayer, but it never changed anything. My life has just gone from one bad thing to another. Look where I am now. Look at me!" She met her new friend's steady gaze. "What must everyone be saying about me now?"

Nita laid aside the two-pronged fork she was using to turn the bacon and reached out to place a small hand over Meg's. "I've heard what they say of you, Meg. There are more people in Wolf Creek who know the truth than not, and I don't know a single soul who blames you for your husband's wrongdoings—or your mother's, for that matter. Most of them admire you for the way you've conducted yourself these past years."

"Admire me?"

"Yes, because no matter what happened, you never lost your smile and you stayed faithful to God. As for looking at you…when I look at you, I see a beautiful woman filled with courage, a woman who's been through a tremendous amount of heartache and pain and has come out of it all with a whole new future ahead of her. No one likes to be the subject of gossip, Meg. I know that firsthand, but the thing is that in time, people tend to forgive and forget. I think Rachel Gentry would tell you that."

Nita gave Meg's hands a squeeze. "Don't give up on God, child. I believe He has good things planned for you."

"I want to believe that, Mrs. Allen," she said, more of the tears she'd held back for so long once again flooding her eyes.

"Keep believing," Nita said, smiling. "He's the only thing that will get us through the bad times. We can't see the whole picture the way He can—thank goodness! Why, I daresay that if we could see our future, it would likely scare us to death. That's why we're told to take one day at a time and not to worry about tomorrow."

"In other words, don't borrow trouble," Meg said, wiping at her eyes with the corner of a dish towel.

"Yes. There's no sense worrying about things that may not happen. Just concentrate on getting better, one day at a time, and deal with the problems as they come."

Nita turned back to her cooking.

Meg had a sudden vivid recollection of the squirrel

Ace had taken her into the woods to see. She finally understood the lesson he'd been trying to get across. The squirrel's home had been destroyed, yet it didn't give up. Instead, knowing winter was coming, it got to work carefully rebuilding its nest, choosing the uppermost branches of the tree, finding the grit and courage to aim high, just as she should.

Despite the hurt and pain in the Gentry family's past, its members had all lifted themselves above the ugliness and aimed not only for happiness, but also for peace and contentment and love. Was that what it meant in Romans, where it said that all things worked together for good to those who loved God? Was that what Libby was trying to tell her?

Meg wondered how He could possibly turn all that ugliness into something of beauty, yet He had done just that in others' lives. Could she hope for that? Was that what was happening with Ace?

It was too soon to say, and he was too hard to read. It was impossible to know if these fledgling feelings were the first stirrings of love. She did know that whoever the man in her future might be, he would need to accept her for what and who she was. She also knew that before she could trust someone wholly, she had to find forgiveness in her heart for Elton. To do that, she needed to pray.

For the first time since the day of Elton's death, Meg prayed for pardon for the lack of sorrow she felt at his loss, and she prayed that the Heavenly Father would have mercy on his soul. When she finished, she felt a sense of peace, and for the first time since she'd realized her marriage was made in hell, not heaven, she felt a glimmer of promise for the future.

One thing was certain. A man who watched squirrels and welcomed the dawning day with open arms and praise to the Almighty was not a man to be feared.

He was a man to be cherished.

Ace, who was standing outside the back screen door with an armload of kindling, heard every word of Meg's conversation with his mother. He'd always been told that eavesdropping was poor conduct, but in this case, he felt it was warranted. He'd always known things between Meg and Elton were bad, but until now, he hadn't known the extent of it. In addition to being beaten, she'd been blamed, ridiculed and made to feel ugly and inadequate. It was little wonder she'd lost her smile and her confidence, not to mention her faith.

He finally understood why she was so apologetic for everything she said and did. To raise Elton's wrath had been to invite his anger. That was why she'd run that day on the plateau.

Though her body was healing, Ace knew she had a long way to go before she was well emotionally and spiritually. What she needed was time, not a man pushing her into something she wasn't ready for.

A muscle in his jaw tightened and he pulled open the door. It was time to face the music and see how much damage his near kiss had done. The minute he stepped into the room, the aroma of the resin-rich wood mingled with the smell of frying bacon, familiar scents he associated with home. Meg sat at the table, a cup of coffee cradled between her palms.

"Good morning." His greeting was intended for them both, but his gaze grazed Meg's as he passed. "Am I interrupting?"

He didn't miss the look of discomfiture that crossed her face.

"Not at all," Nita told him. "I was just telling Meg how good the farm is looking and asking her if she'd noticed."

Ace met Meg's gaze. "And?" he asked with a lift of his dark eyebrows.

"I guess I haven't noticed," she confessed with a passable shrug of indifference.

Nita broke a couple of eggs into the skillet. "It's really amazing what the two of you have done in such a short time. You make a good team."

A good team. His mother's little reminder that she knew how he felt about Meg, he supposed. He wondered if she agreed. It was surprising what two people working toward a common goal could accomplish.

"Meg's good help. She's not afraid of work and she doesn't mind getting her hands dirty, unlike some people."

He noted the soft glow of pleasure in her eyes at his simple compliment. Ace doubted Elton had given her credit or praise for anything she'd done.

They were halfway through the meal when Nita asked, "Are you still going into town this morning?"

He nodded. "It's time to pick up the laundry." He

glanced over at Meg. "Do you feel up to going into town with me, just to break the monotony?"

Caught off guard by the invitation, Meg looked from him to his mother. The pleasure on her face was a sight to behold.

"That's a wonderful idea, Ace," Nita said, smiling at Meg. "An outing would be good for you, and it would give you a chance to visit with some of your friends."

As quickly as it had come, the joy on her face fled. "I think I'll pass."

"Are you sure?" he asked, wondering what had happened to change her mind and her attitude so fast. "I think it might do you good to have a change of scenery."

"Maybe so, but I'm not much of a gadabout. Besides, I…I need to work on Lucy's quilt."

Nita reached out and touched his wrist, forcing his attention to her. There was a warning look in her dark eyes. "Do you mind if I go in with you instead? I need to take the sassafras root I harvested to Gabe. He said several of the ladies were asking for it since it's getting cooler."

"Of course I don't mind," he told her, understanding her silent appeal to stop pushing. He fell easily into her strategy to take the focus off Meg. "And if you're a good girl, I might buy you a piece of penny candy."

"Candy! Oh, licorice, please!"

"Ugh!" Ace said, his mouth turning down at the corners. "How can you stand that stuff?"

"The same way you stand horehound, I reckon," Nita answered, casting Meg a smile.

"What's your favorite candy?" he asked Meg.

He watched color rise to her hairline. Though she seemed to be uncomfortable, she straightened in her chair.

"Um, there was never much extra money for candy, and when I did buy it, I got peppermint for Teddy. El…" She paused and then plunged ahead with a hint of defiance, almost as if she were deliberately drawing attention to her situation. "Elton brought me some chocolate once when he came home from a long…trip. I really liked that."

Ace ground his teeth to keep from saying something he shouldn't. "We'll see if Gabe has some chocolate, then."

"Oh! I never meant to hint that you should—"

"I know you didn't," Ace interrupted. "But you've been pretty good about minding Rachel's orders the past couple of weeks, so I think you deserve a treat."

Without giving her a chance to answer, he turned to his mother. "I need to feed the animals, and then I'll hitch up the wagon. Can you be ready in about twenty minutes?"

"I need to do the dishes and freshen up."

"I'll do that," Meg volunteered. "You go ahead."

"Thank you, Meg," Nita said, reaching out and giving her hand a pat. "You do deserve a treat."

Almost exactly twenty minutes later, Ace helped Nita into the wagon and vaulted up next to her. He turned the rig toward town and clucked to the horse.

"What on earth was that all about?" Nita asked,

smoothing her blue plaid skirt. "She was definitely, I don't know…not at ease with you this morning."

Ace turned to her with a wry half smile. "Probably because I came inches from kissing her."

Chapter Ten

Meg watched Ace and Nita pull down the lane with a heavy heart. She would have loved to go to town. Cabin fever had set in with a vengeance a couple of days earlier. Her initial pleasure at his invitation vanished the instant she realized that she'd have to carry on a conversation with him during the whole hour-long drive to Wolf Creek and back. What could she say to him when she'd practically begged him to kiss her and he'd turned her down?

Muttering beneath her breath at her boldness, she wandered around the cabin, wondering what she would do with herself until they returned. Since she'd finished Lucy's quilt two days earlier, she decided to take Nita's advice and walk down the road to the curve where the house would first be seen by visitors. She wanted to take a look at the improvements she and Ace had made, back when they were a "good team," before she'd made a fool of herself.

When she reached the bend in the lane and turned,

her mouth fell open in surprise. A couple of weeks of hard work and her little farm looked almost prosperous! The piles of brush and fallen limbs that once littered the grounds had been piled and burned, and the fence rows cleaned of scrub brush and weeds. The fall garden looked green and lush.

The fresh coat of whitewash made the house stand out against the foliage that had begun to change to its fall wardrobe. They'd given the outbuildings a coat of white, too, and Ace had painted the window frames of the house with some green paint Gabe had given him after it had fallen off a wagon and part of it spilled.

With the repaired corral and the chicken wire no longer drooping, the improvements were astonishing. All she needed were a few flowers around the front and maybe some green shutters and it would be perfect!

Meg felt her eyes fill with tears and brushed them away with an irritated swipe. It seemed that ever since seeing the evidence of Ace's suffering had freed her of the numbness that enveloped her, tears were always close to the surface.

These tears were happy, though. She actually laughed out loud in pleasure. It was no longer just her little house; it was a place she would be proud to call home, one she would not be ashamed to invite her new friends to visit, the place she would bring up her two children and any others she might have.

Would there be others? Oh, she hoped so! In the sleepless hours of the night, she'd realized that despite Elton's efforts to break her of feelings, there was still much love inside her, but the next time she would have to be very careful about to whom she gave that love. It must be a man who truly loved her back, one she could trust with her heart and her body and her children. Foolishly and too hastily, perhaps, she dared to hope Ace would be that man.

With or without a husband, Meg vowed that she would bring so much love and joy into those four walls that there would be no room for the old memories and the sorrow accompanying them. She promised herself that she would not be weak any longer, that she would stand up for herself and her children and be the person God intended her to be. She knew she would not change overnight.

One day at a time.

Meg spent an hour at her favorite place in the woods, where she felt closest to God, where the cares of the world dropped away beneath the perfection of His creation and she felt so very close to Him. Ace explained that the Celts believed that heaven and earth were only three feet apart. Sometimes, at certain times or certain places, the distance was less. These were places or moments—not necessarily beautiful or serene ones—where people were forced to look at the world in a different perspective. The Celts called them "thin places."

Meg liked the idea of thin places, places when, for a brief time, heaven and earth seemed closer. She'd always felt that this spot in the woods was the tiniest peek of what heaven must be like. Now, basking in the peace she found there, she read her Bible and prayed for herself and, falteringly, once more for Elton.

At midmorning, filled with contentment once again, she went back to the house and did the things mothers did. She swept and dusted and looked through the sweet dresses Abby Gentry's girls had outgrown that had been passed on for Lucy. Some of them were wellworn, but Meg was glad to have them.

Lucy hadn't been walking the last time she'd seen her, and there was no help for everyday wear and tear when a baby was on her knees most of the time. These would be just fine. There were a couple of dresses that had obviously been for Sunday services and would look precious with Lucy's blond hair and blue eyes.

Meg was sitting on the front porch, mending a tear in one of Ace's shirts that Nita had set aside to repair, when she glanced up and saw the dust of an approaching vehicle. It was a buggy, not a wagon, so it wasn't Ace and Nita. Meg set aside the shirt and got to her feet. A wagon, trailing far behind to avoid the worst of a cloud of dust, followed the buggy. She wondered who was coming and what on earth was going on.

Drawn by curiosity, she went down the front steps and started across the grass toward the road, shielding her eyes against the sun. It looked like the doctor's buggy, and Nita was sitting next to Rachel. Why was Nita with Rachel instead of Ace? Was it possible that she was bringing home her babies? Meg wondered as a tentative joy began to fill her. The closer they got, the better she could see. Yes! Lucy was sitting on Nita's lap.

By the time Rachel pulled the buggy to a stop, Meg was almost bouncing up and down with happiness. Her gaze found Lucy first. Her sweet baby girl was nestled against Ace's mother, chewing on the tail of the bow adorning the front of her dress and looking quite pleased to be outside.

Beneath the brim of a new eyelet bonnet, her cheeks were rosy with health and the warmth of the day. Meg ached to snatch her out of Nita's arms and cover her face with kisses; at the same time, she was running toward the buggy, searching for a glimpse of Teddy. She spied him in the backseat, sitting in her aunt Serena's lap. Uncle David sat next to them. Everyone waved and wore wide smiles as they called out greetings.

"Mama!" Teddy cried, struggling to get out of his great-aunt's arms.

"Hold still, Teddy," Serena said in a gentle voice. "Let Uncle Dave hold you while I get out. I'm not sure Mama can carry you just yet. She has a sore arm—remember?"

"I'm fine," Meg insisted, but Teddy nodded and did as he'd been told.

In a few seconds, Meg was kneeling on the ground, unmindful of getting her skirt dirty. Teddy's arms were wound tightly around her neck and hers were holding him so close that her ribs hurt.

"Ouch, Mama," he said after a few seconds. "Don't hug so hard."

With a little laugh that sounded suspiciously like a sob, Meg released him and cradled his precious freckled face in both her hands. "I've missed you so," she breathed and proceeded to cover his sweet face with kisses.

Then she heard an unintelligible sound from her daughter. Giving Teddy a final kiss, she stood and took her baby girl into her arms. She'd grown so much! Meg wasn't surprised to feel her eyes fill with more of those dratted tears. She was getting used to them cropping up with every emotion she experienced.

"Gabe didn't have any chocolate," Rachel said, smiling broadly. "But we thought this might make up for it."

"Oh, yes!" Meg said, rubbing her nose against Lucy's. "This is much better than chocolate."

"She's taking a few steps." Serena slid an arm around Meg's shoulders and gave her a quick hug. "I'm sorry you missed it."

"It couldn't be helped," she said, leaning for a few seconds against the woman who had been her role model for so many years. "I'm just thankful that you could take care of them for me."

"Come on inside," Nita said as she reached for Lucy. "I made cookies yesterday, and I'll fix us some of that cold tea we like so much."

The guests followed Nita up the steps and into the house. Only then did Meg dare to look at Ace.

"I told you that you deserved a treat," he said. For once the expression in his eyes was not guarded. His eyes gleamed with a pleasure that was reflected in his smile. Oh! she thought as her breath caught in her throat. That expression did such amazing things to his usual stern demeanor!

Meg found herself smiling back. "This is a *very* special treat. Did you know they were coming home today? Is that why you asked me to go to town with you?"

He nodded. "We had to come up with an alternate plan when you changed your mind. What happened?"

The challenge in his eyes told her he was probing for the truth. Determined not to be so wishy-washy, she lifted her chin and said, "After…after last night and you going all stuffy on me, I wasn't sure I could carry on a conversation with you for two hours."

Ace regarded her with a lift of his dark eyebrows. "Stuffy?" He glanced toward the house, where Teddy stood with his nose pressed to the screen, waiting for her to come inside. "Go get reacquainted with your little ones," he told her softly. "There's plenty of time to discuss my stuffiness."

The next hour was pure mayhem as they sat around the table and shared cookies and cold tea. Conversation never flagged, and the little house was filled with the hum of a half-dozen voices and peals of happy laughter.

Lucy was content to sit in her mother's lap, munching on sugar cookies and sipping from her glass of tea, while Teddy reacquainted himself with the place in which he'd once lived. After thirty minutes or so, he went to the back door and peered through the screen toward where the sound of Ace's hammering could be plainly heard.

"I want to go out to help the man," he announced to no one in particular.

All eyes turned to Meg. Even her aunt and uncle, who had been responsible for Teddy these past weeks, looked to her for an answer, returning her motherly authority. What should she do? Would Ace mind if Teddy joined him, or would he explode in anger the way Elton had the few times Teddy had wanted to be outside with him?

Meg's gaze sought Nita's.

"Ace won't mind at all," she said, rising. "I'll take Teddy out. We'll take Ace a glass of tea and a couple of cookies."

It wasn't the answer Meg had expected. Ace wasn't used to being around children. She was so fearful that it would all go awry.

"B-but Teddy has on his good clothes" was all she could think to say.

"I'll see that he doesn't get dirty."

Somewhat relieved that Nita would be there to watch over Teddy, Meg cautioned, "Don't let him get in the way."

"He won't."

Once they had disappeared out the door, Serena leaned back in her chair and said, "I couldn't believe how wonderful everything looked when we rounded that bend and saw all the improvements you've made to the place."

Meg knew her aunt was trying to steer the conversation in a new direction. "Nita thought it would be a good idea for Ace to get things ready for winter," she said.

"It looks like he did a lot more than that," her uncle

said with a smile of approval. "Colt is right. Ace is a good man."

"Yes," Meg said, hoping they couldn't tell just how good she thought he was.

The talk turned to what was going on in town. Rachel said that plans were going ahead for Colt and Allison's wedding in January, and that Mayor Talbot was having a conniption because he was losing her as their teacher midyear and had no idea who would take her place. Libby said Blythe would be perfect for the position, but she had no desire to live in Wolf Creek. Dan Mercer and his fiancée, Gracie, were planning a spring wedding, and to Libby Granville's delight, everyone seemed to love the new library.

Nita and Teddy were still outside when the guests started getting ready to leave. Lucy had fallen asleep in Aunt Serena's arms, crying and reaching for the older woman when she'd begun to tire from all the excitement.

Meg didn't miss the pitying glances in the eyes of her guests as she handed over the fussy child without a word. Lucy was asleep minutes later. Meg's heart ached. Her daughter had grown used to finding comfort in someone else's arms. Like everything else in her life that needed mending, it would take time to bridge the gaps between her and her baby girl.

While Uncle Dave and Rachel cleaned up the table, Meg followed her aunt into the bedroom and watched as she placed Lucy in her crib.

"I'm sorry," Serena whispered when the baby was settled.

"There's no sense being sorry. Things are what they are, and it will just take time for us…" Her voice trailed away.

"You need time to figure out who Meg Thomerson is."

"Is she anyone?" Meg asked with a disheartened smile. "Does she even exist?"

Her aunt took her by the shoulders and looked directly into her eyes. "Oh, she exists. She just forgot who she was for a while, and now she's trying to figure it out." Serena smiled. "Not only does she exist, she's a very special person who found herself under the control of a very bad man."

Meg's eyes filled with more tears. "I made some really bad choices, Aunt Serena."

"We've all made bad choices, sweet Meg. The trick is not to make the same ones twice."

"How do I keep from doing that?"

Serena gave her a little shake. "You won't."

"How can you be sure?"

Serena gave her another little shake, this one harder. "You won't, because you are not Georgina. She chose the life she's living. Things might have been different if your father hadn't died."

"What do you mean?" Meg's father had died when she was ten, leaving a void in both her and her mother's lives.

"Georgina wasn't always the way she is. When your father died, she didn't like being alone, so she took up with Charlie. He doesn't care what she does as long as he has his liquor. Trust me. You're nothing like my sister."

"Even though Elton and I had to get married?"

"Yes, even though. And you needn't think I don't know why you took up with him. Everyone saw that Charlie had his eye on you, and he wasn't the only one. You were looking for an escape, and when Elton came along and started wooing you, it was easy for you to believe that he was your way out of what would have become a terrible situation."

Meg's eyes widened with surprise. How could her aunt have known about that? She'd thought she was the only one to see the inappropriate way Charlie had looked at her.

"I'm not blind, child. Thank goodness you got out."

Meg gave a bitter laugh. "I got out, but I only traded one kind of hell for another."

"You had no way of knowing that." Serena gave her another hug. "Let's join the others. I imagine Rachel's ready to get on the road. Give yourself time to heal, Meg. There's someone out there who will be the man you and your children need." She gave her a saucy wink. "From what I've seen and heard, you could do worse than the one who's helping out."

"Ace!" she scoffed. "He isn't interested."

Soft laughter filled the small room. "Remember, sweet Meg, I'm not blind, and I'm not stupid. I see the way *he* looks at you."

Nita joined her to send their visitors on their way. Before the dust had cleared, the two women had headed to the barn. She could spare only a minute since the baby was asleep inside, but she wanted to make sure

Teddy was not aggravating Ace. To her surprise, she found her son with his little hands on his hips, staring up at Ace, who was on a ladder nailing a board in place for what looked like another lean-to.

"Mama, Ace is making a surprise!" he shouted, grabbing her around the knees.

"I see that." She ruffled his hair and looked from him to Ace. "What are you doing?" she asked.

"Fixing a place outside for you to do the laundry that's partially protected, so you won't be at the mercy of the weather quite as much this winter," he explained. "It'll have a roof and three enclosed sides. I'm hoping that if you build the fires near the open end, the smoke will go out, but a little of the heat just might stay in." He shrugged. "I'm no carpenter and it isn't a perfect solution, but maybe it will help. At least you'll be out of the rain."

For a moment, Meg was stunned speechless by the thoughtful gesture. She couldn't recall Elton ever doing anything for her simply because he knew it would make her life easier.

"Thank you," she said. "I appreciate it. Any kind of protection will be better than what I've had."

"That's what I thought."

"I think Teddy and I will go inside to check on Lucy and think about what to fix for supper," Nita said, stretching out a hand to the toddler. "What sounds good to you, Teddy?"

"Pink beans," he said, placing his hand in Nita's. "They're the bestest beans in the world."

Meg and Nita exchanged smiles. He'd always loved navy beans.

"I think that can be arranged, even though I didn't put any to soak this morning."

"Soda," Meg offered as the two started toward the house.

Nita turned. "Baking soda?"

"Yes. You've never heard of baking soda to help them cook faster?"

"I can't say that I've ever run across that in any of my Cherokee or Irish recipes," Nita confessed.

Meg smiled back. "I'll be in in a moment to show you what to do."

"I'll be looking forward to it."

Silence descended on Ace and Meg after Teddy and Nita went to the house.

"Did Teddy get in the way?" she asked, hoping to get a feel for what Ace thought of her son.

"No more than any three-year-old boy who wants to help," he said. "Mother said you were worried about him coming out here."

"Yes."

"Why? Because Elton would have been furious to have a kid in his way, or he didn't want to keep an eye on him?"

"Yes to both of those reasons. He had no patience with Teddy—with either one of them, for that matter."

"Doesn't sound to me like he had much patience for anything," Ace commented, reaching for more nails.

"You're right. He was like a tinderbox and a piece of flint. Anything and everything could set him off."

"I'm not Elton." A muscle in his jaw tightened.

"You've told me that before," she reminded him.

"And I'll keep telling you until you believe it."

How could she tell him that she did believe it, but that her history had left her a little gun-shy? It would be a long time before the new lessons she was learning were such a part of her that she would no longer worry or question the little everyday irritants and expect them to explode into full-blown quarrels. What she could do instead was thank him.

"I really do appreciate everything you've done for me, Ace," she said at last. "I can never repay you."

"So you've said before," he told her, tossing her words back at her as he hammered another nail into the end of a board. "I don't want any pay except to see you get better."

"I am."

"I know, and I'm glad."

She drew in a shaky breath as he came down the ladder. It seemed imperative that she tell him how she was feeling, how she was changing. She leaned against the barn wall.

"That day…the day you and Colt and Dan found me and I was hurt so badly, I hardly felt it. It's like I was dead inside, like Elton had killed the very thing that made me who I was."

"Who you *are*."

"No!" she snapped with a sharp shake of her head. "I'm not that woman anymore. I won't ever be that scared, weak woman again." One corner of her mouth hiked up in a wry smile. "In a strange way, I guess I can thank Elton for that."

Ace took a step closer. "I'm not Elton, and not all men are users, Meg."

"I know. You've shown me that. You've shown me that I don't have to be afraid of saying what I want or feel." Tears filled her eyes. "I don't have to be afraid."

"All I've done is help with a few chores."

"You've done more than that," she argued softly. "You're a man who's been through some of the same things I have and you've learned a lot along the way, things you've passed on to me."

"Like what?"

"Like, don't give up. Don't ever give up. Rachel said we should try to find the good that's hidden in the bad. You and Nita are the part of the good. She's so kind and so wise, and you… You've taught me that with God, all things *are* possible, even forgiving the ones who caused our pain."

She gave a little laugh. "I admit I'm having a little trouble with that one, but as Brother McAdams says, it will come."

"And it will, in time."

She nodded. "I've learned, too, that the Lord is able to heal broken hearts and shattered souls. Especially shattered souls."

"Souls are His specialty," Ace reminded her.

"Yes," she whispered. "I always knew that, but I'd just more or less given up on hope and trust and…and life. I don't think I could have come as far as I have in such a short time without you to help me along the way."

"Don't try to make me some kind of white knight," he cautioned. "I'm just a man with all the usual bad habits."

Meg stood there staring at him, wanting to tell him that he was much more than that to her and that she dreaded the time he would leave and not come back, and that even though she was determined to be strong, she wasn't sure she could go on without his reassuring, supportive presence.

"I'd better go inside and show your mother what to do with that baking soda," she said instead, taking the coward's way out.

The new Meg was a little afraid of being that daring.

A week passed, and then two. As he always had, Ace went home at night to take care of their place; Nita was staying nights for a while, sleeping in Teddy's narrow bed to keep an eye on Lucy. Teddy slept with Meg. As much as she hated imposing on the older woman, Meg was glad for her help. Chasing after two little ones was harder than she'd expected, especially since Lucy was finally walking and wanting to explore everything. It had taken Meg less than twenty-four hours to realize she wasn't up to her former strength just yet.

Teddy settled back into his life with his mother without any problem. Lucy was harder. Aunt Serena was all she'd known for weeks, and it was evident that she missed her, probably as much as Serena missed Lucy.

Gradually, though, Meg felt her life returning to

normal. No, not normal. The life she'd shared with Elton had in no way been normal. Instead, like the squirrel, she was rebuilding her nest and cautiously building a new life.

The days things felt overwhelming and frightening, Nita would remind her to put her trust in the Lord. That simple command was hard for a woman who felt more secure if she were in control. Nita said that like everything else in her life, it would take time.

Another week passed. Meg had promised Ace that she would do her best to start each day with a positive attitude and thankfulness, so even though the weather was growing colder, she started taking her coffee and Bible with her to the back porch first thing in the mornings. She hoped the quiet time while the children still slept would give her the optimistic attitude she needed to tackle the day ahead.

She was a little surprised at how easily she fell back into her old routine and amazed that with every faltering prayer and every moment she spent with the Word, she felt more peace and strength filling her.

To her amazement, both the children were quite taken with Ace. Teddy, who'd become Uncle Dave's shadow during the weeks he'd stayed with him, was at an age where he needed a man to look up to, and Uncle Dave was one of the best. With her uncle out of the picture, Teddy had latched on to Ace in a way he never had his own father.

They had fallen into the habit of Ace regaling Teddy with some folk tale or another at bedtime. Meg couldn't believe how adept he was at mimicking an Irish brogue and the high girlish voices of the ladies and the various facial expressions that accompanied the tales of haughty princesses, lazy beauties and enchanted lakes that brought smiles and laughter to everyone.

She didn't know if the growing closeness between the two was a blessing or another problem she'd have to deal with when Ace and Nita stopped coming around. She pushed the troubling thought aside. That was in the future, and she was doing her best to take one day at a time.

Even though Ace was not what any woman would call handsome, he was very attractive in a stark sort of way, which was the only reason Meg could figure out that Lucy was so taken with him. She was a female, after all, and whether or not they would admit to it, he was the kind of man most of the fairer sex found appealing. Of course, it might be the gentleness of his rare smile or the softness of his voice when he spoke to her.

At almost every meal, Lucy held up her arms for Ace to pick her up, and he always did. He blew on hot food and fed her things from his plate that her chubby hands could handle. When she made some sort of mess and he scowled at her in mock ferocity, Lucy just giggled, showing off her eight little teeth, as if to say she knew he was harmless. If children and dogs were the best judges of character, Ace passed with flying colors.

They hadn't yet talked about his "stuffiness" or anything else serious since soon after they'd almost shared a kiss. He'd finished the laundry lean-to and spent most of his time trapping. Meg had been busy with the children. Everyone was working hard, and her life was settling into one she found she liked. Perhaps she liked it too much.

As a treat, everyone was going to ride into town with Ace the next morning when he went to deliver the laundry. Meg was looking forward to the trip, especially since she'd have Nita and the children as buffers to ease any strain between her and Ace.

She'd been sticking back a little money every week, hoping there would be enough—after making a land payment to Nate Haversham at the bank and seeing if Gabe had any shoes that would see Lucy through the winter—to treat everyone to pie at Ellie's. She was also looking forward to visiting Libby Granville at the library and checking out some more books. She also thought she'd worked up enough nerve to speak to Libby about some things that had been bothering her.

She was so excited about the upcoming trip she could hardly contain herself. It had been so long since she'd been around anyone but Ace and Nita. Her anticipation had rubbed off on Teddy, and even though he usually fell right to sleep after his story, tonight was different. By the time his eyes drifted closed, Meg was exhausted, but she knew it was far too early to call it a day.

She shut the bedroom door behind her and found Nita thumbing through one of the magazines Libby had brought.

"Finally asleep?"

"Finally." She noticed a glow outside the kitchen window and looked inquiringly at Nita.

"Ace built a fire," she explained. "He likes sitting outside, even in the dead of winter."

Meg could imagine what he'd say if she were to ask him why. He would tell her about finding peace beneath the vast space after being confined behind bars for so long, or feeling closest to God when he was enjoying His creations. Or he might simply say that he liked to be alone.

"Why don't you wrap up in a quilt and join him?" Nita suggested.

Memories of the times she'd tried to connect with Elton flashed through her mind, followed almost immediately by the memory of Ace telling her time and again that he wasn't Elton. She knew that, but still, the thought of imposing on his alone time was a bit scary.

"Go on," Nita urged. "He won't mind. I'll make you each a cup of sassafras tea with honey to keep you warm."

Meg took a deep breath. "Are you sure?"

"Of course I'm sure," Nita told her, making a shooing motion toward the door. "Go. Get the quilt off my bed."

Fearful that she might be overstepping her bounds, Meg nonetheless decided to do just that. After all, she was not the old Meg anymore. The new Meg needed to be more forceful, less fearful. Besides, Ace was too polite to say anything, even if he did feel as if she were intruding. Taking Nita's suggestion, she tiptoed into the children's room and got the quilt.

Chapter Eleven

Ace was staring into the fire when he must have heard the latch of the door catch. He looked up and watched as she made her way down the back steps. Knowing he was watching every step she took made her very uncomfortable. Trying to ignore the butterflies in her stomach, she settled onto one of the big chunks of wood that doubled as a stool. It was closer to his than she would have liked, but moving it would only draw more attention to the awkwardness they'd struggled with the past weeks.

"Kids down for the night?" he asked.

His voice was as smooth and dark as the sky spread out above them. She gave a little shiver that had nothing to do with the chilly air and drew the quilt closer. "Yes. I think between your story and the excitement over tomorrow, Teddy was just overly excited."

"I'm sorry."

"Oh, no! I didn't mean to put the blame on you. It's just one of those things that happen every now and then when you have children."

"You're a good mother."

The compliment caught Meg off guard. No one except her aunt had ever told her that before. She felt pleased and strangely humbled. She loosed a soft, wry laugh into the night. "I don't know if I'm doing a good job or not, but I'm trying."

"That's all anyone can do."

"I hope they aren't bothering you too much, demanding so much of your attention," she said, daring to put her fears to the forefront.

He turned to face her, and the light of the fire gilded his angular features with molten copper. "Lucy and Teddy? Not at all. I remember being as curious as Teddy about everything when I was his age, and Lucy is such a sweetheart that no one could be angry at her about anything."

"Elton could."

The words escaped before she could stop them. Meg wished with all her heart that she could call them back, that she could reach a point where everything in her present life was not a comparison to the past.

"That was too bad for him," Ace said.

The awkwardness passed and that peaceful silence they'd shared as they worked together stretched out between them. An owl hooted nearby, and a pack of coyotes began to yip in the distance.

Meg decided to raise a topic she'd wondered about for more than three long weeks—probably longer than that. It was a very personal topic, and probably one that was highly improper for her to bring up, but she hoped to gain some insight into the workings of the mind of the man with whom she feared she was falling in love. Taking a deep breath, she plunged headlong into uncharted waters.

"You've never married."

The statement caught Ace completely off guard. He was surprised and wasn't sure he wanted to comment. "No."

Meg looked at him curiously. "I know it's none of my business, but why? It's pretty clear that you'd make a great husband and father."

He couldn't tell her that he'd cared for her since the first time he'd seen her, and he couldn't say that for three long weeks he'd thought of little else but the moment he'd almost kissed her.

Though he regretted passing on the chance to see if her lips held the sweetness they promised, it was best for everyone that his sanity had returned in time. He knew that she'd wanted that kiss as much as he did, but he was also aware that sometimes in situations like theirs affections got misplaced. He didn't want her to make the mistake of thinking she cared for him when in reality it was nothing but gratitude.

"How many women want to get involved with a man who's been in prison?"

She frowned. "I don't think people think of you in that way. More than likely they think of you as the man who rescued me and my children and saved Colt's life."

Ace nodded slowly. "Ah, so that's what you're calling it now instead of me killing your husband," he said, determined to make her see the reality of what had happened.

"That's not how it was. It was self-defense. Everyone says so," she argued. "Besides, you saved lives besides yours."

"Trying to make me a hero again, Meg?"

"You're my hero."

As soon as the words left her mouth, Ace saw that she regretted them. So did he. He was no hero, and no one knew it any better than he did. Still, he wished the words were true.

He leaped to his feet so fast she gasped. Turning his back to her, he stared into the fire as if he thought he could find some sort of answer in its flickering depths. That failing, he drew in a couple of deep lungfuls of air to clear his mind and refocus his thoughts.

"The fair maiden isn't usually afraid of her hero," he said mockingly without turning to look at her.

He heard her small, embarrassed laugh.

"If you're no hero, I'm certainly no fair maiden, but I am still a little fearful."

"Only a little?"

"Only a little."

"What else do you want from me, Meg?" he asked, needing to know, yet fearing the answer, since he knew that any way she responded would not lead to the conclusion he wanted.

"What do you mean?"

"What do you want besides my…help?"

"For starters, I want you to tell me what's wrong with me."

He turned to look at her. "Wrong with you? I'm not sure I understand."

"Well," she said with a hesitant shrug, "Elton...was never happy with anything I did, and you...you were going to...to k...kiss me and you stopped, so I figured there's something wrong with me." She'd stood as she spoke, leaving the quilt behind. She tipped back her chin to a determined angle as she faced him.

"Are we about to have the conversation about my... stuffiness?" he asked, unable to suppress a hint of a smile.

"I believe we are," she told him, moving closer. "After what I went through growing up, I'd be the last person to look down on anyone that way. We're not responsible for our parents' sins and they aren't responsible for ours.

"That may be what the Bible says, but that doesn't stop people from feeling differently."

"You have a point," he told her, knowing that she was right.

"All right," she said, forging ahead in a way that surprised him. "You said the timing was bad. Why?"

"Because it was. Elton—"

"Had only been dead a short time," she interrupted. "I know that. I thought you were saying in a nice way that I was too bold."

"You, bold?" he asked with a lift of his eyebrows.

"Well, I did encourage...things. It's just that I haven't loved Elton for a very long time, so it didn't seem too soon at all to me."

He didn't know whether to laugh or cry. What a

muddle! "Look, Meg," he said, trying once more to make her see the reality of their situation—or maybe it was himself he was trying to convince. "When people go through difficult incidents together, their thinking can go awry and they sometimes misinterpret a situation."

"Did I misinterpret?" Without allowing him time to reply, she took another step toward him, looking up at him in the dim light of the fire. "I don't have much experience with men, but it felt...right."

Ace closed his eyes. He was doomed, he thought, unaware that he reached out and curled his hands over her shoulders. Without knowing quite how it happened, he realized that he was holding her in a close embrace. Her arms were tight around his middle and her cheek was pressed against his chest. In the sweetness of that moment, when he let down his guard to reveal his own vulnerability, he knew without a doubt how much he loved her.

With a sigh of surrender, he closed his eyes and rested his chin on the top of her head. Her arms tightened around him and he wished she could stay in his arms forever, shielded from any harm. Safe.

"What am I going to do with you?" he asked, more to himself and the night than to her.

Love me.

Meg wanted to say it, but she knew she couldn't make him love her any more than she could force the sun to rise in the west. He would either return her feelings or he wouldn't.

She understood all that, but none of it mattered. Not now. Instead, she pressed closer. She was so wrapped up in the mixed emotions racing through her she almost missed what he said.

"No."

"What?" she asked, drawing back to look at him.

Ace tucked a silvery strand of her straight blond hair behind her ear. "You didn't misinterpret."

Did this mean that he cared for her, too? Oh, she hoped so! Even though she had more healing to do before she was truly whole, Meg was pretty sure her feelings for him wouldn't change, but there was no guarantee that he would ever feel more than this... whatever it was, for her.

She couldn't let this moment pass by. It might be the only thing she had to remember him by. "Then don't be stuffy," she begged. "Please."

"Meg..."

She curled her fingers in the fabric of his shirt. "Please."

He gave another of those soft moans, and then she felt his lips touch hers.

For such a hard man, the touch of his mouth was incredibly soft. A revelation. Accustomed as Ace was to physical demands, his lips communicated controlled longing as well as tenderness. She felt cherished, special, as if she had worth to him. It was her turn to groan in protest when his hands slid to her shoulders and he stepped back, lifting his mouth from hers.

Meg's lips felt as if they'd been branded by his kiss. Was the wonder still coursing through her veins reflected in her eyes? Did he feel it? She stared at him, waiting for him to comment or to do something to let her know what he was feeling, what he'd felt.

No. She knew. For once he wasn't hiding behind his expressionless shield. He looked as overwhelmed as she felt. He might have been reluctant to kiss her, but she was no innocent miss who didn't know when a man's emotions were involved. His had been, yet she couldn't help wondering if she had somehow disappointed him as she so often had Elton. She wanted to ask him, but figured she'd been brazen enough for one night.

The sound of the door closing sent them jumping apart. Nita was coming down the steps with the tea. Had she seen them?

"Are you two freezing?" she asked, handing them each a large cup.

"It's not too bad," Ace said.

Was it Meg's imagination, or was his voice huskier than usual?

"I'm warm enough," Meg added.

Nita crossed her arms and tipped back her head to look up at the sky. "Isn't it gorgeous?" she asked on an exhaled breath.

"It is," Meg agreed, following her example.

"I never grow tired of looking at it."

Meg didn't want to admit that she couldn't recall the last time she'd really looked up at the night sky. Probably not since before she married. Once she and Elton had tied the knot, she'd been too busy with work and babies, or just too plain worn-out to want to sit outside, drink tea and stargaze.

She remembered when she was about fifteen or so, Aunt Serena had told her to look up at the night sky. As Meg had been trying to take in its vast beauty, her aunt had told her that if God could make all of that from nothing, He could take care of any problems they might have.

Funny that she'd forgotten that until this moment. That she hadn't remembered such a wise statement was a shame, just as it was a shame that she had so seldom looked up. She vowed to do better.

"Well, I'll leave you two to your visiting," Nita said, turning back toward the house and pulling Meg's attention back to the present.

Once the door had closed behind her, Meg said, "She's a wonderful woman."

"She is," Ace agreed. "She thinks you're pretty wonderful, too."

"I can't imagine why."

"Can't you, Meg? How can you think of what you've accomplished in spite of everything you've been through and not know that there are few women who could do the same?"

"The same way you can't see that in spite of everything you've been through, you're a pretty remarkable man, I suppose," the new, bold Meg dared to say.

He didn't reply, and there was no hint of what he was feeling on his face. For several seconds they stood looking at each other and Meg was tense with anticipation that he might kiss her again.

Finally, when the silence stretched out unbearably, she took a sip of her sassafras tea and pasted a false smile on her lips. "So tell me again why you've never married."

"Because until now I've never met a woman who was everything I wanted and needed."

Meg froze. It felt as if the world were suddenly empty of air. He couldn't possibly mean her, could he? Once again she was afraid to ask. So much for her newfound courage.

"Why do you look so confused?" he asked. "After that kiss there can't be any doubt in your mind who I'm talking about or how I feel."

"Are you saying that you care for me?" Her voice was so small the vast darkness almost swallowed it up.

"Yes, but that doesn't mean I'm ready to do anything about it."

He sounded defeated.

"Why are you acting as if…caring for me is a bad thing?" she asked. "You must know that I…I care for you, too."

Ace flung the contents of his cup into the night and set the mug on the log. "Do you, Meg?" he asked. "You've spent almost four years in a marriage that was little more than a prison. Now you've been let out and the freedom must be overwhelming. Maybe you just fancy that you care for me because I'm the first man to treat you well."

She opened her mouth to deny the charge, but realized he had a point. The knowledge that Elton would never deal her any more grief *was* liberating in ways she was only now beginning to understand. She could do or be whatever she wanted, go wherever she pleased, without fear of punishment. But Ace was right. Sometimes that newly found freedom was a little frightening. How could he know that?

Because he's been where you are.

He could be right about something else. *Was* she mistaking her feelings for love when they were nothing but gratitude? She didn't think so, but how could she know for sure? Her head spun with conflicting emotions as she struggled to put all the pieces together.

"You say you care for me. Why don't you want me to care for you?"

"You're very vulnerable right now, Meg. Everyone keeps saying it, but I'm not sure you really grasp that you can't get over the things you've been through in a matter of weeks."

Her mind whirled. Something else to consider. Maybe she should give more thought to what both he and Aunt Serena were saying. Maybe she did need more time to recover from her past, time to figure out who she was and what she wanted to do with her life. She was trying to build a future. She couldn't make any more mistakes.

"It may take years," Ace was saying, "and until you can stand on your own two feet and know in your heart and your mind that you don't need a man to take care of you, I'm not sure you'll be ready for involvement with someone else."

Ace was up half the night reliving his conversation with Meg as well as the kiss. It was everything he'd expected, which was why he'd done his level best to nip anything more between them in the bud. A romance between them would never work. She might say she didn't blame him for Elton's death, but he wondered if she could ever truly forget it. Was that something she'd bring up every time they got into an argument?

Besides, he had his own reasons. As much as he cared for her and wanted to make her his wife, he couldn't bear the thought of putting her and those sweet kids in a position where they would be talked about behind their backs, especially after he'd heard Meg tell his mother how much she hated being the subject of everyone's conversation.

He remembered a talk he'd had with his father once after a particularly nasty incident in the town where they'd lived at the time. Yancy had been heartbroken because Ace and Nita had been the subject of whispers and ridicule. Ace, who had been fourteen or fifteen, had confronted his father.

"Why did you marry her if you knew people would make fun of her—and you?" he'd demanded, getting right up into his father's face. "Why didn't you marry an Irish girl?"

Yancy's handsome face was etched with pain, but he didn't back down from Ace's anger. "Because I never met an Irish girl who made me feel the things your mother does," he said.

"If you just want to get married, it makes little difference whom you choose, but if it's love you're looking for, lad, it just happens, usually when you least expect it. I wasn't looking for love or a wife when I first saw your mother, but from then on, I knew I'd never be happy without her. It was either make her my wife or be miserable the rest of my life."

"So you decided we should all be miserable."

"I wasn't thinking of that. I only thought of us sharing a life together. Yes, it's been challenging at times, but I have no regrets beyond the fact that you're the one who suffers most."

That was the moment that he'd told Ace that the things in life defined you, destroyed you or helped mold you.

Ace's mother, who had been listening, had added that she had no regrets, either. "Love can soothe a lot of hurts, Asa," she'd told him. "And if love finds you, you should embrace it and be glad."

At the time, suffering as only a young person could, their answers seemed selfish. Now he understood what they'd meant, but the difference was that he wasn't sure he could place that burden on any woman. Ever.

He knew what he needed to do, but decided that it wasn't something that needed doing at that moment. There were things he had to finish before he bowed out of Meg's life. He fell asleep wishing things were different, recalling the sound of his blunt challenge to her hanging in the cool night air.

When Ace woke, a gray dawn was just creeping over the landscape. As he rose and stretched, he heard the shuffle of the horse's hooves, the muffled snorting of the pig they would slaughter in a couple of weeks and the rustle of chickens in the nearby coop.

He glimpsed a barn owl overhead, a ghostly gray silhouette gripping something in its talons.

There was already a light in the kitchen and he figured his mother was up making the morning coffee. Grabbing a rough muslin towel from a stack of his belongings, he walked down the frosty trail to the creek to take a bath in the cold water. Once he was done, wide-awake and shivering, he donned clean clothes and made his way back to the house.

When he passed by the still-glowing embers of the fire, a rush of memories bombarded him. He could feel the warmth of Meg's slight body pressed so closely to his and the touch of his lips on hers. Gritting his teeth, Ace stomped up onto the porch and stepped through the back door. The aroma of fried chicken made his mouth water. Chicken at breakfast?

His mother and Meg were up and busy. Nita was setting the table and Meg was stirring gravy. They both looked up when he entered the room, but his mother was the only one who offered him a smile of welcome. Meg just looked at him with a combination of hurt and confusion in her eyes.

Ace stared back at her, hoping his own misery didn't show. Even though his heart was revolting against his will, he was convinced that he was doing the right thing by not encouraging her to believe there could be anything more between them than there already was.

"Kids still asleep?" he asked.

"Yes," Meg said, dragging her gaze from his. "I thought I'd wait until breakfast was ready to get them up. They had their baths last night, so it won't take long to get them ready."

"No hurry. We have all day." He went to the shelf hanging on the wall, took down a cup and poured himself some coffee from the big granite pot that sat in the middle of the table.

"I'm not sure all day will be long enough for Teddy," Nita said. She gestured toward the coffeepot. "That should still be hot. I just moved it from the fire a bit ago."

"It'll be fine," Ace assured her, pulling out a chair.

"I fried some chicken earlier and made some extra biscuits. I thought I'd treat us to some cold sarsaparillas from Gabe's and we could take it to Jackson's Grove and have a picnic down by the creek at lunchtime."

Ah. *That* was why he smelled chicken. "Sounds good," he said. "I bet Teddy will love it."

"I hope so."

"He's really looking forward to the day," Meg said without looking up from her chore. "He loves going to the mercantile and looking at all the penny candy. It takes him forever to choose."

"That's a mighty big decision for a boy that age," Nita said, smiling.

"It's a pretty big decision for boys of any age," Ace told her and earned a brief laugh.

"What about you, Meg? Do you have a hard time choosing candy?"

"Not really. I'd much rather have a piece of Ellic's pie, which I'm planning on us all doing this afternoon. I've been saving my mending money," she explained.

"After all you've done for me the past few weeks, a little treat is the least I can do for the two of you."

"That isn't necessary," Nita said, but Ace knew better than to say anything. Meg Thomerson was a woman with a lot of grit and pride. How else could she have done what she had since her marriage?

"Necessary or not, we're having pie and coffee. It's settled."

Nita looked at Ace and he shrugged. He'd already tangled with the tenacious Meg, and his only option the night before had been to toss out a challenge and retreat.

Teddy sat next to Nita in the backseat of the wagon, and Meg held Lucy on her lap. Both children seemed content to watch the passing scenery, and Teddy asked a dozen questions about things he saw along the way.

The late October day was autumn perfection. A gentle breeze turned the colorful leaves into a shifting mosaic of glorious reds, rusts, hues of yellow and dark purple. A dove sang its mournful song, promising more rain, and patches of black-eyed Susan and purple aster dotted the swaying knee-high grasses that grew alongside the narrow road. It was a picture-perfect day for the hour-long trip. Meg dreaded winter coming, when she would have to make the twice weekly journey alone in the wet and cold.

Nita, at least, was a good traveling companion. Ace was quiet, speaking only when a comment was directed to him. The ride into town passed quickly, and by the time the buildings of Wolf Creek came into view, Teddy was literally bouncing up and down on the wooden seat.

Knowing that the boy wouldn't be happy until he got to go to the mercantile, Meg was pleased when Ace looped the rig's reins around the hitching post. He helped the ladies and children alight near the door and said he was headed to the jail to visit Colt since he wasn't one for shopping.

Gabe Gentry, the store's owner, turned when he heard them at the doors. The usual batch of old men sat around the potbellied stove, engrossed in their daily game of checkers. They barely glanced up when the four entered. A blue spatterware coffeepot sat atop the stove, sending out the pleasant aroma of coffee.

"Nita Allen and Meg Thomerson!" Gabe said, coming around the counter where he'd been applying a feather duster with some vigor. He was smiling the smile that had set many a feminine heart aflutter before he'd settled down with Rachel earlier in the year.

Nita greeted him with a soft hello and a smile.

"Hello, Mr. Gentry," Meg said.

"Call me Gabe."

"Oh, I couldn't," Meg protested.

"Well, I understood from Rachel that you're her newest friend, and anyone my wife calls a friend usually calls me Gabe."

"That's very nice of you," she said, a bit discombobulated by his sincerity. "I'll consider it. How's Rachel?"

"She's wonderful, but then, everyone knows that. A better question might be how you are. You're looking very well."

"It's been a long rough road," she told him, "but I'm feeling better every day, thanks to your wife and Nita and Ace."

"I knew they'd be a blessing to you if you'd let them," he said.

Gabe glanced over at Teddy, who was slowly inching his way toward a counter, where large jars of brightly colored candy were lined up for display. Gabe winked at Meg and Nita.

"Take your time, Teddy," he said. "There's no hurry." He turned his attention to Lucy. "She's really growing, Meg. And she's so pretty. Looks like you."

Meg felt herself blush to the roots of her hair. "Thank you."

"We're all sort of hoping for a girl this time," Gabe said, reminding them of Rachel's pregnancy. "Even Danny." The mention of his son brought a gleam of pride to Gabe's eyes.

He glanced from Meg to Nita. "So, is there anything special that you need, or did you come in for Teddy to buy candy?"

"Actually, I was hoping you had some shoes in Lucy's size. She's grown so fast that she doesn't have anything to see her through the winter."

"I bet we can find something," he said. "Nita, I have some new printed calico that came in last week if you want to look it over."

"Thanks, Mr. Gentry."

Gabe shook his head at her continued formality and led Meg to the section of the store that displayed shoes. In the end, Meg chose sturdy brown shoes in a size a little larger than Lucy needed at the moment so that she could wear woolen socks to keep her feet warm and in hopes that she could at least use them until the following spring.

Gabe was down on one knee and lacing up the second shoe when he looked up at Meg. She knew instantly that something was on his mind. Without warning, a frisson of alarm shot through her. She stilled, every sense on alert, as her mind thought of and culled half a dozen possibilities.

"What is it?" she demanded, unable to draw a decent breath for the sudden panic unfurling inside her.

"Your mother and Charlie are in town," he told her. "I thought you might want to know."

Dread, so heavy it threatened to suffocate her, rose up inside Meg. "Where are they?"

"I saw them go into Ellie's earlier, but they headed down the street toward the old newspaper office a bit ago. I guess they wanted to check out the new library."

Somehow, Meg dredged up something that resembled a laugh. "To my knowledge, Georgina Ferris and Charlie Green have never read a book in their lives."

Gabe tied Lucy's shoe and stood. "I'm sorry. I didn't want to ruin your outing, but I thought you might want to know. Maybe you can avoid running into them."

"I certainly hope so. And thank you, Gabe. I am grateful for the warning."

She and Nita spent another thirty minutes or more looking over things in the store. Meg knew the older woman suspected that something had happened, but she didn't want to ruin Nita's day, so she kept quiet.

They walked through the store, taking turns carrying Lucy, marveling over the slipper-shaped tub and the collection of pretty laces and buttons on the dry-goods shelf. Meg ran her hand lovingly over the green-and-white enamel stove. Teddy was fascinated by a carved wooden tool set that he said was "just like Ace's."

Meg and Ace had already had a set-to over him letting Teddy call him by his nickname; Ace argued that he was hardly the "Mr. Allen" type. She also knew Teddy was becoming very attached to Ace, and she was already starting to worry about what would happen to the child when Ace left and never came back, which, in light of their devastating conversation the night before, she was convinced would happen sooner rather than later.

"They left the library," Gabe said with a guilty smile. "So if you plan on going there, now might be a good time."

Meg smiled back. "I don't expect you to spy for me, but thank you. I think I'll pay you for our purchases and we'll head that way."

Several minutes later, they entered the new library. The former newspaper office was hardly recognizable. The plaster walls were lined with head-high shelving that was filled with books, more than Meg could imagine anyone owning. The library appeared empty, and Meg was glad, since it meant she could visit without fear of disturbing anyone.

Libby Granville was sitting behind a mahogany desk, a pair of wire-rimmed spectacles perched on her nose, reading a newspaper. She looked up when she heard Teddy say, "That's a lotta books!"

"Meg! Nita!" Libby cried, getting to her feet and rounding the desk. "What a wonderful surprise!" She hugged each of them in turn.

"I'm returning the books you brought, and I thought I'd get one or two more, if that's all right."

"It's more than all right," Libby said. "Teddy, there's a chalkboard over there on the wall. Why don't you draw us a picture while I show your mother some books she might like?"

Teddy's eyes lit up with pleasure. "Look, Mama, I'm in school, too," he announced proudly. No one bothered to correct him.

"Your mother just left," Libby said.

Nita looked over at Meg. "So that's what's wrong."

Meg gave her an apologetic smile. "Gabe told me she was in town, and I didn't say anything because I didn't want to ruin your day. I'm hoping we can avoid her."

"This day is our treat," Nita said. "I'm not going to allow anyone to spoil it."

Meg sighed. "You don't know my mother."

Chapter Twelve

"Come on," Libby said, deftly changing the subject. "There are a couple of books over here I think you might like."

"I'll keep an eye on Teddy and Lucy," Nita offered.

"Just put Lucy down and let her roam. There isn't much in here for her to get into."

Libby led Meg to the far end of the room. When they reached the spot where the books for Meg were shelved, she said, "I'm so sorry."

"There's nothing to be sorry for," Meg assured her. "I can deal with my mother. I've had a lot of experience."

"I'm sure you can."

They spent the next several minutes discussing the merits of some titles Meg might enjoy. She finally settled on *Vanity Fair* for herself and *The Adventures of Tom Sawyer* to read to Teddy.

"Something's bothering you," Libby said, once Meg had made her decisions. "Is there anything I can do to help?"

"You may be the only person who can help."

Libby looked at her with raised eyebrows.

Meg took a deep breath to work up her nerve and plunged in. "I'm worried, Mrs. Granville."

"Libby," she corrected her gently. "What are you worried about?"

"My children's futures."

"That's normal," Libby said. "All mothers worry about that to some extent."

Meg shook her head. "It isn't the everyday getting by that worries me—there's nothing wrong with struggling to make ends meet—but I'm so afraid that Teddy will grow up to be like his father. How do I keep that from happening? I want him to be a good man, not one filled with hate, and anger and dishonesty and...and cruelty. I—I hoped that since our circumstances were similar, you might be able to tell me how to keep that from happening. Your boys turned out just fine, even though they lived with their father for so many years."

To Meg's surprise, tears sprang into Libby's eyes. "Oh, Meg," she breathed. "I see now why you thought I might be able to help you, and you're right. Lucas Gentry and Elton Thomerson might have been two peas in a pod. I was devastated when Lucas forced me to leave Caleb and Gabe with him. I prayed over the same fears you're going through every day for twenty years, and the only assurance I had that they weren't like Lucas was an occasional letter from one of the hired hands or a note from a friend."

Libby gave a sad shake of her head. "I'm afraid I

can't offer you any help, but you do have an advantage I didn't. You're still able to be a mother to your children and influence them every single day."

"You're right," Meg said. "I'm glad for that, but I've made some bad choices."

"We've all made some bad choices," Libby told her with a wry smile.

"How do I stop Lucy from making the same mistake you and I made?" she asked the older woman. "I want her to be smarter than I was. I want her to know when a man is lying to her, and if she does choose poorly, I want her to be strong enough to walk away without looking back, no matter what people might say about her. How can I do that? How can I keep her from being like me, or like my mother, for that matter?"

After a lengthy pause, Libby said, "I don't think there are any guarantees when it comes to bringing up children. It's unfortunate, but making mistakes is how we gain wisdom."

Meg thought of her mother's life. From the time she began to understand what was going on in her house, she'd prayed not to be like Georgina and had tried her best to emulate her aunt. She said that to Libby.

"I suspect that all we *can* do is discourage the bad things we see and encourage the good, the way your aunt Serena has done with you. You made a mistake, Meg. That's different from choosing a life of wrongdoing."

"I know, but I still worry."

"Of course you do. That's what mothers do best. And we can also be good examples." Her quick smile caused little crinkles to fan out at the corners of her dark eyes. "Children do watch and imitate what we do, you know—good or bad."

Meg thought of how Teddy had started taking on the way Ace stood and tried to help him with whatever project he was working on.

"I'm convinced that the most important thing we can do is bring them up to love the Lord and pray and trust that He will be with us and them. Even then, sometimes they can go astray. But it's possible that people who grow up in terrible circumstances can become wonderful people, too. Like you."

She gave Meg a gentle smile. "Yes, it was a mistake to marry Elton, just as it was a mistake for me to marry Lucas. No one I know blames you for your husband's wrongdoings, Meg, and they certainly don't blame you for your mother's. In fact, it seems that almost everyone in town has great admiration for you."

"What do you mean?"

Libby reached out and placed a soft hand over Meg's, the one that clutched the books. "You're a beautiful, hardworking woman filled with a lot of courage, Meg Thomerson. Don't forget that. Everyone knows that you love your children, since it's clear that you take such good care of them and work hard to provide for them."

Meg pressed her lips together to still their trembling.

"My advice is not to look too far into the future. That can be terrifying. You just concentrate on getting better one day at a time."

One day at a time. That seemed to be everyone's

approach to her getting better, so it must surely be the best way to approach life. They couldn't all be wrong, could they?

Meg stopped by the bank and made her land payment and then made it a point to visit Hattie, to thank her for her continued business during her recuperation. When Meg and her companions stepped through the door of the boardinghouse, they were greeted by a lovely tune. The sheriff's twelve-year-old daughter, Cilla, was at the upright piano, her fingers moving over the keys with a confidence and skill that could come only from hours of practice. Hattie, who owned the boardinghouse and gave piano lessons to Colt's daughter, Cilla, sat in a nearby chair, her index finger moving through the air in time with the rhythm, nodding and smiling. She looked up when Meg, Nita and the children stepped through the pocket doors that led from the front hallway to the parlor.

"Why, hello, ladies! What a surprise," Hattie exclaimed, getting to her feet. Cilla's fingers stilled on the piano keys, and she turned to look at the newcomers.

Both women said their hellos and Meg's gaze moved from Hattie to Cilla. "I'm so sorry to interrupt your lesson, Cilla. That was lovely. I don't know anything about music, but it seems to me that you've come a long way in a very short time."

"Thank you, Miss Meg," she said with a smile. "That's what Miss Hattie says. And you didn't really interrupt. We're almost finished anyway."

"What was the song you were playing?"

"One of my pa's favorites, 'Lorena.' His birthday is coming up and I wanted to surprise him, so I've been working really hard on it."

"Well, he'll be very surprised and pleased, I'm sure."

"How about some coffee and cookies?" Hattie suggested. "Cilla brought some sugar cookies she made yesterday."

"Oh, thank you, but I really don't mean to intrude. I just wanted to stop by and thank you for standing by me while I've been on the mend."

Hattie gave her cackling laugh. "Well, that was no problem. There's no way I could do all that laundry myself and not be run plumb ragged."

She held out a hand to Teddy and spoke to Meg. "Now, don't be silly. Come on into the dining room for that coffee. Teddy here is looking very disappointed, and we can't have that, can we, young man?"

Smiling, Teddy shook his blond head and placed his hand in hers. Meg glanced at the clock hanging on the wall. It was an hour before they were supposed to meet Ace. She knew Ace, unlike Elton, wouldn't be upset if they were a few minutes late. He'd just go in and talk to Gabe while he waited. Meg sighed. It looked as if they had no alternative but to have cookies and coffee, not that it was a hardship in any way.

Cilla joined them, and much to Meg's surprise, Lucy wanted the young girl to hold her. Though she looked uncomfortable, Cilla obliged, and Lucy promptly grabbed at the pink bow in Cilla's hair. She looked taken aback, but sighed in resignation.

"I guess I may as well get used to it. I imagine my pa and Miss Allison will be having a couple of these when they get married."

The three women broke into laughter. "I imagine they will," Hattie said.

It felt good to laugh, Meg thought. Really good. Maybe this was one of those unexpected blessings she was supposed to look for.

"You may think you won't like having a new baby brother or sister," Nita told her, "but I can tell you from experience that even though they may drive you batty from time to time, there's nothing like being the *big* sister. You can be a help to Allison, and that baby, whether it's a boy or girl, will think you hung the moon and stars."

"Really?"

"Really."

Cilla looked pleased and spent the rest of the visit playing with the two children. When it was time to go, Meg and Nita thanked their hostess for the wonderful refreshments and prepared to leave. Hattie and Cilla followed them to the door. Meg was almost to the steps when the young girl called, "I'm so glad you're all right, Miss Meg. My brother and I have been praying for you."

Meg felt her throat tighten. There *were* people who cared about her. "Thank you, Cilla. Are you looking forward to the wedding?"

"Yes, ma'am. Miss Allison is going to make me a

new dress. She still has no idea who they're going to get to take her place at school."

"Well, personally, I think it's silly that they won't let married women teach!" Hattie snapped. The spinster boardinghouse owner had never been shy about speaking her mind on any topic.

"Well, maybe things will change one day," Nita offered.

"Maybe."

"Hattie, we've really enjoyed this," Meg said. "It was good to see you again. You, too, Cilla. And I want to thank you again, Hattie, for being such a good friend and customer."

"Oh, pshaw!" Hattie said, waving her arms as if to shoo them off the porch. She looked at Nita. "You send that good-looking boy of yours over before you go. I have some things that need to go back with you."

Nita smiled. "I will."

Sheriff Colt Garrett tipped back his chair, slung his booted feet onto the top of the desk and laced his fingers behind his head, his favorite pose. "So how are things going out at the Thomerson place?"

"Everything's going well," Ace said with a slow nod.

"Rachel says things are looking good out there."

"Meg has been helping me with some cleanup and repairs. It does look a lot better." He frowned. "I can't believe Elton let the place go the way he did."

"Elton had bigger fish to fry," Colt noted with a dry smile. "How are you and Meg getting along? She was in a pretty sorry state when we found her, and she wasn't too happy about the idea of having you help her on the farm."

Ace leaned back in his chair and folded his arms across his chest, resting one ankle on the other knee. "When I first got there, she was like a cornered wild animal—scared and distrustful. She cringed away from me every time I got near her, but lately, she isn't so jumpy. I think she knows I'm no threat."

"That is improvement."

Without any warning, an image of Meg from the night before drifted through Ace's mind. She hadn't drawn away from him then, and she hadn't been the least bit jumpy.

"What?"

Colt's sharp question brought Ace's thoughts back to the present. He glared at his friend, who was looking at him with a knowing smile. "What?" he echoed.

Colt's grin broadened. "You had a sappy look on your face for a minute there."

"Sappy look?"

"Yeah. Like you're thinking about something that makes you ridiculously happy." The tough sheriff actually blushed. "The only reason I recognized it is because I've gotten pretty used to seeing it staring back at me in the mirror every morning when I'm thinking about Allison."

Ace knew exactly where Colt was going with the conversation. "Let me assure you, I wasn't thinking about Allison," he quipped back, determined not to let his friend interrogate him the way he did his prisoners.

"Come on, Ace. Tell me what's going on with you and the Widow Thomerson. I've suspected for a long time that you were smitten, and now I have no doubts."

"You need to mind your own business," Ace cautioned.

Colt hadn't gained his reputation as one of the best lawmen in several counties by giving up. "As a concerned friend, it is my business. So what's going on?"

"Nothing."

"Liar."

Ace glared at Colt for several seconds, and seeing that familiar determination in his tawny eyes, he exhaled a loud breath. "I'm in trouble."

"How so?" Colt asked with a satisfied smile.

"As crazy as it sounds, I think she's starting to… care for me."

Colt lowered his chair and rested his forearms on the desktop. "Why do you think that, and why would it be a problem? I know you had to deny how you felt as long as Elton was in the picture, but he's gone. There's nothing to stand in the way of you courting her if that's what you both want."

Ace didn't say anything for a moment. He wasn't used to having anyone to confide in, but he knew that Colt had suffered in the past, just like everyone else. Maybe telling another man his concerns would help him get a different perspective on things.

Instead of easing into the subject, Ace plunged headfirst. "I kissed her last night, and she let me."

"I'd say that's a pretty fair indicator that she's interested," Colt said with a lift of his sun-bleached eyebrows. "I thought that was what you'd hoped for."

Ace leaped to his feet and paced the small room. "It was, but I didn't expect it to happen."

"I see," Colt said, but the confusion on his face said that he didn't see at all. "So if you care for her and she's learning to trust a man again and seems to care for you, why are you so upset?"

"Because she's been hurt so badly by Elton, and I'm the first man to come along who's shown her the way a woman should be treated, and I'm afraid that whatever she thinks she feels is only gratitude."

"Well, I have no way of knowing how she feels, but I do know that love will tie you in knots," Colt said with a sage nod. "It will make you weigh every word either of you has ever said and think of all the ways those words might be taken another way. When you're in love, you don't know which way is up."

"Who said anything about love?" Ace snapped.

"What else could we possibly be talking about?" Colt replied. "The only thing I can tell you is that time will tell you both if what she feels is real love or not."

The conversation hung in the air for a few minutes as both men digested it. "Why couldn't I have fallen for a pretty Cherokee girl?" Ace asked finally. "Life would have been a lot simpler."

"What do you mean?"

"I grew up in a mixed-race family. I know what it's like to see a father devastated about the way his wife and son were treated. I know firsthand how hard it can be for a kid torn between two cultures. If I truly love someone, wouldn't it be wrong to put her or any kids we may have through that?"

"If you haven't asked your mother if she would change anything, maybe you should," Colt suggested. "I'd also say that the decision isn't all up to you. The lady has a say in it, too."

Meg watched Ace striding down the covered sidewalk; he was looking neither to the left nor the right. Her heart skipped a little beat at what a magnificent portrait of self-confidence and dignity he made in his Levi's and chambray shirt. No one would ever suspect that he'd once been a tormented man who questioned his very existence in the world.

More than anything she'd wanted in a long time, she wanted to run to him and have him envelop her in his strength and calm, knowing that he would protect her from any harm that came her way.

Just then, he saw her standing there watching him. He seemed to pause midstride for just an instant, as if he were acutely aware of her. Even from a distance, the intensity radiating from him was like a bolt of lightning to her senses. In that moment, she knew that whether or not it was too soon, she loved him. Now and forever.

The muscle in his jaw was knotted, and there was no smile of welcome on his face. Nothing gave the slightest hint that he felt the same except the sudden heat in his light blue eyes. A need blazed there that he was unable to hide, even with his many years of impassiveness to lean on.

Other than brief greetings, no one spoke. Nita seemed acutely aware of the tension between them, yet wisely stayed quiet. They loaded everyone into the wagon and set out for Jackson's Grove, where the folks of Wolf Creek had all their major events, like the spring picnic, the box-lunch auction, the ice-cream social and the fall harvest celebration, which would be coming up in two more weeks.

Ace drove through the slight trail that wove through the tall grasses toward the grove of trees. A hawk dipped and soared in the cloudless cerulean sky, riding the shifting currents of air as it searched out its midday meal. Sun-dappled shade welcomed them as he pulled the wagon beneath the trees.

Ace tied the horses to a sapling and rounded the wagon to lift Meg down. Their gazes met, hers questioning, his once more unreadable. Suppressing a sigh, she leaned forward, placing her palms on his chambray-covered shoulders. His hands went to her middle, and she realized with a bit of a start that even though she'd put on a couple of pounds, she'd lost so much weight during her recovery that he could almost span her waist with his big hands.

Just weeks ago, she would have stiffened at his touch and thought of what hands that size could do to a woman. But this was Ace. Instead of tensing up as she once would have, she smiled at him and murmured a soft "thank you."

The spell binding them shattered, and they set about unloading their picnic. Nita instructed the children to stay in the back while she spread a quilt beneath a peeling, white-barked sycamore tree whose golden leaves rustled in the gentle autumn wind. Then she and Ace lifted them from the wagon. Soon they were seated in a circle, plates in their laps, enjoying Nita's fried chicken, biscuits and dewberry jam, and the wedge of red-rind cheese and cold sarsaparillas she had purchased at the mercantile.

Ace tied a dish towel around Lucy's neck and coaxed her into tasting the cheese. The minute it hit her tongue, she made a terrible face, shuddered and promptly spit it out. She looked at him as if to ask why he'd done something so terrible to her and said, "Nasky." *Nasty.* The word Meg always used to deter Lucy from putting things into her mouth that she shouldn't.

Everyone laughed, which of course Lucy loved. She joined in, clapping her tiny hands in glee. The poignancy of the moment filled Meg with both joy and sorrow. This was what a real family should be like. Parents and grandparents together, enjoying each other, enjoying the life God had given them.

She knew suddenly that of all the things she could wish to have in the future, this was what she wanted, what she and her little family needed. She dipped her head and blinked fast and hard to hold back her tears. Families should not have fathers who attacked and robbed people and tried to kill them, or mothers who tried to smooth over outbursts of rage and blame and bore the brunt of misplaced anger. "Are you all right?" Ace asked in a low voice.

It had been a good day. She would not let memories of the past ruin it. She raised her head and smiled at him, knowing that her eyes were shining with tears. "I'm fine."

She broke off a piece of buttery biscuit and put it in Lucy's mouth. As she munched happily, Ace pulled all the meat, gristle and the tiny, sharp bone from a chicken leg and handed the large bone to her.

Ace had promised Teddy that he would let him fish for a while. With their stomachs full, he took the cane fishing pole from the rear of the wagon and led the boy to the nearby creek. Meg helped Nita pack up the picnic items in the now-familiar basket. Lucy was rubbing her eyes, and Meg decided to try to let her have a short nap before they drove the short distance back to town for their promised treat at Ellie's.

Nita decided to try her hand at fishing and left Meg and Lucy alone. Wearing a contented smile and marveling at what a wonderful day it had been, she stretched out next to her baby daughter and began to sing "Froggie Went a-Courtin'" in a hushed tone. Lucy was asleep by the end of the third verse. A gentle breeze tickled the leaves overhead, and stippled sunlight danced across Lucy's plump cheeks. Smiling and running a finger along their sweet curves, Meg closed her eyes…

She knew she was dreaming because she was looking down on herself as she lay in her bed, sleeping. The spot next to her was empty. How long had he been gone this time? Would he come tonight? She tossed restlessly, and the Meg watching moaned as her chest tightened in anxiety.

From somewhere far away, she heard laughter. She

felt the presence of someone next to her and knew her
husband had come home. Something grazed her face,
and she clenched her eyes tight and swatted at it, even
knowing that her protests would anger him.

"Meg."

The timbre of his voice was deep, melodic. Soothing. Nothing at all like Elton's voice. Once again, she
felt the brush of something against her skin and reached
out to slap it away. She didn't want to open her eyes
and look at him.

"Wake up, Meg."

This time the voice penetrated the veil of sleep
cloaking her. It wasn't Elton's. Her eyes flew open and
she found herself staring into a familiar blue gaze. Ace
was next to her on the quilt, propped up on one hand. In
his other he held a stalk of wild wheat that had turned
golden brown. As she looked up at him and tried to
get her bearings, he tickled her beneath her chin with
the piece of wheat.

"What are you doing?" she asked breathlessly.

"Trying to wake you. You've been asleep for almost two hours."

Her eyes widened. "Oh, no!" she cried and then
glanced over at the sleeping baby to see if she'd awakened her.

"I hated to bother you, but if you want to have your
pie at Ellie's, we need to get a move on. I want to get
home in time to take care of the animals before it gets
dark."

Home. Meg looked up at him, wondering if her place

was beginning to feel like home, or if it was just a chance choice of words.

"I'm sorry. I never meant to fall asleep."

"Don't be," he told her, getting to his feet and offering her a hand up. "You needed the rest."

Without even pausing, Meg placed her hand in his and let him pull her up. As she stood, her foot caught in the hem of her skirt and she stumbled into him. His arm went around her. All her senses were besieged by the essence of him. His unique outdoorsy scent. His touch. His strength.

One hand rested on his forearm; the other was against his chest. The muscles beneath her palms were rock-solid. She looked into his eyes and saw cautious awareness. Drawing in a shaky breath didn't help. Instead of calming her, she inhaled the warm scent she always associated with him. She imagined she could hear the beat of his heart, but realized that it was more likely the blood thundering in her own veins.

"Where's Teddy?" Her voice was little more than a whisper.

"He and my mother are on their way. She was trying to land a pretty big perch when I came to wake you."

As if on cue, Teddy came running up from behind Ace, calling, "Mama. Mama. I caught a fish, but it was too little to keep."

Relief warred with disappointment at the interruption. She forced a smile she hoped showed pleasure at his announcement. "That's wonderful, Teddy."

"Ace says we can fish another day before it gets too cold."

"Good." She looked from him to the other adults standing nearby. Nita was watching her closely. She bent to wake Lucy. "Let's clear all this up and head back to town. I'm craving a piece of Ellie's chocolate pie."

Chapter Thirteen

The trip back into town took less than five minutes. Ace was tying the rig to the hitching post, and Meg and Nita were unloading the kids from the wagon, when a feminine voice spoke from behind them.

"Well, well, look who's in town for a nice little family outing."

Meg froze. She would recognize that voice anywhere. It belonged to none other than her mother, Georgina Ferris. Meg cast an anguished look at Nita, who glanced at the newcomer and said, "I'll take the children on inside if you like."

"Please," Meg said through stiff lips.

Nita held out her hand and Teddy obediently placed his into it, sparing his grandmother nothing but a brief glance.

"Oh, don't take them in," Georgina whined to Nita's back. "Let me have a look at them. I haven't seen them since right after Lucy was born."

And that was just how Meg wanted it.

Nita paused, glancing from the older woman to Meg. "Take them on in, please." She glanced at Ace, who was standing on the other side of the gray mare, clenching his hands so tightly in the horse's mane that his knuckles were white. The expression on his face resembled a dark thunderhead before a storm.

Meg gave him a shaky smile and braced herself for the scene to come. She turned slowly to face the woman who had given birth to her, but had never been a mother. The man who had taken her father's place in her mother's life stood beside Georgie. Tall and gaunt, the sack suit Charlie Green wore hung on his thin body and looked exactly like the sack from which it took its name. The two of them had always reminded Meg of what she imagined nursery-rhyme character Jack Sprat and his wife might look like. She smothered a nervous giggle at the thought.

Charlie's gaze was fixed on Ace.

As usual, Georgina was dressed far too flashily for Wolf Creek. Her bright emerald green dress was sewn from satin and trimmed with delicate lace. Quick to indulge her every appetite, she'd always been overweight, but Meg thought her mother's face looked thinner than the last time she'd seen her. Still, whatever style statement she hoped to make with the shelf bustle was undermined by the extra pounds it added. Meg was relieved to see that the bodice was made more or less decent by the lace tucker edging its low cut.

Her straight blond hair, so much like Meg's, was twisted and curled into an elaborate style that was inappropriate for a woman her age. A satin hat, the exact color of her dress and adorned with a cluster of pink velvet roses and three pheasant feathers, sat at a cocky angle atop the tortured mass. A fake emerald hat pin held it in place.

Her face was dusted with powder at least a hue too light, and her eyebrows were enhanced by a charcoal stick. Bright color rode high on her cheekbones, and lip rouge in a deep carmine hue gave her lips a full, pouty look.

"Hello, Georgie," Meg said, calling her mother by the name she preferred over "Ma." Her voice held a definite chill as she acknowledged her mother's companion. "Charlie."

Addressing her mother once more, she said, "I heard you've been ill, but you're looking…like your old self."

"Can't keep a good woman down," Georgie said with a cheeky grin. "I heard you were in town, and I was hoping to run into you." She held her arms wide. "Come give your mama a hug."

Meg stood firmly in place. She didn't think she could have moved to save her life. The small act of rebellion made her the focus of Charlie's attention.

"You heard your mother, girl. Get over here!"

Without a word, Ace stepped around the hitching post and took his place beside Meg.

Georgie's nostrils flared in anger, even though the green eyes that looked Ace up and down held a glimmer of admiration. Her mama had never failed to appreciate the attributes of an attractive man.

"I think we passed the hugging stage years ago,

Georgie," Meg said, praying that she could hold herself together for a few more minutes.

"Still have that mouth on you, I see," Georgie said with a put-upon sigh.

When Meg had gotten old enough to understand her mother's behavior for what it was, she'd felt no qualms about taking Georgie to task about it. All it had earned her was a smack across the face and a moment's satisfaction.

"I heard about Elton's…murder." Georgina coughed delicately into a lacy handkerchief and then cast a look of wide-eyed innocence at Ace. "Is this who killed him?"

Even from two feet away, Meg felt the coiling of angry tension that vibrated through Ace's body. Without thinking, she reached out, her hand finding his unerringly. She meshed her fingers with his. He didn't pull away, but he didn't return the pressure, either.

Georgina's knowing gaze moved from their clasped hands to Meg's face, a shrewd smile curving her painted lips.

"Do you speak?" Charlie taunted, ever the agitator.

"When I have something to say."

"If you heard Elton was murdered, you heard wrong, Georgie," Meg said, hoping to correct her mother's impression and defuse the antagonism between the two men. She was pleased to hear that her voice shook only the tiniest bit. "But yes, Ace is the one who saved Sheriff Garrett's life. And probably mine."

Georgina shifted her gaze from Ace to Meg. "I did hear that you were hurt pretty bad, poor thing, but it looks like you're doing just fine now. You need to put a little meat on your bones, though. You're as skinny as a scarecrow. Men don't like bony women."

Once again, she shot Ace a sly glance. Heaving an exaggerated sigh, she shook her head in a display of sadness as fake as the emerald holding her hat in place. "I tried to tell you to think twice before you married Elton, baby girl. Those Thomerson men all have simply *terrible* tempers."

"You may recall that there was a reason or two that I married him," Meg reminded her, determined to hold her own with her mother. She pinned Charlie with a hard, accusing look.

"Oh, yes," Georgina said, tapping her lips with a long fingernail. "Teddy was on the way."

She glanced at Ace, and when she saw no surprise on his face, she changed tactics. "So you're sharing all your deep dark secrets now, are you? Well, bravo! I've always thought it best to get everything out in the open if you hope to have a good understanding with your man."

Answering would be futile. Instead, Meg watched her mother warily.

Georgie's cool gaze never left Meg's as she waggled her gloved fingers at Charlie. "Run along and get the wagon, Charles. I'm almost done here."

Meg's heart began to race. Georgie had decided to stop toying around. She intended to draw blood. Who knew what she might say or do next?

Charlie's glare moved from Meg to Georgina, but

he did as she asked. No one spoke until he was on the other side of the street.

"I promised my children a treat, Georgie," Meg said. "I need to go." Never releasing Ace's hand, she turned to do just that.

Before she could take more than a step, cruel fingers bit into her upper arm and hauled her back around. She inhaled sharply at the venom she saw in her mother's eyes.

"Don't go high and mighty on me, missy," she said in a low, harsh voice. "You might fool the town with your little story about him—" she gave a jerk of her head toward Ace "—staying at the farm to help you, but you don't fool me. Blood will tell, darlin'. You'll always be that wicked Georgie Ferris's daughter. Like it or not, you're just like me."

Meg's blood ran cold at the thought. A trembling seemed to start in her very soul. "You're wrong, Georgie. I'm nothing like you. I'll never be like you."

"Think what you will. Everyone knows the apple doesn't fall too far from the tree." Her eyes narrowed. "And let me tell you another thing. There may have been a lot of men in my life, but I never lowered myself to carry on with the likes of him!"

Her meaning couldn't have been clearer to Meg. Georgie was saying she'd never shared her favors with an Indian. She released Meg's arm, giving her a little shove that pushed her against Ace.

The curve of Georgina's lips was an awful parody of a smile. She grabbed up the emerald satin of her skirt and stomped across the dusty street.

Meg was too stunned to do anything but watch her go. Georgie had always liked a grand exit.

As soon as Georgina Ferris walked off, Ace felt the tension in him begin to slip away. Standing there listening to the venom spewing from the loathsome woman's lips and not taking up for Meg—and himself—was one of the hardest things he'd ever done, but something told him that handling her mother was something Meg needed to do herself. Besides, it wasn't his place. He was only the hired help.

He pulled his hand free and took her shoulders so that he could turn her to face him. Faint tremors still shivered through her, the result of her anger and pain. As she looked up at him, a single tear slid down her pale cheek. Unable to deny himself the need to touch her, he reached out and brushed away the moisture with a calloused thumb. He ached to pull her close and offer her whatever comfort she would allow him to give and knew he couldn't.

"Are you all right?"

She tried to smile and failed. "Not really."

"Would you like to go home?"

She drew in an unsteady breath. "No," she said with a defiant lift of her chin. "I'm choosing not to let my past shape my feelings or my life anymore. Today is a day for fun and treats, and I won't let Georgie Ferris ruin that for me."

This time her smile was steadier. She shook out her skirt, lifted her chin and smoothed back the silky strands of golden hair that had come loose from her braid. Then, looking as confident as her mother, but in a different way, she caught up her skirt and strode toward the wooden walkway, tossing him a resolute look over her shoulder.

"What kind of pie do you think Ellie has today?"

There wasn't much talk during the trip back home. The children were exhausted from their exciting day. Always planning ahead, his mother had brought some quilts to make a pallet in the back of the wagon, where she snuggled with Teddy and Lucy, since the temperature dropped steadily as the sun slipped toward the horizon.

Meg sat next to Ace on the front seat, lost in thought. That was good, since he had a lot to say and it wasn't the time to say it.

His heart felt as if it had been shredded. He'd known that reality would set in sooner or later, and on some level, he'd suspected that things would become clear to her when they showed up in town together. He'd never imagined it would be Meg's mother who would point out the very obvious truth.

The encounter with Georgina proved beyond a doubt what he'd been trying to make Meg see about his background and how people would treat her if they allowed their feelings for each other to grow into something strong and lasting.

She'd had enough heartache and pain in her life, and as much as he knew he loved her and wanted nothing more than to make a life with her and her children on her little farm, he knew it was impossible. He'd hurt enough people he loved in his lifetime, and he refused to add Meg to the list.

It was time to move on. He'd done pretty much everything he'd promised to do. Maybe he'd implied he'd stay longer, but there had been no set time frame. She was much better physically, and with his mother around to help with things, Meg would be okay.

The only thing left to do was decide when he was going.

Well, Meg thought, staring down at the hands clasped in her lap. Today had certainly been one for the books! A wonderful day in many respects, but the run-in with her mother had almost ruined everything.

She thought of Georgie's insinuation that there was more between her and Ace than him helping her through a bad spot. Did the fact that she and Elton had been forced to marry incline other people to believe the worst of her? For the first time, she began to really consider how a person's actions, both good and bad, could affect not only their lives, but also the lives of everyone they knew. Like the way her mother's sordid life had colored her own decisions. How her mistake with Elton would be talked about even when her children were grown.

Sometimes even good things had bad results. Irishman Yancy Allen had loved a Cherokee girl enough to marry her, yet the world had looked down upon that union and the child born of it. Those things had influenced Ace. Poor Yancy had had no idea that something as simple as loving someone would cause heartache years later for his own flesh and blood and a woman he didn't even know.

Meg sighed and knew without looking that Ace had shot her a curious glance. She knew him well enough by now to know a lot of things about him, like the fact that Georgie's comment about Meg "carrying on" with him was a weapon chosen to inflict pain on them both. Her mother knew—had always known—what to say to cut Meg to the heart.

When would she stop letting Georgina Ferris hurt her? When would she find the courage to rise above her past and stop thinking of herself as inferior? Ace said she was courageous, that she had done well at making the best of things, but she still felt shame every time she thought of her mother's way of life and the way Elton's escapades would be fodder for the town's gossip mill for years to come, bringing misery to her and their children.

Ace said he didn't want her to suffer the way he and his family had suffered. Well, today should have shown him that his past was no worse than hers. She *was* beginning to understand what he meant when he told her she needed time to heal and to make certain she didn't need anyone before choosing to share her life with another man. She had no desire to rush into anything. She'd done that once. She needed to talk to Ace about what she was feeling. Really talk.

When they reached the farm, Ace unhitched the mare and took care of the evening chores while Nita sliced bacon and fried it for their dinner. Lucy was whiny, and Teddy was cranky. Meg got them ready for bed early and fixed Teddy a quick sandwich with the bacon and the leftover biscuits, while Nita fried Lucy an egg.

After the children ate, Meg brushed their teeth and tucked them in. They were both asleep by the time Ace finished outside. Like the ride home, the meal was mostly silent.

It wasn't until he finished and went out to his bed in the barn and Meg and Nita were cleaning up the supper dishes that the older woman finally turned to Meg and said, "Maybe it's none of my business, but I'm curious about what happened after I took the children inside Ellie's."

Meg finished drying a plate and turned to face her. "My mother did what she's so very good at doing. She made me feel small and unimportant and…dirty."

"She must have hinted that there was something going on between you and Ace," Nita said.

"How did you know that?"

"No offense to you, but I've known a few people like her during my life and they all seem to think alike and act alike. Deep down, they're unhappy, and everything they do is meant to make someone else feel bad so that they can feel better about themselves."

Nita's comment gave Meg pause. She'd never considered the idea of her mother being unhappy, especially when everything she did said otherwise. "She told me I was just like her, that the apple didn't fall far from the tree. Because of Elton, I guess, and what she thinks is going on between me and Ace."

Instead of taking offense, Nita laughed. "I've only known you a short time, child, and I can say with no hesitation that you are nothing like your mother—if she's anything like the rumors about her."

Urging a half smile to her lips, Meg turned to stack the plate with the others. "Thank you, Nita. And let me tell you…she's all and more that you've no doubt heard."

"Well, that's too bad for you. But it's even worse for her."

Meg gave Nita a sharp glance. "What do you mean?"

"Only that she's missed out on a lot of things by going out of her way to alienate you, and I imagine the older she gets, the more she realizes that."

Confusion clouded Meg's eyes.

"First of all," Nita said, "she's missed out on knowing a wonderful woman. I know how special my relationship with Ace is, and I can only imagine that if I had a daughter it might be even more special. What's really sad is that she's missing out on all the sweet and funny things Teddy and Lucy do, and they're missing out on knowing what it's like to go to Grandma's house."

Meg had never considered the things Nita mentioned. She'd been too wrapped up in her own disgust over her mother's way of life and her shame in knowing that the whole town knew about how Elton had abused her. There'd been no room for worry about anyone or anything except how to get from one day to the next the best way she knew how. Ace and Nita Allen had opened her eyes to a lot of things. Like never considering how her mother had been robbed of many of life's joys by choosing the lifestyle she had.

"Thank you, Nita," she said, giving the older woman a brief hug.

"For what?"

"Being you, I guess." She folded the dish towel and placed it on the edge of the counter. "Will you listen for the kids for me? I need to talk to Ace."

As she expected, Meg found Ace sitting near the fire he'd built between the house and the outbuildings.

"Have a seat," he offered, gesturing toward the hunk of wood next to him. "I wanted to talk to you about today."

The statement took her by surprise. She'd made up her mind to try to explain how sorry and ashamed she was of Georgina's behavior. She hadn't expected him to raise the subject first. She sat on the stump and pulled her shawl closer.

"I'm sorry you had to see that this afternoon," she told him, focusing her gaze on the blazing fire. "I'm afraid Georgie brings out the worst in me."

"Because that's what she sets out to do."

"What?"

"She's jealous of you."

"Jealous?" Meg echoed, turning to look at him. "Why would she be jealous of me?"

"Because she doesn't have the courage you do."

Meg shook her head, not understanding at all.

"Right or wrong, you found a way out of the nightmare that living with her must have been." His gaze probed hers in the flickering light of the fire.

"If I hadn't gotten out of there…" She left the sentence unfinished.

She heard a soft hiss as he released the breath he'd been holding. "So," he said, picking up his train of thought. "You got involved with Elton and more or less jumped out of the frying pan into the fire. As you've said, a bad choice. It takes a lot to rise above a situation like that, especially when you know everything's a mess because you made bad choices."

"Like you said, from the frying pan to the fire," Meg told him in a cynical tone.

He nodded. "Maybe. But you still did a good job with what you had to work with. Your mother, on the other hand, was too weak when your father died to do what you did. It was easier to let her problems drag her down even deeper."

He paused, and Meg knew he was trying to figure out how to make his point without bringing up Elton's death.

"Now that things are different, you have a whole new life stretching out before you with new opportunities, new dreams and new choices."

"I hope I do better this time."

Ace got to his feet and kicked a log closer to the flame. A shower of sparks flew upward. "That's what I wanted to talk to you about."

She heard something in his voice she couldn't put her finger on but didn't like.

"The quarrel with my mother?"

"No. The things she said."

Meg gave a shaky laugh. "You have every right to be angry. I was. Am. It was pretty embarrassing for her to imply there's more between us than there is. Nita says Georgie likes making other people look bad so she can look better."

"That's because she's unhappy. But that's not what I'm talking about."

Hearing that her mother was unhappy from both Ace and Nita was an eye-opener. There must be some truth to their claim, since they shared the same view.

"Then what is it?" she asked.

He turned to face her. "What about the other things she said? She made it pretty clear that she didn't hold Indians in high regard."

"Oh, well," Meg said, waving a dismissive hand. "That was just Georgie trying to hurt me again."

"And me," he added in a low voice.

Meg sobered in a heartbeat. She'd been so wrapped up in her own anger that she'd given no thought to how her mother's oh-so-casual comment had wounded Ace.

"I'm sorry."

Ace turned to her again. "I'm not. It brought back a lot of memories I thought I'd put behind me. And it was a very good example of what life with me would be like if I were selfish enough to ignore my common sense and make you my wife."

Meg felt as if her own heart stopped beating for a second or two, and then, when she'd thought the statement through, joy flooded her and she could breathe again. He'd just said that he cared for her and wanted

to marry her! And then she recalled that little word *if.*
If I were selfish enough...

She got to her feet and went to stand in front of him,
so close she could feel his warmth. Reaching out, she
placed a hand on his chest. For an instant, he stiffened at her touch but then relaxed, almost, she thought,
against his will. His heart beat strong and steady beneath her palm.

"You want to marry me?" she asked in a voice filled
with wonder.

"More than anything this side of heaven."

"Then I don't understand. You must know that I
feel the same."

"Meg—"

"No!" she said, holding up a hand to silence him.
"Don't try to make me believe that what I feel for you
is gratitude or that it's too soon after Elton's...death to
feel the things I feel, or that I'll always think of you as
his killer. Of course I feel gratitude for all the things
you've done for me, but it goes beyond that. I've never
felt for anyone what I feel...for you."

He grew very still, and she saw him swallow hard.

The tears started then, and with an agonized groan,
Ace pulled her into his arms and rested his cheek
against the top of her head.

"My parents and I went through the same sort of
thing your mother put us through today, and believe
me, it never gets any easier. You deserve better than
that."

She held him tighter, needing the strength she found
from just touching him. "I'm strong!" she whispered

in a fierce voice. "If you love me, I don't care what people say."

He tipped her head back so he could look into her eyes. "You are strong, Meg Thomerson. You're one of the strongest women I've ever known. But the taunts won't go away, and hearing them won't get easier. I know. It won't work, Meg."

All the progress she'd made the past weeks, all the joy she'd felt throughout the day, vanished like the red sparks shooting up into the inky darkness. She felt as numb as she had when she first woke up at Rachel's. "But you overcame all that, and your parents loved each other in spite of it."

"I overcame it, but not until I went to prison and almost killed my parents with grief. I don't want that for our children. I won't have it for you."

The finality she heard in his voice left no room for compromise. Still, she was used to fighting for everything good in her life, and she wanted a life with him. "What if it's what I want?"

Ace took her face in his hands and looked her directly in the eye. "You've said you don't blame me for Elton's death, and I do believe you, but whether or not you forgive me doesn't matter. Whether or not God forgives me doesn't matter. What matters is that I can't forgive myself."

"I don't understand," Meg said.

"From the first minute I saw you, I loved you." He shook his head. "I'm a pretty practical man, but nothing about that moment was ordinary. I felt as if something in you was calling out to the most basic part of me and we were connected in some way. Maybe that isn't love, but whatever it was, it was pretty overwhelming.

"After that, every time I heard what Elton had done to you, I wished him dead." He released his hold on her and sat back down, burying his face in his hands for long seconds. When he looked up, he faced her almost defiantly.

Seeing the agony in his expression hurt too much, so Meg closed her own eyes and plunged her clenched fists into her pockets to still their trembling.

"I've relived that day a thousand times," he said. "I see him shooting at Colt and then turning the rifle toward me. And as we're looking down the sights, eye to eye, I see that gloating smile of his, and I remember all the terrible things he'd done to you and how he jerked you up by your broken arm."

He drew in a deep breath. "I know the facts say that I did the right thing. I saved Colt and myself, but the truth is that when I pulled that trigger, I wanted him dead. God have mercy on me, but I'm glad he's dead. How can we base a marriage on that?"

His words washed over her, dousing her with a chilly splash of reality as she struggled to grasp his burden of blame while floundering around in her own. How often had she wished Elton was dead? And what about the fact that, like Ace, she felt no sense of loss, only a liberating sense of relief?

It was a sobering moment. Meg pressed her fingertips to her throbbing temples. Maybe he was right. Maybe they could never be happy with Elton's death always standing between them. It seemed that, once again, joy was just out of reach.

She needed to confess her own guilt. She opened her eyes, expecting to see him sitting on the log. No one was there. She heard the crack of a twig at the edge of the forest and turned to see a tall figure disappear into the canopy of darkness.

Just like that, he was gone.

Breakfast was a solemn affair. Meg had hardly slept and Nita looked as if she'd spent a few wakeful hours, too. At one point, as she lay next to Teddy's small, warm body, Meg had heard low voices coming from the kitchen. She'd thought about getting up and demanding to know why Ace had walked away from her, but realized that between them they'd said about all there was to say. If he wouldn't accept her forgiveness and love, she had nothing else to offer.

Nita didn't say what she and Ace had discussed, but she was quiet, unlike her usual cheerful self. They ate oatmeal with butter and brown sugar along with fried biscuits, dressed the children and went out to start the laundry.

It would take longer to fill the tubs today, since Ace wasn't there to carry the water buckets.

"Where did he go?" Meg asked the question as she and Nita built the fires at the end of the three-sided enclosure Ace had built. He'd constructed a low fence about halfway back to keep the children safe from the fire. It kept them under Meg and Nita's watchful eye while giving them ample room to play.

"Here and there," Nita said with a shrug. "He said something about going to Oklahoma for a while. Then... I don't know."

Meg's heart sank. It seemed he intended to put as many miles between them as possible. "Did you try to stop him?"

The smile Nita gave her said without words that she'd learned long ago that there was no stopping her son when he got something into his head. "He's done this all his life," she said at last. "It's his way of working through things, finding his peace, if it's to be found."

Thinking of how she did her best thinking when she was at her quiet place in the woods, Meg understood. "When is he coming back?" Is *he coming back?*

"I never know," Nita told her. "He's always just showed up when he has his mind clear."

Meg wondered if he would just show up this time, or if the things standing between them were so insurmountable that he would never find his peace.

"Did he tell you what happened?"

Nita didn't look up as she fed another log to the fire. "Yes."

"Would you think I was a horrible person if I told you that even though I've reached the point of feeling sorrow for the fact that Elton died in sin, I haven't been able to dredge up even the smallest bit of sadness or regret that he's dead? Some days I think I'll drown in that guilt, so I understand exactly how he feels."

"Did you tell Ace that?"

"He left before I had a chance."

"Maybe if he knew that, it would make a difference, but I'm not convinced that guilt is his problem. I think driving a wedge between the two of you made it easier to leave."

Meg looked up sharply.

A gentle smile curved Nita's lips. "I know you love my son, and I know that when you love someone, that love blinds you to many things. Asa loves you enough that he doesn't want you and the children to go through the things he and I did while he was growing up. Though it may seem insignificant to you, he lived it, and he still remembers that pain."

"He told me that, and I understand. Don't forget that Georgie Ferris is my mother. People have looked down on me and talked about me all my life, and it only got worse when I married Elton. I'm used to it. Nothing would really change if Ace and I…were together."

"I thought you might say that." Nita sighed. "I have nothing to tell you to help you except to give him time. He might come to see things differently. I can't say." She dumped the two buckets of water they'd already carried from the well into the cast-iron kettle. "In the meantime, he wants me to stay with you to help with the children. Would that be acceptable?"

Meg's eyes filled with tears. "What about things that need doing at your place? And what about your animals?"

"He'll see to it that they're brought here."

"Then it will be more than acceptable. I'd consider it a blessing to have you here."

Chapter Fourteen

When Meg awoke the morning after her talk with Nita, the older woman's animals were in the pens alongside her own. Since they must have arrived in the dead of night, she suspected that Ace had delivered them, and she wondered if he'd spoken with his mother again. She had enough pride not to ask, and Nita didn't volunteer anything except "Looks like Ace got the critters moved without any problem."

They finished up the ironing by noon, and Meg asked if Nita minded watching the children while she went to town to deliver it. She didn't want Lucy out in the chilly air, since she had picked up a runny nose and cough.

Meg couldn't help comparing this trip to the last one. Instead of driving in sunshine and birdsong, gunmetal-gray clouds hung low in the sky. There had been casual conversation between her and her companions on their last trip to town, and Teddy had been so excited he could hardly contain himself. Her own heart had been light, and her future seemed to hold a promise of better things. Ace had taken that hope with him.

My grace is sufficient to you.

The words she'd read so many times drifted through her mind, a reminder that she was putting her trust and hope in the wrong person. Jesus was the one her faith and future happiness should rest on, not Ace.

All she'd done since he left was bemoan the fact that it wasn't fair to finally find love and lose it, and to stew about what would happen to her now that he had gone and how she could ever hope to live her life without him. Just like the women in the romance novels of which she'd grown so fond.

Not once had she prayed about their unusual situation or the many things that needed discussing with the Lord. She had not thanked God for sending Ace and Nita to her when she so desperately needed love and help. She hadn't thanked Him for allowing her to know a man who had shown her what real love between a man and woman should be. She had not asked the Lord to show them both a way to leave their pasts, along with their guilt, behind, nor had she prayed for strength and faith enough to conquer their fears so that they could have a life together.

For the remainder of the trip to Wolf Creek, she prayed from the depths of her heart, not only confessing her own faults and weaknesses, but also asking for forgiveness and giving thanks for the many blessings in her life. She thanked Him for this chance to learn to stand on her own two feet.

When she finished, she felt that perhaps for the first

time since the day that had changed her life that her heart was in the right place as she'd talked to the Lord. By the time the buildings of town came into view, Meg felt better than she had in months, perhaps years.

Thankful that she beat the rain, she made short work of delivering the clean laundry to Hattie and Ellie, both of whom asking where Ace was. She received a couple of strange looks when she confessed that she had no idea. Before heading home, she stopped by the doctor's office to pick up some cough syrup for Lucy.

As Rachel was writing the dosage on the label, she said, "I hear you ran into your mother outside of Ellie's the other day."

"You heard right."

"Ellie said you were white as a sheet when you came in."

"I probably was," Meg said with a little laugh. "Conversations with Georgie are never pleasant."

Rachel handed Meg the brown bottle with a shake of her head. "I don't understand her. Under the circumstances, I think I'd be trying to mend my bridges instead of burning them."

"What do you mean?" Meg asked, frowning.

Rachel pressed her lips together, looking as if she'd brought up a subject she'd rather not discuss. "I'm sorry. I should never have mentioned it, but I just supposed she'd told you when the two of you talked. She's sick, Meg."

"Sick?" A parade of thoughts marched through Meg's mind. She'd heard a few weeks before running into Georgie in front of the café that she was ill, but she'd looked fine when they'd met on the street. A little thinner and a bit pale, perhaps, but healthy enough. Or had the flush of color in her cheeks been a bit too bright? "What do you mean, sick? What's the matter with her?"

"Consumption," Rachel offered in an almost apologetic tone.

Consumption! Just hearing the word struck terror in Meg's heart. It was commonly known that anyone diagnosed with that disease had been handed a death warrant.

"How long has she had it?" she asked, feeling a bit queasy.

"I have no way of knowing for sure. Serena told Georgina that she needed to see what was going on, since she'd been running a fever and had a nagging cough and lack of energy for such a long time. At first your mother thought it was a cold, even though she was coughing up blood from time to time. Then she'd get better for a while. When that happens, the patient thinks they're on the road to recovery, but another setback is inevitable."

"Is she bad?"

Rachel nodded. "Not as bad as she'll get if she doesn't change her diet and get some exercise. So far, she's fighting that. You know your mother likes her food, and I've tried to caution her about overeating. Even though her breathing is difficult, she would benefit from spending time outside as long as the temperature is stable. Moderate exercise would be good for her, as well. Contrary to what everyone believes, some people do recover. Sadly, most don't."

Meg's head was spinning as she tried to absorb what Rachel was telling her. She and her mother had been at odds for her entire life, yet to hear that her time on earth was limited was disturbing. "I've heard that moving to a warmer climate can help."

"It can if the move is undertaken early in the disease's progression. Most people, including your mother, wait until things have gone too far for a move to make any difference."

"How…how long can someone live with it?" Meg asked around the unexpected lump in her throat.

Rachel gave a slight, noncommittal shrug. "If the disease is active, time can vary from a few weeks to a few years. The average time is about eighteen months."

"Georgie?"

"Oh, Meg!" Rachel shook her head. "I have no way of knowing that. God will take her when it's her time. I do know that her cough is getting progressively worse and so is the amount of blood mixed with the phlegm. She's started having night sweats, too, which can happen at any time, but it's usually a good indication that the disease is well established."

They talked about her mother's condition a bit longer, and then, feeling as if a rug had just been pulled out from under her, Meg rummaged around in her pocket for the money to pay for Lucy's medicine and pressed it into Rachel's hand. "Thank you for telling me, Rachel. You're a good friend."

Rachel placed the coins on a nearby table. "I know

things have been…rocky between you and your mother, but if you ever hope to mend the rift between you, I wouldn't wait too long to do it."

Torn by conflicting emotions and a depth of sorrow she was hard-pressed to explain, Meg gave the gray her head and the wagon barreled down the bumpy roads toward home. Still, she barely beat the rain. She'd no more than unhitched the mare, rubbed her down and fed her and run back to the house when the cold drizzle started to fall. After giving Lucy a spoonful of the cough syrup, Meg and Nita followed their evening routine of preparing supper and tending the children as needed.

To add to Meg's distress, Teddy and Lucy were unusually demanding and whiny—Lucy because she was miserable with her cold and Teddy because he was missing Ace. Telling him that Ace had things he needed to take care of in a faraway place did little to ease his tears.

Meg, who tried to never let her feelings spill over into her interaction with her children, snapped at Teddy. She could tell by the concerned looks Nita was giving her that the older woman wondered what was wrong. Only when she started talking about the upcoming Thanksgiving holiday and how much they would enjoy that big old Tom turkey Ace had shot and hung in the smokehouse did Teddy quiet and eat.

After cleaning up the supper dishes, the two women got the children settled and donned their own bedclothes before they sat down in the rocking chairs near the fireplace. Nita added another log to the fire and Meg carried the lamps from the kitchen to the small parlor area, placing them to make reading easier.

They had fallen into the habit of mending or reading for a while each evening before weariness or the increasingly cold nights sent them in search of their beds.

Meg was doing her best to concentrate on the words of her most recent choice from Libby's library when Nita looked up from the patch she was sewing on Teddy's denim pants. "I was going through that pile of worn-out clothes you'd set aside for rags, and I think with the feed sacks we have between the two of us, we could piece another quilt."

Meg glanced up from the book she was having such a hard time getting interested in. "Really? That would be wonderful. I've pieced tops before, but I'm afraid I've never done any actual quilting. It wasn't on Georgie's list of skills, and somehow I never learned from Aunt Serena, either."

"I can show you how, and I have quilting frames at my place. It's a good way to pass the time when it gets really cold."

"Thank you, Nita," Meg said sincerely. "I'd love to learn."

"From the way you already handle a needle, I expect you'll pick it up in no time."

"Thank you," Meg said again. Instead of going back to her reading, she clenched the book tightly in her hands and stared at her friend, wondering whether or not to tell her about her mother.

"What's the matter, child?" Nita asked. "Since you

got back from town, you've been as pitiful as I've ever seen you."

"It's my mother."

"Don't tell me you two had another squabble."

"No. I didn't see her, but while I was getting Lucy's medicine, Rachel told me that my mother is—" Meg couldn't stop the little crack in her voice "—dying. She has consumption."

Meg told Nita everything Rachel had confided about her mother's condition and the progression of the disease.

"Did she say how long she has?"

"No," Meg told her with a shake of her head. "She did say that the disease is active and, from the symptoms Georgie is displaying, that she's probably had it for some time. She says there's a treatment called the Golden Medical Discovery that might be beneficial. She's going to look into it, and she claims that a lot of people have recovered with the proper diet and care. Unfortunately, my mother isn't one to do anything other than what she wants."

Meg ended her tale with Rachel's admonition that if she wanted to make her peace with her mother, she should do so.

"Will you go see her?"

"I know I should, but how do I know she wants me to come see her? She's treated me so badly, and Charlie…" She gave a little shudder. "Charlie gives me the creeps."

"Well, that's up to you, but regardless of how she's treated you or even how you feel about her, she is your mother. She carried you inside her body for nine months, and from what I hear, she came close to dying when you were born. That's something."

Meg knew Nita was right, but still, she needed to think on things awhile. Refusing to give Georgie any more thought for right now, Meg asked, "Have you heard from Ace?"

"No, child. Not a word," Nita told her.

Meg didn't doubt Nita, but there had been times, especially when he'd first gone, that Meg imagined she could feel his presence. Times she stopped what she was doing and looked around, as if she expected to see him come striding out of the woods. She supposed she was being fanciful, but remembering how he had secretly stayed nearby to keep an eye on her, she felt justified in indulging in the harmless fantasy—another of those romantic notions with its roots in her choice of reading material, no doubt. Of course, back when he was staying in the lean-to, the temperatures weren't dropping into the thirties at night.

"Do you usually fix a big Thanksgiving dinner?"

The question pulled Meg away from her troubling thoughts. She looked at Nita in astonishment. She'd never fixed a traditional dinner. Elton was seldom home, and she had no family other than Aunt Serena, and she'd been unable to make the long trip to her place alone with two children in tow.

"No. Never."

It was Nita's turn to look amazed. "Well, we can't have that! Thanksgiving was one American tradition that Yancy embraced wholeheartedly, probably because there was food involved," she said with a tender smile.

"My Irishman did love his victuals. We'll have that turkey Ace smoked. I prefer to bake my Thanksgiving turkey so I can make dressing from the broth, but I'm sure it won't be any hardship to eat this one. And we'll have sweet potatoes and turnips and pecan pie…"

Meg listened to Nita planning the holiday with a sad wistfulness. This was what she'd missed by not having a mother who was interested in a family. She vowed right then and there that she would not do to her children what Georgie had. She would make every day special in some way and she would be the best mother she possibly could.

Meg thought about her conversations with Rachel and Nita throughout the remaining days of October and into November. Between her unexpected grasp of her misplaced faith, her failure to turn things over to God and hearing the story of her mother's illness, she had more to consider and even more to pray about. She continued to pray for God to soften the hardness of her heart so she might have a future free of the hostility that had taken root there. Maybe when God had healed *her*, she could make peace with *them*.

Her bitterness toward Elton seemed to be easing. Either her prayers were bearing fruit, or the passage of time and the forging of new memories and experiences were as beneficial as everyone said they'd be.

Though she'd never imagined it, forgiving her mother was proving to be harder than letting go of her anger at Elton. How did one let go of a lifetime of heartache, shame and resentment?

She wasn't sure. What she was sure of was that by failing to give Elton and Georgie the mercy she should, she could never hope to have the joy she wanted for the future. That would be like building a house on a rotten foundation.

Thanksgiving arrived, and with it a light sprinkling of snow that glittered like diamond dust over the brown grass and bare tree limbs. Meg knew the skimpy layer would be gone by midmorning, but it made the start of the day even more unusual.

Even though Meg and Nita were determined to make this a special day for all, they decided to take Rachel's advice and pamper themselves by sleeping later than they normally did.

They had the centerpiece of the meal under control since the turkey was already smoked. A whiff of the hickory Ace had used teased their nostrils every time they passed by the large ironstone platter where the bird rested.

Nita had made the pecan pies the evening before, filling the little house with the wonderful aromas of butter and roasting nuts. The sweet potatoes would be baked in the Dutch oven later in the morning, and the turnips, which would be mashed with fresh butter, wouldn't take long to cook. Turnip greens simmered gently over the fire, and the aroma of the bacon used to flavor them mingled with the other mouthwatering smells.

They ate at noon on the dot. It seemed to Meg that the simple country fare tasted far better than usual, which she credited to her company. Lucy and Teddy seemed to get into the joyful spirit, and Teddy offered to say the prayer of thanksgiving for their blessings.

Meg was surprised at how grown up he sounded as he thanked God not only for the food, their house and all the animals, but also for Nita and Ace. When he prayed for Ace to come home, Meg couldn't help the rush of tears or the way her breath caught at the knowledge that Teddy had come to look up to Ace, to depend on him. To love him. And no wonder. Ace had been more of a father to him than Elton had ever been. She dreaded the day Teddy realized that Ace wasn't coming back.

After the noon meal, Nita suggested that they go for a walk in the woods and find things to decorate for the upcoming Christmas holiday. Meg's heart overflowed with love for the pretty older woman who'd come into her life so unexpectedly and, through her willing spirit, patience and gentle ways, had made herself an important part of their lives.

The walk in the woods was filled with fun and laughter, and even Lucy, bundled up against the chill air, giggled when her faltering steps sent her tumbling into the leaves. Holly and pine and cedar were plentiful, but Nita explained to Teddy that the fragrant branches would dry out and turn brown if they picked them too early, so they didn't take anything home except some huge pinecones. Nita said they would pile them in one of her baskets with some greenery and tie a bow on the handle. Teddy had great fun picking up the pinecones and placing them gently in the tow sack she'd brought.

When they came to Meg's special place, memories of the last time she'd been there with Ace slipped into her mind, like the water rushing over the rocks of the creek. She could almost smell the smoke from his fire.

On impulse, she took a stick and knelt to stir the remains of the fire. There, beneath the gray ash, were small glowing embers. He'd been here! She didn't know long ago, but recently enough that the fire hadn't grown fully cold. Knowing it was insanity, she stood and peered into the thick undergrowth, turning in a full circle as she searched the woods. She saw nothing except naked scrub, fallen leaves and an occasional lichen-covered boulder.

"What are you doing, Mama?" Teddy asked, looking up at her curiously.

Meg's guilty gaze found Nita's. Nita Allen knew exactly what she was doing.

"J-just looking for some more holly," she fibbed. "I don't see any, but it's getting colder. I think we should start back."

"I agree," Nita said. When Teddy began to whine, she added, "We'll have some milk and pie when we get back, and then I think we all need a Thanksgiving nap. Look! Lucy is rubbing her eyes."

With Teddy somewhat mollified, they started the tramp back through the woods. On the way, Meg spotted a sprig of mistletoe the wind must have blown down. For some reason it reminded her of the day

Ace had plucked the twig from her hair. She realized just how far she'd come since then. On impulse, she picked it up.

When they reached the house and the others went inside, she paused on the front porch for just a moment, wishing there were some way she could let Ace know that she wanted him to come back. Finally, unable to think of anything else, she suspended the piece of mistletoe on the dinner bell that hung from one of the porch posts. Then she opened her arms wide the same way he did when he welcomed the sunrise. She turned slowly from one side to the other.

Was he out there?

Would he understand?

Would he care?

Ace had no problem following the little quartet through the woods without them being aware of him. He was close enough to see most of what they did but far enough away that their conversations were inaudible. He couldn't help smiling when he saw Meg sit back on her heels and stir the ashes of the fire, one of the tracking hints about which he'd told her. The smile faded when she looked around at the bare forest. Looking for him.

What was she feeling? Anger that he'd left without telling her he was going? He had no idea. Even more important, he had no idea why he'd come back. Nothing had really changed except the season.

After spending a few days getting things settled, he had made the long trek to Oklahoma, intending to spend some time with his aging grandmother and to put as many miles between himself and Meg as possible.

Though the distance was great, everything about her followed him. Images of her seldom left his mind. He heard her rare laughter in the rustling of the trees, imagined he could smell the clean scent of her hair on a sudden gust of wind. His heart ached to hold her. His spirit cried out for her. He wasn't sure he would ever be able to banish her from his mind or his heart. A long, empty life stretched out before him.

Feeling lower than a snake's belly, needing the benefit of her wisdom, Ace told his grandmother everything about Meg, from the first time he'd seen her in Wolf Creek to his last memory of her when he'd left her standing by the fire.

It hadn't taken long for Amadahy to set him straight.

The tiny birdlike woman with the heart of a bear had exhibited no remorse when she'd told Ace in no uncertain terms that he was acting like a fool for using excuses to drive Meg away. He wanted to argue in his defense, but no one argued with Amadahy. They listened until she finished and then they thanked her.

"You are a fool, Asa Allen," she told him, her dark eyes narrowed as she squinted at him through the smoke of a clay pipe. "Do I hear you saying that you fear that perhaps you killed this man because you cared for his woman?"

Ace, who was sitting at her feet with his arms around his knees, squirmed at the disapproval in her voice. "No. I know I had no choice but to protect myself and my friend. I know I jerked the gun because Elton's bullet nicked my arm. I wish things could have been different, but that's not what's bothering me."

"Tell me."

Ace met her gaze squarely. "I was glad he was dead, Grandmother, and that is not the way a Christian or an honorable man should feel."

"We feel what we feel, right or wrong. You tell me you don't want her and her children to go through what you and your mother did. Times are changing, and your woman's ways are different than ours. Just as your mother's was, her heart is involved. She should have a say in what she is willing to endure to have a life with you. You tell me that she has been through many troubles and that she is strong."

"Very strong."

Amadahy gave a shrug of her narrow shoulders. "Who can say? Perhaps those troubles have strengthened her even more. Perhaps they were preparing her for the trials she may suffer as your wife."

Ace felt like Teddy looked when he got a scolding from Meg.

Amadahy pointed the stem of the pipe at him. "It is the way of men to talk, my son. They will talk and talk about everything and everyone. They have talked about you more than most, perhaps. It has taken you many years to find out who Asa Allen is, and for the first time, the Creator has given you peace with yourself."

She paused long enough to take another long draw on her pipe while Ace tried to figure out where she was headed with this conversation. He didn't have to wait long.

"I think it is possible that it is you who is afraid of more talk. I think that maybe you like living in the shadows of the woods instead of out in the world so that no one can criticize you."

The no-nonsense statement had taken Ace aback. Was that what he'd been doing?

"You have much to offer. Stories and hard truths. Knowledge and love. Much love," she had told him. Then she'd told him to leave her, that she was weary of talking.

He'd left the reservation soon after his talk with his grandmother, and during the long journey home, he'd given serious thought to her comment about the things Meg had gone through making her stronger. Could he dare to hope that Amadahy was right?

He blew out a disgusted breath, making the air around him fog. He wasn't ready to deal with that just yet, so here he was, a grown man hiding in the woods and the barn, watching for a glimpse of the woman he loved as she spent time with her children. The children he'd come to love.

He was standing at the edge of the clearing, hidden by a persimmon thicket, watching as his mother and the children traipsed into the house. He saw Meg stop on the porch and look out at the woods again, almost as if she sensed his presence. Then she went to the dinner bell and placed something on the metal bracket that held it. Stepping back, she spread her arms out and turned slowly from side to side, as if she were welcoming someone. The way he welcomed the sun.

Ace frowned. What was she doing? After a while, she let her arms fall to her sides and turned to go inside. Later, when the landscape turned dusky dark, he stole through the gloaming to see what she'd left on the bell.

Mistletoe! His heart began to race as he considered the implication of the small gift. She'd left him kisses. Smiling a silly smile, he counted the berries. Nine kisses. He closed his eyes and thought of the feel and taste of her lips and what it would be like to have the right to kiss them every day for the rest of his life.

He moved quietly through the twilight to the barn, still making no move to go to her. Amadahy was right about his living his life on the fringes. It was much easier that way. The simple truth was that he was scared of what it would mean if she said yes. He was afraid that they would think her a fool for marrying a man with no future for the second time.

He knew how men thought. Many would say that since Meg had married so soon after Elton's death, she'd probably been carrying on with him while Elton was in jail. They would drag out his old sins and parade them through town. Hers, too. Without a doubt, they would be the focus of everyone's talk, at least for a time.

His grandmother was right about another thing.

About this at least, he was behaving like a fool.

Chapter Fifteen

Two mornings later, Teddy was sleeping later than usual, and Meg was feeding Lucy her oatmeal when she heard hoofbeats thundering down the road. She gave Lucy's mouth a swipe, set her on the floor and went to see what was going on. Nita joined Meg at the window. At first she couldn't tell who the rider was, but finally realized it was the sheriff.

Memories of other times she'd seen Colt Garrett coming down the road set off an immediate feeling of alarm. Her anxiety eased when she remembered that the law would not be coming after Elton ever again. Going to the door, she stepped out onto the porch, hugging herself against the biting chill of the air.

"Mornin', Colt," she said. "Come on in out of the cold and have some coffee."

"Mornin', Meg. Coffee would be great," he said, dismounting and striding up to the porch.

"What are you doing out and about so early?"

"Rachel sent me," he told her, whipping off his hat and gesturing for her to precede him.

The uneasy feeling returned. Why on earth would Rachel send the sheriff at such an early hour?

Nita handed Colt a mug of coffee. He took it from her, but his eyes never left Meg.

A feeling of doom seemed to be closing in on her. "What is it, Colt?" she asked.

"It's Georgie, Meg. She's real bad and asking for you."

In spite of the ill will between Meg and her mother, there wasn't an ounce of hesitation as she prepared to go to Georgie's side. She didn't recall ever being summoned by her mother for anything but a scolding. Colt hitched up the wagon while she got ready, and then he tied his horse to the back and drove her to the Ferris place while Nita stayed with the children.

The ride to the little house located on a back road a couple of miles outside of Wolf Creek seemed to take forever. Meg recognized Rachel's buggy and another tied to the hitching post, an unfamiliar horse next to them. When Colt knocked, Meg's aunt Serena opened the door. A frisson of alarm tripped down Meg's spine when she saw the preacher standing near the fireplace.

"I'm glad you came, Meg," Serena said with a weary smile and a brief hug. "I wasn't sure you would. She's been asking for you."

After Meg greeted the preacher, her aunt took her by the hand and led her across the gaudily decorated parlor to a closed door. A dozen questions swirled through Meg's mind, but one stood out. Why was the pastor at her mother's house?

The door opened to a small bedroom at Serena's light rap. Rachel welcomed Meg with a hug, but her attention was on the woman who lay so still beneath the pile of quilts.

As she approached the bed, she could see that Georgie had lost a considerable amount of weight since she'd run into her outside of Ellie's—how many weeks ago? It was the first time Meg remembered seeing her mother without the benefit of her powder and paint.

Hectic color heightened her cheeks and there were dark circles beneath her eyes. Even so, her unadorned face was truly beautiful with its softly winged brows, straight nose and prettily shaped lips. Pain squeezed Meg's heart. What a shame that the world had not seen this Georgie Ferris. What a shame that she had been so insecure and dissatisfied in who she was that she'd found the need to create another person.

Meg's guilty gaze sought Rachel's. "I…I thought there would be more time."

"There probably would have been, if she hadn't contracted pneumonia. With her lungs already in distress, it's just too much."

Meg looked from her aunt to the doctor. "Pneumonia?"

Rachel actually smiled. "That's the good news in all this."

"How can that be good news?" How could her mother's pneumonia be to her advantage in any way?

"She sent for Brother McAdams a few days ago," Serena said. "She said she wanted to make things right with God—with everyone—and insisted on being baptized in the creek."

"But it's freezing outside!"

"We all argued with her," Rachel said, "and Gabe even offered to fill one of his slipper tubs so we could do it inside." She gave a humorless smile. "You know your mother as well as anyone, and there was no changing her mind."

That was a fact. Once Georgina Ferris made up her mind about something, there was no swaying her.

"There's nothing we can do?" Meg asked.

"I'm doing what I can. I've been putting poultices on her chest and giving her flaxseed and slippery elm tea when she can take it, but I don't think it's doing much good," Rachel told her apologetically.

"I came to check on her," Serena offered, "and even though her cough was worse, I assumed it was the consumption. Maybe if I'd fetched Rachel sooner…"

"I don't know if that would have made any difference at this point," Rachel said when Serena's voice trailed away.

"Where's Charlie?" Meg asked, realizing she'd seen no sign of the man who'd been such a terrible influence on her mother.

"That's another good thing. Georgie sent him away the day she sent for Brother McAdams. Said she never wanted to see him again."

"Should have done it years ago."

The observation, spoken in little more than a breathless whisper, came from the woman on the bed.

"Mama." Meg was at her side in an instant and took one thin hand in hers.

Georgie smiled up weakly at her daughter. "Thank you for coming. I wouldn't have blamed you if you hadn't."

"Don't talk," Meg said. "Save your strength."

"I brought you here to tell you some things."

"It doesn't matter," Meg insisted. "All that matters is that you get better." Tears began to slip down her cheeks. "I should have come when I first heard you were sick. I'm sorry, Mama."

"You're like me that way," Georgie said with a twist of her lips that was meant to be a smile. "Bullheaded. And just for the record, I'm the one who's sorry."

A severe coughing spell interrupted whatever it was she was about to say. Meg didn't miss the streaks of blood on the scrap of white cloth Georgina tossed into a wooden box at the bedside.

When she was in control once more, Georgie said, "I'm ashamed to say that when your father died, I was so miserable I wanted to die, too. And then along came Charlie, and he was fun, and he made me forget my unhappiness for a while. I came to depend on him for a lot of things, including the roof over my head for a time. And then when his money ran out and he began to ask me to do…things I should have been ashamed to do, I did them to make him happy."

Meg closed her eyes, but she couldn't close her ears. "You don't have to tell me this."

"Yes," Georgina said, fighting for every shallow breath. "I do. That's one reason I tried to put as much distance between us as possible by goading you and pushing you off on Serena every chance I got. I knew she and Dave would give you the background you needed to live a decent life."

"And the other reason?" Meg asked.

"I admit to being a weak woman, Meg," she said, her grip tightening. "But I've never been stupid." Her smile was as dry as dust. "Well, maybe a little stupid when it came to Charlie. I saw how he and his buddies looked at you and I knew what he had on his mind. I didn't want that for you, so I kept picking those fights. The good Lord knows I wanted you gone, but I never meant to drive you into Elton Thomerson's arms."

Meg forced a short laugh. "Believe me, I was well aware of Charlie, and I wanted out, too, and if it hadn't been Elton, it would have been someone else."

She sighed. "I have to give the devil his due. Elton had a way about him that was hard to resist. By the time I started figuring out what kind of man he really was, I was pregnant with Teddy, and I was stuck."

Georgie gave a reasonable try at her signature snort of disgust. "You should have just walked away and let the gossips talk. They did anyway."

"You're right," Meg said. There was no sense telling her mother that every time she'd threatened to leave, Elton had told her he would find her and drag her back and make her sorry she'd gone. Meg didn't say a thing about that. It was in the past. Instead, she and her mother shared a smile for the first time since… She couldn't remember when.

"I'm proud of you, Meg," Georgina said.

Meg shook her head, denying that she deserved the compliment. "I've made mistakes, too, Mama."

"You have. Everyone does. But you've worked hard to overcome them, and you've turned out to be a good person despite who your mama or your husband was."

"Thank you for that," Meg said, blinking fast. "That means a lot."

Georgie looked at her sister. "I want to thank you for all you've done, Serena. Despite everything I've been and done, I never doubted your love for me." Her voice was barely louder than a whisper.

"You're my sister," Serena said, as if the simple statement explained it all.

Georgie smiled at Serena and gave her attention back to Meg. "I wish things had been different. I wish I'd been different, because I've always loved you and I threw you away for a man who wasn't fit to breathe air."

Tears filled the green eyes, so much like Meg's. "I've made my peace with God and I know He's forgiven me. I pray that someday you can, too."

Meg didn't recall ever seeing her mother any way but feisty and difficult. The genuine contrition in her manner was something Meg had hoped for through the years, but never thought she'd see.

Her mother was saying goodbye.

"I have forgiven you," Meg said, and the moment the words left her lips she knew it was true.

Georgina Ferris died three hours later.

When Meg left for town, Ace lost no time going to talk to his mother, who was overjoyed to see him.

She wasn't the only one. Lucy toddled over to him and grabbed the fringe on his leather pants, begging him to pick her up.

"Where's Teddy?" he asked, doing just that and letting Lucy smear wet kisses on his cheek.

"Still sleeping."

"It's just as well," Ace said in a low voice, bouncing the baby on his knee. "I can't stay long and don't want Meg to know I'm back just yet."

Nita set a cup of coffee in front of her son and took a seat across from him. "How is my mother?"

After Ace assured her that Amadahy was as well as could be expected for her age, she asked, "Did she offer you any new thoughts about you and Meg?"

Ace flashed one of his rare smiles. "She told me I was a fool."

"I'm afraid I would tend to agree."

Ace laughed softly, trying his best not to wake Teddy. Until recently, he hadn't had much to laugh about. He told his mother what he'd confessed to his grandmother about being fearful of the slurs people might sling at him and Meg if they married. "She told me that Meg should be allowed to make the decision whether or not she wanted to go through that."

Nita nodded. "I agree. Two hearts are involved in this thing called love, and two hearts should come together in every decision."

Ace only nodded. "Grandmother also asked me if my concern was really for Meg or if I was fearful of facing the gossip again myself. She told me I've been hiding from the pain that life hands out by avoiding people."

"And?" Nita asked gently.

"I think she's right. Now I just have to see if I'm man enough to be the man Meg thinks I am."

Serena, the preacher and Rachel offered to take care of the funeral arrangements, which would happen in two days. Serena and Dave would pay for the casket.

Colt offered to drive Meg back, but she thanked him for his trouble and told him that she was fine and didn't want to bother him to make the extra trip.

As Meg made her way back home, she thought of the conversation with her mother. As wrong and as hurtful as Georgina's treatment of her had been, she had been doing her misguided best to give Meg a chance for a decent life.

Unfortunately, things hadn't worked out as planned; in fact, they often didn't. Ace was right. God gave everyone choices every day. Good or bad, our lives reflected those choices. Meg had assumed that she was more or less free of her mother's influence since she seldom had contact with her. That couldn't be further from the truth. The truth was that Georgina Ferris had influenced almost every choice Meg had ever made.

No more feeling sorry for yourself, Meg Thomerson. No more blaming God for the bad things that had come her way. In the end, whatever had happened in her past was the sum of those choices, and there was nothing to do about them once they were made, except to live with the results.

Meg took a deep breath of the cold air and realized that making the choice to forgive her mother had lightened a burden she'd carried for a long time. It was not a decision she'd regret.

She prayed all the way home, and by the time she reached the little whitewashed house, her sorrow over her mother's death was tempered by the fact that Georgie had made the choice, however late it might have been, to make things right with the Lord.

The moment she walked through the door, Nita must have known what had happened by the look on Meg's face. She'd come to know the older woman so well over the past weeks that she had no qualms about telling her everything her mother had said as they shared a cup of tea.

"It's good that you went, then," Nita told her, giving her hand a pat.

"It is," Meg agreed, "but I should have gone when I first heard she was sick."

"There's no sense fretting and blaming yourself over the things you should have done," Nita said. "The important thing is that you got there in time, and you resolved your differences."

Meg nodded. "Today made me aware of something else, something I know but more or less ignored, I guess." She gave a short, almost embarrassed laugh. "It's something that, maybe more than anyone, I should be aware of."

Nita regarded her with a questioning look.

"We aren't promised tomorrow, so there's no sense

in ruining today with anger or blame or regrets. We need to tell people we love them and make our apologies when we need to and just…welcome every potential source of love that crosses our path."

"It sounds as if you've got things figured out," Nita said.

"Well," Meg said with a crooked smile, "I'm at least getting there. And I've made up my mind what to do about Ace."

"And?"

Meg straightened her shoulders as if she were preparing to go to battle. Maybe she was. "He's taught me so much about forgiveness and regaining faith and trust. I don't think I would be where I am today without his steadiness."

She faced Nita with tears shimmering in her eyes. "We love each other, and that is a rare and wonderful thing. It may never happen to either of us again, and I'm not going to let him toss it away because of what people might say. We have to trust that the Lord will give us enough love and courage and patience to weather any storms that come our way."

Nita laughed at the determination in Meg's voice. "I think my son is a fool if he doesn't realize how fortunate he is to have you."

Meg blushed. "Thank you," she said almost shyly. "And I want to say that in very different but equally important ways you have helped my heart to heal. You have been more of a mother to me than my own ever was, and for that, I will always love you, Nita Allen."

* * *

Despite the cold, dreary day that threatened rain, Georgina's graveside service was better attended than Meg had expected. Friends and people from town and church who had offered Meg work and friendship despite her mother or her marriage came to sing and listen to the minister's final remarks. These gentle souls wanted to show their support for Meg if nothing else.

She was flanked on one side by the Gentry brothers and their families, and by Colt and Dan with their fiancées on the other. For some crazy reason, Meg expected that Ace would miraculously show up to help her through this latest trial. Even though she'd stood on the porch every day since Thanksgiving with her arms outspread in welcome, she'd seen no sign of him and he'd made no effort to contact her.

She couldn't help her disappointment, but she didn't really have any proof that he was anywhere in the vicinity except that the morning after she'd placed the mistletoe on the arm of the bell bracket, it was gone. So Meg swallowed her unhappiness and managed to be gracious to those who came to offer their condolences after the short service.

Thankfully, Ellie had closed the café for the afternoon. There was so much food, Meg and her small family could never hope to eat it before it went bad, so she invited those at the cemetery to join them at Ellie's and asked that she and the preacher see to it that the remainder was divided among the needy families in town.

By the time Meg got back to the house, the spotty showers had moved through the countryside and the weather had turned colder. She was glad she'd taken up Nita on her offer to stay at home with Teddy and Lucy since the weather was so inclement. The day would have been far too cold and exhausting for them.

She unhitched and cared for the horse and then grabbed the two baskets of food she'd brought home. The weak afternoon sunlight was making a valiant effort to push aside the clouds, a subtle reminder that this dark time would pass and the sun would shine on her again.

As she made her way up the back steps, she couldn't help wondering again if Ace was nearby. If only there were some sign that he was back, she could breathe much easier.

She saw it just before she reached the door. There, where she couldn't miss it, the sprig of mistletoe hung from the doorknob by a piece of soft doeskin. Meg set the baskets down and untied the thin strip of leather carefully. The small leaves were a little drier, and the berries were a bit more shriveled.

For a moment, she just stood there while pure joy bubbled up inside her. He was back, if he'd ever gone. Did this mean he was willing to talk, to meet her halfway, to at least discuss the possibility of loving each other without looking for problems that might never arise?

She reached for the door handle and stopped. Was he inside? Wearing a wide smile, she pushed through the door and stepped into the kitchen. Nita, who was rocking Lucy, looked up.

Teddy, playing with his blocks near the fire, saw her and leaped to his feet. "Mama!"

Meg barely had time to set the baskets on the table before he flung his small body at her and grabbed her around the knees. She knelt down and hugged him, but her hopeful gaze rested on Nita.

Nita knew what she was asking. "I haven't seen him since the day your mother died. He came while you were gone and we talked," she confessed.

Meg pressed her lips together, wondering what that meant. Why did he refuse to speak to her? Would he leave again?

After giving Teddy and Lucy the attention they felt they deserved after her absence, she carefully placed the mistletoe on the mantel. Trying her best to mask her misery, she unpacked the food and set it on the narrow table.

Talking to Nita would be futile. Meg doubted his mother knew much more than she did. Ace was too good at holding his cards close to his chest. She sighed and told Nita she would tend to their animals for the night. Changing into an everyday skirt and shirtwaist, she grabbed her shawl and tromped through the soggy grass to the barn. To her surprise, she found that the pig, which still hadn't been butchered, was munching on dried corn. All the other animals had full buckets of water, feed and a little hay.

Annoyance warred with a cautious joy. What on earth was he doing? Meg wondered, planting her hands on her hips and turning to look around the small enclosure. What kind of game was he playing? Why did he refuse to show himself?

Well, two could play his cat-and-mouse game, she thought crossly. "I know you're here somewhere, Ace Allen, and just so you know, I will find you. You can't run or hide from what I feel for you or what you feel for me any more than either one of us can escape our pasts."

She strode out into the gloom of the approaching dusk and headed for the chicken house. The chickens were already shut up, and just inside the door she saw the small basket she used for egg gathering. It was full. Picking up the basket, she left the henhouse and closed the door behind her.

Halfway to the house she stopped and called out in a testy voice, "I've learned to stand on my own two feet, just the way you said. I can do my own laundry." It took her longer without his help, but it got done, just as it had before.

"And I can figure out how to get things done I can't do or don't know how to do," she called out. "I *certainly* don't need anyone to feed my animals. Not that I don't appreciate it," she added.

"In short, I don't need a man to take care of me, but I want one. I want you. I want you for my husband and a father for the two children I have and for any that we might have."

Nothing but silence greeted her. She gave a little growl of annoyance and stomped through the mire to the house. At the bottom of the steps she turned.

"I've forgiven my mother and Elton and even myself

for the stupid things I've done. God has forgiven me, too. So I have a clean slate, and starting tomorrow, I'm rebuilding my life, my home, just like that squirrel you showed me. I want you to be here to build it with me."

With that, she turned and went up the steps. At the top, she turned once more. "I've even forgiven you for acting like a ninny and going away."

From where he watched her in the haymow, Ace smiled. This was what he'd wanted from the first. This Meg was well on her way to being whole, perhaps for the very first time. Uneasiness over the future churned in his gut, yet he was eager to see what it would bring. Wherever she went, however she chose to start her new day, Ace knew he would be there.

Morning dawned cold and crisp. It was far too chilly for Meg to sit on the porch with her coffee as she'd grown accustomed to doing; those days were probably over until spring.

She'd lain awake throughout the night, reliving every conversation she'd ever had with Ace, trying to remember the things he'd told her, the tenderness of his actions.

She knew he cared for her, and she felt as if she could make him see that it was pointless to fight their feelings—if only he would give her a chance to tell him the lessons she'd learned from her mother. Nevertheless, she had a plan.

Careful not to wake Teddy, she washed up in the gray light of dawn. She dressed in her prettiest blouse, brushed her long hair up into a loose coil atop her head and cleaned her teeth. Then she slipped on her sturdy shoes, since she'd be making a trek up to the plateau.

Ace was a creature of habit in many ways. Her heart told her that that was where he'd be, waiting for the sun to rise on a new day. Just before she left the room, she picked up the piece of mistletoe and nestled it in the swirl of hair pinned on top of her head, grabbed her Bible and left the house.

The cold air made it harder to breathe, and by the time Meg got to the top of the hill, she was panting a little. She'd timed her ascent just right. The sun was just painting the morning sky and the wisps of cloud in a glorious pink, gold and lavender palette.

She stopped at the edge of the woods and drew her coat more closely around her. He wasn't there.

For a moment, disappointment shot through her, and then, knowing that this was her best time to find him, maybe her only time, she strode briskly to the big boulder. She flipped through the pages until she found the passage she'd marked the night before. Then, in a faltering voice, she read loudly, "'In his favor is life—weeping may endure for a night, but joy cometh in the morning.'"

Very carefully, she closed the Bible and placed it on the rock. She spread her arms wide to the sun as it climbed over the treetops, and then she turned slowly, a gesture of love and welcome, for the new day and what it held. And for Ace.

* * *

And Ace, who was watching from the cover of the trees, knew that having the love of this strong, unbreakable woman would be well worth any pain that might come with it. He smiled when he saw the mistletoe in her hair, an invitation if he ever saw one. He couldn't wait to hold her and to give her those nine kisses. Maybe more.

Giving a little whoop of joy, he ran to her.

* * * * *

Dear Reader,

I hope you're enjoying our time in Wolf Creek. I certainly am. I appreciate so much all your wonderful comments on the books so far. Lord willing, I'll keep trying to write about imperfect people who may have lost their way but find it again, stories that uplift and resonate with you in some way.

Wolf Creek Widow deals with a very serious topic. Domestic violence/spousal abuse is not new to society but a plague that's been around since the beginning of time.

Meg Thomerson has been crying out to have her own story ever since she was introduced as a walk-on character in the first book. The problem was finding the right man and the right circumstances to bring her happiness. As I got to know Ace Allen better and started thinking about the challenges he'd dealt with in his life, I realized his circumstances made him the perfect man to help her on her road back to joy and real love. I hope I've handled this subject in a way that shows its seriousness while also offering hope.

If you know someone suffering from spousal abuse, the National Domestic Violence Hotline is available 24/7 and has a list of 5,000 agencies and resources across the country to provide help and support.

I love to hear from readers. If you have comments or questions, please contact me at pennyrichardswrites@yahoo.com.

Blessings always,

Penny Richards

A DADDY FOR CHRISTMAS
Christmas in Eden Valley
by Linda Ford

Chivalry demands cowboy Blue Lyons help any woman in need, so he offers widow Clara Weston—and her daughters—shelter and food when they have nowhere to go. And whether he wants it or not, Clara and her daughters are soon chipping away at his guarded heart.

A WESTERN CHRISTMAS
by Renee Ryan & Louise M. Gouge

In two brand-new novellas, Christmas comes to the West and brings with it the chance for love, both old and new.

HER COWBOY DEPUTY
Wyoming Legacy
by Lacy Williams

Injured and far from home, sheriff's deputy Matt White finds love in the most unexpected of places with a former childhood friend.

FAMILY IN THE MAKING
Matchmaking Babies
by Jo Ann Brown

Arthur, Lord Trelawney, needs lessons in caring for children, so he decides to practice with the rescued orphans sheltering at his family estate. A practical idea...until he meets their lovely nurse, Maris Oliver.

LIHCNM0915